'For the time being, it may be useful to engage yourself to me...'

Harriet jumped to her feet in consternation. 'No, no!' she cried, shaking her head in protest. 'I have not run away from one groom simply to have another thrust upon me!'

Biting her lip, she confronted her hosts. 'I am sorry—but I do not wish to marry anyone. I want to go to my grandfather. If you cannot help me I must leave...' Her voice trembled.

'Please sit down!' Sandford's voice was curt. 'Perhaps you could do me the courtesy of hearing me out? You mistake the matter. I assure you there is no question of marriage!'

Dorothy Elbury lives in a quiet Lincolnshire village, an ideal atmosphere for writing her historical novels. She has been married to her husband (it was love at first sight, of course!) for forty-five years, and they have three children and four grandchildren. Her hobbies include visiting museums and historic houses, and handicrafts of various kinds. *A Hasty Betrothal* is Dorothy Elbury's first novel for Mills & Boon® Historical Romance™.

A HASTY BETROTHAL

Dorothy Elbury

MILLS & BOON®

First published in Great Britain 2004
Large Print edition 2004
Harlequin Mills & Boon Limited,
Eton House, 18-24 Paradise Road, Richmond, Surrey TW9 1SR

© Dorothy Elbury 2004

ISBN 0 263 18192 8

Set in Times Roman 14 on 15¼ pt.
42-0704-88381

Printed and bound in Great Britain
by Antony Rowe Ltd, Chippenham, Wiltshire

A HASTY BETROTHAL

Dorothy Elbury

Chapter One

'*Hell and damnation!*' cursed Robert, Viscount Sandford, as he pulled his horses hard over to avoid a seemingly inevitable collision with the coach that had suddenly appeared from around the curve ahead.

Driven at speed by a reckless youngster with no heed
for the safety of either the terrified passengers or any
other road user, the vehicle was swinging perilously
from side to side as the ageing coachman attempted to
wrest the whip from the young blade's hand.

Having eagerly accepted the fistful of guineas from
the would-be professional, the driver was now regretting his impetuous gesture and was determined to reinstate himself into his rightful position before they
reached the next stage, where the mealy-mouthed pro-
prietor would be sure to report him for this breach of
contract. Luckily, the man's skill with the ribbons was
still with him and, as the coach swayed on into the
distance, Sandford could see that it did indeed seem to
be slowing down as he carefully brought his own pair
to a sweating, trembling standstill.

'Jump down and hold the heads, Tip,' he commanded. 'We'll have to walk them for a bit until they calm down. Damned coachmen—I wish to God they'd refrain from giving the ribbons to these young whipsters!'

'Whoops! Guv—looks like he hit something!'

Tiptree, Sandford's groom and one-time batman, pointed to the verge some distance ahead, where a figure lay sprawled in an untidy and apparently motionless heap. Leaping lightly from his seat at the rear of the curricle, he went to the head of the nearside chestnut, talking gently and stroking its nose while Sandford sprang from the driving-seat and strode quickly up the road to see what had occurred. Tiptree followed more slowly, leading the horses and the carriage to where his master was bending over the prostrate form.

'Nasty bump on his forehead, sir,' he offered. 'Wheel must have clipped him as it passed—or maybe he hit it on one of these here stones when he fell?' He crouched beside the viscount and helped him to straighten the crumpled body.

'Why, 'tis only a lad!' he said, as Sandford took the thin wrist in his hand, feeling for a sign of life. 'A stableboy, by the look of his kit! Is he dead, sir?'

'No, he's still breathing—we'll have to get him to a doctor. Dammit! That means more time wasted! Lift him into the curricle, Tip, then we'll see if there are any dwellings hereabouts.'

This feat eventually achieved by Tiptree, Sandford climbed back into the driving-seat, steadying the lad against him with one arm, and, holding the reins loosely in his other hand, commanded Tiptree to walk the horses on. Once or twice, the groom thought he heard a low moan coming from the boy and hoped that the youngster was not going to cast up his accounts over his lordship's driving-coat, for, as sure as eggs were definitely eggs, Kimble would blame him, as usual, for any extra work incurred from this trip. Kimble was his lordship's new valet and prided himself in keeping his lordship 'bang-up-to-the-mark' as the saying went but, luckily, Kimble was still at Beldale, where Sandford had left him contentedly reorganising his master's wardrobe.

The viscount, having purchased his colours some ten years previously, had distinguished himself with honours at the Battles of Corunna and Ciudad Rodrigo and had risen to the rank of Lieutenant-Colonel but, close on the heels of the victory at Waterloo, had received from home the tragic news of the death of his twin brother, Philip, in a carriage accident, and had straight away resigned his commission. His younger brother's death had left Sandford as their father's sole adult heir, so the earl had persuaded Sandford that his army days must, perforce, be over. He must now devote his energies to the Beldale estates and, hopefully, settle down.

The viscount's brother, whom Sandford had always laughingly referred to as 'Farmer Phil' because of his love of the pastoral, had left a young widow, Judith, as well as two little children. During the past year Sandford had become uncomfortably aware that this lady's mother cherished the thought that he must surely now take his opportunity to marry the girl with whom both brothers had fallen in love as striplings, her father's property having neighboured theirs. Sandford, unfortunately for the dowager, no longer carried the willow for his pretty sister-in-law, having long since recovered not only from that particular sickness, but also from several similar afflictions over the intervening years.

Now that Napoleon was safely ensconced on St Helena, many of the viscount's former comrades had also left their companies and returned to England. Sandford had recently been enjoying a spirited reunion with some of his fellow officers in London when he received an urgent summons from Beldale that his father had fallen from his horse and suffered a serious injury. The viscount and his groom were now on their way home with all the speed they could muster.

This present delay would not serve to improve his lordship's frame of mind, thought Tiptree, as he surveyed the grim expression on Sandford's face. His long military service with the viscount had earned him a special place in his master's affections and he had learned to judge his moods to a nicety.

'Looks like an inn of some sort ahead, sir!' he called, but Sandford had noted the ramshackle building and was already lifting the unresisting victim on to his shoulder and preparing to climb down.

'Bring the carriage into the yard and see to the horses,' he instructed, as he strode to the closed door, at which he kicked violently. 'Landlord! Ho! Open up within, I say!'

Moments passed as he eased his now-groaning burden more securely across his shoulder. Again he hammered and shouted and finally, to his relief, he heard the rattle of door-chains and the screech of an iron bolt being drawn back. The door opened, but only fractionally, to reveal a tousled-headed old woman who regarded him with rheumy eyes.

'We'm closed for business, sir,' she mumbled fretfully, attempting at the same time to shut the door in his face.

'Open up, I say!' demanded his lordship curtly. 'There has been an accident. This youth is injured and I shall require assistance.'

He pushed at the door firmly and the old dame stepped aside fearfully, recognising the Voice of Authority when she heard it, but still she shook her head apologetically as she attempted to grasp his sleeve.

'Sir—sir,' she stammered, 'There baint no one here but mysen. My old Sam—he took ill and died a sennight since and I been waiting for our Jem to come back from the soldiering...'

Sandford interrupted her. 'Then I shall deal with the matter myself. Get some water heated and show me to a couch of some sort.'

He nudged the old woman firmly along the passageway until, realising the futility of her protestations, she shakily pointed him in the direction of the 'best' parlour where, ducking to miss the lintel, Sandford backed into the room and deposited his once more silent burden effortlessly upon a couch. Then, reaching for a cushion, he gently settled the boy's head on to it and smoothed back the ragged mud-spattered hair from the grimy face.

After some moments the reluctant innkeeper, followed by Tiptree, hobbled into the room carrying a bowl of hot water and a towel.

'My eyesight baint too good, sir,' she wheezed, as she dipped one corner of the linen into the water. She was about to attempt to bathe the boy's forehead when Sandford took the cloth from her and proceeded to wipe the filthy brow himself.

'We're soldiers ourselves, ma'am,' he explained, as he examined the ugly swelling which could now be clearly seen on the boy's temple. 'I've had to deal with many such incidents—aye, and worse,' he added, almost to himself. Then, 'Could you rake up some victuals, do you think? Cold pie or bread and cheese will amply suffice.'

He turned to Tiptree, who was examining the patient for broken bones. 'Well, Tip, what have we got, do you think? Is the boy done for?'

'Shouldn't think so, Guv,' said that worthy cheerfully. 'Thing is, though, what we have here ain't exactly a boy!' He pointed to the unbuttoned shirt, beneath which the beribboned top of a cotton camisole could be clearly seen.

'Good God!' exploded Sandford, stepping back in dismay. 'Cover him—her up, Tiptree, for God's sake!'

He snatched a rug from a nearby chair and together they made a half-hearted attempt to make their patient decent as she gradually stirred and focused a pair of dazed green eyes upon them.

'Wh-what are you doing?' she protested faintly and tried to sit up. 'Oh, my head! Wh-where am I—what has happened—who are you?' She fell back on the cushion in pain and confusion, gripping the rug tightly to her chin as she regarded her rescuers with understandable apprehension.

Sandford stared down at the girl in frowning consternation. No rough serving wench, as he immediately realised on hearing her voice, but surely no young lady of any breeding would appear in public, wearing such shocking attire?

'You must forgive us, ma'am,' he said curtly. 'You were hurt at the roadside—we brought you here—thinking you to be a boy!'

The girl flushed slightly, but a wan smile crossed her face. 'Yes, well—I am in disguise, you see—could you help me up, do you think?' She swung her breeched legs gingerly to the ground and Tiptree grabbed her arm as she swayed forward.

'Oh, dear,' she groaned. 'I seem not to be quite myself—perhaps I should sit for a moment or two.'

Sandford controlled his impatience with difficulty as the girl stared up at him in silent expectation, waiting, he supposed, for him to make the first move.

'Allow me to present myself, ma'am,' he eventually managed. 'Sandford of Beldale at your service—Tiptree here is my man. You must forgive my haste—but I am on most urgent business and I have no time to waste, so I beg you to acquaint me with your destination and I shall see to it that you return home as quickly as possible.'

'Oh, no! You don't understand!' the girl retorted crossly, as she once again attempted to rise. 'I have run away—they were trying to force me to marry— Did you say *Sandford*?' She looked up at him, amazement in her voice. 'Not Colonel Sandford? But yes! I can see that you are indeed he!'

She was, at once, on her feet and staring hard at his countenance.

'I can claim that honour, ma'am,' Sandford replied stiffly, 'but you have the advantage—should I know you?'

'Well, you hardly would—even if you remembered—in this outfit,' countered the young lady, deftly straightening her clothing. 'Allow me to introduce myself—Harriet Cordell—Sir Jonathan was my father—you will not have forgotten him, I'm sure.' She looked at him confidently.

Sandford nodded slowly. 'No, indeed. Our paths crossed many times in Spain. So you are Major Jon's daughter?'

He surveyed the grubby apparition before him and Harriet had the grace to blush.

'But what scrape is this that you are in? Your parents settled in Lincolnshire, as I recollect? How do you come to be in Leicestershire—and in this rig? Is it some sort of wager?'

'No. It is as I said—I have run away from my home. I took the stableboy's clothing and left yesterday morning before the house was up. I have walked *miles and miles* and I slept last night in a hayloft after the owner had put the horses to bed!'

She looked about her in sudden concern. 'Did you recover my bundle? My purse and gown are in it—I don't see it here.'

Sandford glanced at Tiptree, who shook his head. 'We had our hands full with you, miss,' he said apologetically. 'I'll go back down the road and take a look, sir, shall I—but I doubt it'll still be there. It's a busy road.'

At the nod from his master he left the room.

Just then the landlady re-entered, bearing a tray of refreshments, which Sandford, stepping forward, took from her hands, at the same time sending a warning frown to Harriet to remain silent.

'Thank you, ma'am,' he said cheerfully. 'Our patient has recovered. This fare will set us up and we will all be on our way without delay. Here's for your trouble.'

He pressed some coins into her hand, ushered her out of the door and returned to the table. Selecting some of the cold pie and a piece of chicken, he handed the plate to Harriet and instructed her to eat the food.

'And no missish airs, if you please,' he commanded sternly. 'A seasoned campaigner, such as you are, will be well used to eating what's to hand. You spent your youth in the train, I collect?' He helped himself to some food and sat down at the table, regarding her with undisguised curiosity as he ate.

'I admit to having little appetite,' Harriet acquiesced politely. 'And I do have the most throbbing headache, but I shall do my best to take some nourishment. We—Mama and I—learned that lesson in the Peninsula. As you say, we often travelled with the baggage-train, along with the other wives and families. Our quarters were generally quite good, however, and we had our abigail, Martha, with us. Papa went out to Gibraltar when I was tiny and, of course, we went with him, for we had always stayed together...' Her voice trembled slightly and she took a sip from the glass he had poured for her, pulling a face.

'Ugh! Porter! I could never become accustomed to that!'

She was immediately comforted by the sight of his quick grin and covertly studied her rescuer. Throughout her childhood she had listened in awe to the many tales of his daring exploits, so was intrigued and, she had to admit, not a little nervous at meeting her one-time hero at such close quarters. She recollected having been presented to him at a ball in Lisbon, but this had been in her youth and she doubted that the great man would recall such an insignificant incident.

Having cast off both his driving-coat and jacket, Sandford was now in his shirtsleeves, riding breeches and top boots, all of which displayed his good shoulders and strong limbs to advantage. Although not precisely handsome, the viscount was blessed with regular features, crisp brown hair and a pair of steady grey eyes with which he now sat and frowningly surveyed her as she nibbled at her pie.

There was a tap at the door and Tiptree entered, empty-handed. Harriet jumped up and started forward.

'Oh, no! Don't say you could not find it! Now I am in the suds!' She spun round to face Sandford. 'I wonder, sir—could I prevail upon you to advance me some money? I need to get to the staging post, you see. I am going to seek out my grandfather. I am sure he will help me...' She broke off lamely. 'What must you think of me? I will tell you the whole, if you can spare me your time?'

Sandford sighed resignedly. 'My business is most pressing, to be sure, but I cannot just walk out and leave you here. Tiptree, come and eat while I hear Miss Cordell's tale.' He rose from his chair and seated himself on the window settle next to the couch Harriet had just chosen.

'I will be quick, for I can tell that your time is precious,' she said gratefully. 'You may have heard that Papa was injured at Nivelle and we returned to England before Napoleon escaped from Elba, so we were not involved in the Belgian campaign—much to Papa's fury. He had been hit in the chest and never really recovered and he—he died last year, before the victory. Mama was totally to pieces and our neighbour—who farms the land next to ours—was so very helpful to us, arranging the funeral and organising the farmworkers to carry on and—so many things I shan't tire you with. Anyway, somehow she grew to depend upon him and his advice and, just after Easter—three months ago— she agreed to marry him. Would you believe it, after being married to Papa for more than twenty years! *I* think Sir Chester is quite the most odious of men and as for his son—words fail me!'

Harriet clenched her fists and her slim frame shuddered. 'That was it, you see. Sir Chester had married Mama, thinking that she was wealthy—but Papa had left everything to me, in trust until I am twenty-five or marry. Mama has the interest from the trust and a generous competence, of course. Papa was not a rich man, but we were always secure, and he had also inherited the family farm when his cousin died. However, to the point; when he discovered that it will be another five years before I inherit the estate, Sir Chester started pushing his horrid son at me and throwing us together at every opportunity—he was determined to make a match, but I was very unco-operative, I can assure you! Two days ago I overheard them planning to abduct me and force an elopement, so I knew I had to get away before I found myself Mistress Gilbert Middleton!'

She was obliged to stop to compose herself and Sandford took the opportunity to ask, 'You mentioned a grandparent—he lives in Leicestershire? Perhaps I can take you to him?' but Harriet shook her head and, after taking a deep breath, hurriedly continued with her explanation.

'Mama's father—he is a Scottish landowner, but she eloped with Papa when she was eighteen and she has had no contact with him since. I understand that he lives somewhere to the north of Edinburgh...'

She then looked hopefully at Sandford, who had risen to his feet and was reaching for his jacket. Laying her hand upon his arm, she beseeched him urgently, 'Please, my lord, will you lend me some money so that I can continue my journey? I was trying to reach Grantham for the staging-post. I believe the coaches leave for Edinburgh at six every morning. We cannot be far away, if you would be so kind as to convey me there?'

'Absolutely not!' retorted Sandford, shrugging into his driving-coat. 'You, my dear Miss Cordell, will accompany me to Beldale where my mother will see to you. You must see that I cannot possibly leave you here alone in this inn. As for allowing you to travel by public stage to some unknown destination—you must be all about in your head still, if you imagine that I will do that! Now, tidy yourself and wash your face while Tiptree sees if the old dame has a cloak or something we can persuade her to sell!'

Somewhat incensed at his lordship's overbearing dismissal of her project, but suspecting that her protestations would be in vain, Harriet allowed herself to be bundled into the viscount's curricle and, wrapped in the hooded cape procured from the landlady (who had made herself a considerable profit from the morning's unexpected activities), resentfully succumbed to her fate.

The journey to Beldale was completed almost in silence, with Harriet and Sandford each engrossed in their own thoughts, and Tiptree, seated behind them, wondering if his lordship had allowed his concern for his father's welfare to overset his usually sound judgement.

Sandford was, ruefully, wondering much the same. His mother would have had enough on her plate, he realised, without this additional complication, having hardly had time to mourn her son. Now to be faced with a serious and possibly life-threatening injury to her beloved husband must require all of Lady Caroline's resources. From her hastily scribbled missive he had gathered that Beldale had been thrown, or had fallen, from his horse while returning from estate rounds and had lain helpless in the woods for some hours. His failure to arrive at the stables had eventually alerted the grooms but, although a search party had then quickly located the injured man, it appeared that drenching rain had exacerbated his condition. He had been given the best medical attention available but he had slipped in and out of consciousness as a raging fever had taken hold. His physician had voiced his worst fears and, after a frantic three days, Lady Caroline had reluctantly sent for her son.

Sandford, having lost the precious time he had gained from his headlong dash out of the city, concentrated on his driving and, for most of the journey, refrained from making any sort of conversation until, leaning forward to spring his horses on a straight section of road, he happened to glance sideways and noticed Harriet's white and set face.

'Not so far now,' he announced bracingly. 'We turn off at the next village and then it is a mere three miles to the lodge.'

Harriet nodded glumly. Still feeling the effects of the bump on her head and gradually becoming more aware of other painful areas of her body, she found herself growing increasingly nervous at the thought of the forthcoming interview with the Countess of Beldale. Although her upbringing had been an uncommon one, leaving her with a lack of some of the more usual feminine accomplishments, it had taught her to be very self-reliant. Her common sense now warned her that it was going to be difficult to justify clothing herself in male garb, whatever provocation had led her to do so. Hadn't Mama and Martha frequently been obliged to remind her that she was a lady and that, even in extreme circumstances, she must always endeavour to behave as such?

It had never been her intention to allow anyone of consequence to see her in her disguise. She had supposed that, as a stable lad, she would pass unnoticed on the roadside and that, hidden from view behind some barn or other, she could have changed into her carefully folded good dress and covered her hastily cropped hair with her ample bonnet before boarding the coach for Scotland. She had brought away a purse full of guineas so had expected to travel in reasonable comfort once she reached the staging route. She had not, of course, allowed for this disastrous turn of events.

Having spent her formative years following the army on the continent, she believed that she was well able to take care of herself. She was a skilled and daring horsewoman, having learned her craft under the unforgiving eyes of the grooms and cavalry officers of her father's regiment with whom she had been quite a favourite, with her swinging amber ringlets and her slim, boyish figure. Always willing to attempt the impossible, she had usually managed to remain steadfastly cheerful in the most disheartening conditions.

Not quite so cheerful at the moment however, she saw, with very mixed feelings, that the carriage was negotiating a narrow curve running through a small, picturesque village. The sun was already nestling down into the puffs of cloud above the nearby hills and its light was fading quickly. She held her breath in admiration as Sandford turned his horses into a broad carriage-drive with hardly a check, raising his whip in response to the lodge-keeper's salute as they swept through the high, wrought-iron gates.

She was unable to appreciate the extent of the parkland flashing past her and, in reality, was in no mood to do so for, as the cream stone façade of the elegant house came into view, her apprehension increased.

The great front doors were already on the point of opening as the carriage reached the steps and an elegantly attired lady of mature years was hastening out to meet Lord Sandford who, having cast the reins at Tiptree, had leapt down from his perch and was taking the stone steps two at a time with his hands outstretched.

'Father? How is he?' he cried, anxiously clasping his mother's hands. 'I am not—too late?'

But her ladyship was smiling. 'Robbie—oh, my dear! His lordship has rallied!' she replied joyfully. 'But I'm so glad that you have returned! The physician is with him now—come along, quickly. He will be wanting to speak with you.'

The countess urged her son into the hallway as she spoke and, throwing his driving-coat to a waiting footman, Sandford bounded up the wide, curving staircase. Halfway to the landing he checked, turned and, with his hand on the banister, exclaimed, 'Good grief! I almost forgot—Miss Cordell ! She is still in the curricle!'

She was not. When the groomsmen had taken the horses' heads, Tiptree had handed Harriet down and she had nervously climbed the steps in Sandford's wake, expecting him at least to account for her presence but, with increasing agitation, she realised that she herself would once again be responsible for the difficult explanations. She stepped hesitatingly into the well-lit hall as Lady Caroline turned in puzzlement towards her, then stiffened momentarily as she heard her ladyship's gasp of astonishment.

'Sally! Sally—can it be? But, no! Of course not!'

The countess stepped forward quickly to peer at Harriet's face.

'Please remove your hood, my dear—oh! Your hair! But the colour—and that face! Surely I would know it anywhere—Robbie! Come down at once! Who is this young lady—where is she from?' She drew Harriet to the middle of the hall as Sandford slowly and reluctantly descended the stairs.

'Forgive me, Mama,' he replied, as Harriet agitatedly clutched the shabby cape around her, terrified that her disguise would be revealed both to the countess and to the several impassive servants on duty.

'This is Miss Harriet Cordell. She requires our assistance in a rather delicate matter—shall we go into the salon?'

He took his mother's arm and propelled her gently into a nearby withdrawing-room, signalling Harriet to accompany them. As the door closed, he drew the countess to a sofa and took up his stance by the fire-place, indicating a nearby seat to Harriet, who perched herself very gingerly on its edge, keeping the front of the cape closely about her breeched legs.

Lady Caroline waved her hand impatiently at her son. 'What is this all about?' she demanded. 'This is Sally Rutherford to the letter—I should know! We were bosom bows at our come out. I don't understand!'

She stared helplessly at Harriet, who was herself in total confusion at the older woman's words.

'I am Harriet Cordell, ma'am,' she stuttered. 'My father was Major Sir Jonathan Cordell—my mother Sarah is the daughter of Lord Douglas Ramsey…'

She stopped as Lady Caroline clapped her hands in delight.

'Ramsey! Well, of course! He married Sally—I was her bridesmaid—he took her off to Craigburn and we never met again. We corresponded, to be sure, but she died in childbed—I always believed that her child died with her. Ramsey refused to answer any letters and I supposed him to have gone into a decline. He was much in love with Sally,' she finished sadly.

There was a moment's silence. Harriet cast her eyes up pleadingly at Sandford, who seemed to be studying the pattern on the carpet with great interest. He cleared his throat and his mother looked quickly towards him and smiled.

'Oh, dear,' she said. 'I am being maudlin, aren't I? Do forgive me, my dears.' She turned to Harriet and patted the seat next to her. 'Come and sit by me, my child, and tell me your tale. I can see that Robert is fretting to go to his father and I feel that he will be of little use to us until he has done so.'

Harriet was only too pleased to comply with her hostess's request and waited until Sandford had left the room before reciting her misadventures once more. The countess interrupted her flow only to clarify certain points and then sat, nodding her head in sympathy, until the tale was told.

'—and what I have to do now, ma'am,' Harriet spoke firmly, 'is to ask if you will advance me the money to seek out my grandfather or perhaps…'

'My dear child!' Lady Caroline recoiled in distaste at the very idea. 'I shall write to Lord Ramsey myself. Indeed, I should have done it years ago. Firstly, however, we must see to your dress—Mathilde will find you something.'

She pulled at the bell-rope beside the fireplace and, almost immediately, a footman appeared at the door.

'Oh, March—send for Mathilde and tell Mrs Gibson to have the Rose room prepared for a lady guest.' She turned once more to Harriet. 'I expect you are famished too—have cook send up some substantial refreshments, March.'

The footman bowed and left the room.

'We still keep country hours for our meals, my dear, and had our dinner at three o'clock, but I dare say a hearty supper will be welcomed by both Robert and yourself?'

Harriet nodded. Tired and aching, she was happy for the moment to place herself in her ladyship's hands and, very soon afterwards, she found herself conducted upstairs to a delightful rose-coloured chamber over-looking the gardens at the rear of the house.

Meanwhile, Sandford had hastened to his father's bedchamber where he was admitted by Chegwin, the earl's elderly valet.

The viscount learned that the crisis had occurred during the early hours of that morning when Beldale had at last rallied and his fever had lessened, although he was still incoherent and weak from the blood-letting upon which Sir Basil, his physician, had insisted.

Chegwin had defied all attempts to remove him from his master's side throughout his illness, refusing all offers of help with either the feeding of the patient or the changing of dressings, resting only when Lady Caroline herself was with his lordship.

'I am glad to see you home, my lord,' he welcomed Sandford softly. 'His lordship is sleeping, but he is no longer as restless as he has been these past days.'

Sandford took his seat by the big four-poster bed and contemplated his sleeping parent gravely. The pale, lined face looked so much younger in repose and his heart softened as he recalled the days of his childhood when he and his twin had accompanied their father around the estate, proudly riding alongside him and always taking his fine example as the pattern-card for their future lives.

He was at a loss to understand how his father, an excellent horseman, had come to take such a toss. The bridleway through the woods on the far side of the estate was a wide and open one and Sandford assumed that the earl would have been riding at a gentle trot. His lordship was over seventy, it was true, but had always been of a hale and hearty disposition and fully active in all outdoor pursuits and had, hitherto, managed his large estate with enjoyment and gusto. Now, the viscount was beginning to wonder if Philip's death had affected the earl more than he had at first supposed.

After his son's untimely death, Beldale had been closely involved with his daughter-in-law's business affairs. To be sure, she had an excellent estate manager in their cousin Charles Ridgeway, but the earl had deemed it his duty to oversee his grandson's inheritance and this was one of the reasons he had felt it necessary to insist upon Sandford's quitting his military career.

During the past year Sandford had become increasingly aware of the fact that his presence at Beldale was likely to be of a permanent nature and that he would have to set about relearning the task of running the estates. He had grown up here, of course, and had dabbled in such matters before the yearning for a military life had sent him on his travels. He had always loved the place and its people, if not quite as wholeheartedly as Philip had done, he ruefully acknowledged, but was gradually coming to realise that there would be few regrets, especially after all the carnage and suffering he had recently witnessed.

The viscount now became aware that his father's eyes had opened and were trying to focus upon the figure at his bedside. A frail hand reached out and felt for Sandford's own and the viscount bent to hear Beldale's whispered words.

'The horse—he fell—something...' His voice tailed off and he sank once more into his drugged slumber.

Sandford drew his head back, puzzled. Chegwin came to the bedside and confided, 'That is how he has been, my lord, and always the same words. Is he worrying about his horse, do you suppose? Smithers tells me that the poor beast had to be destroyed—two legs were broken, I understand. His lordship has not been informed, of course. Would that be causing such restlessness, sir?'

Sandford shook his head doubtfully. 'I should hardly think so, but certainly it is odd that he constantly dwells upon it.'

He stood up, gently unclasping his father's hand as he did so, saying, 'I shall speak with Smithers myself. You are doing very well here, Chegwin. Please accept my deepest gratitude.'

The old manservant bowed, concealing his pleasure at the young master's words. 'We do our best, sir,' was his reply, but there was a smile on his face as he closed the door after Sandford's departure.

The viscount made straight for the stables, seeking out the head groom who was locking up for the day. Smithers confirmed the valet's story that Cobalt had been destroyed. He himself had attended to the horse immediately after his master had been carried away from the scene of the accident.

'Threshing about in great pain, so he were, sir,' he said sadly, shaking his head. ''Twere a real shame that—a grand old lad, he were. But both his front legs was broke, you see, sir, so couldn't do otherwise.' He looked anxiously at Sandford, knowing that his actions had been correct and wondering where his young lordship's questions were leading.

'Absolutely right, Smithers. I am not doubting your judgement. I just needed to clarify a few points in my mind. Did you notice anything odd about the fall?'

Smithers rubbed his chin and frowned. 'I couldn't see how his lordship came to fall at all on that path, sir, him being such a bruising rider, and Cobalt could have fetched him home blindfolded, as you know. But there it is, sir, his lordship had shot over Cobalt's head—that were obvious from how he was lying—and the horse had gone down on both front legs from the look of the cuts on his knees. Likely a hare or some such startled him is my best guess and I did give it a lot of thought, sir,' he said, shifting uncomfortably. 'Even went back the next morning to have a good look round. Still don't get it, though.' He shook his head again.

'Don't concern yourself, Smithers.' Sandford clapped the groom on the back. 'I'm sure that you did all that should be done in the circumstances. You can show me the spot in the morning, just to satisfy my curiosity. As you say, the fact that his lordship fell at all is a mystery. Now, finish up here quickly and get to your supper.'

Turning on his heel, he left, going at once to his rooms where, with Kimble's disapproving assistance, he quickly changed out of his travel-stained garments before descending to join his mother once more.

The countess was awaiting his return with some eagerness, although she was unable to shed any further light on his father's accident, describing only the injuries he had suffered. A blow to the head causing severe concussion and a broken ankle were the main problems, but the old gentleman was covered in bruises, too, and it would be some time before he was himself again. She was just too glad that Sir Basil, his lordship's physician, was now quietly confident that his patient would make a good recovery and she was overjoyed when Sandford informed her of his intention to remain at Beldale and take over his father's reins until Lord William had fully recovered.

By now, having had ample time to formulate her own ideas for Harriet's salvation, Lady Caroline then turned the conversation to that particular problem.

Chapter Two

Harriet sank gratefully into the luxury of the bath, which had been quickly filled by a procession of maid-servants and allowed the last of these, a plump, apple-cheeked damsel, who introduced herself as 'Rose', to wash and rinse her shorn locks.

'Rose?' she asked, in amused curiosity. 'Isn't that the name of this chamber, also?'

The smiling maid nodded, dropping a curtsy. 'Mrs Gibson thought it would be easier for you to remember, miss.' Wrapping a huge, soft towel around Harriet, she helped her from the bath. 'I'm to be your maid during your stay, if you please.'

Rose proceeded to carry out her duties with neat, precise actions, fetching undergarments and a gown from various sources within the room and, finally, taking up a pair of scissors from the dressing-table, set about restoring some sort of shape to Harriet's hair.

''Tis a lovely colour, miss,' she said, brushing back the now shining, red-gold tendrils. 'Who cut it last I can't imagine, but I can just about coax it into that new style they call the "Titus". Luckily you have sufficient curl in it. There!' She stepped back triumphantly to view her handiwork.

Harriet was amazed at the transformation. The curly crop certainly suited her elfin features and, somehow, made her limpid green eyes look larger than ever. The bronze silk gown Mathilde had 'found, from somewhere' accentuated her creamy skin and was of far better quality and design than any she had ever owned. The bruise on her forehead was becoming more obvious and was deepening in colour, but Rose had carefully arranged the curls to disguise it and had woven a spray of artificial lily-of-the-valley through the rest of her hair.

'How very clever of you, Rose,' she said in delight. 'I will be very glad to have you as my maid. It is clear that you have a real talent.'

Rose's ample cheeks flushed with pleasure and Harriet acquired her first loyal friend in the Beldale household. Trained not to ask questions of their superiors, the servants knew better than to query the unexpected arrival of a young lady in strange garb, without luggage or possessions, and, although Rose was bursting with curiosity about her new mistress's background, it was more than her job was worth to exhibit such interest. Mrs Gibson had instructed her to bundle up the dirty, rough clothing and hand it straight to her, and Mathilde, her ladyship's maid, had brought articles from Lady Caroline's own boudoir, although Rose was sure she recognised some of the items as having belonged to one or other of Lord Sandford's young nieces who were often in the habit of visiting with their mamas.

The gown was certainly one that had belonged to Lady Sophie, Sandford's youngest married sister, for Rose herself had been set to mend the flounce when her ladyship had discarded it after a recent visit with her young family.

Summoning up her courage, Harriet descended to the hall and was escorted by a patently admiring March to the small salon where her hostess was to be found in deep conversation with his lordship. They both turned at Harriet's entrance and she could not help a feeling of smug satisfaction at seeing the expression of frank amazement on Sandford's face as he took in her transformed appearance.

'My dear,' said Lady Caroline, holding out her hand. 'You look delightful—but I knew that you would. Do please join us and take some refreshment. Robbie—pour Harriet a glass of wine, if you please.'

Sandford complied, taking sidelong glances at his one-time urchin as he did so. He handed the glass to her with a small bow and a practised smile, saying, 'I see I rescued a nymph. No doubt the gods will reward me!'

Harriet flushed uncomfortably at his mocking undertone.

'Who can tell?' she responded dismissively. 'I myself am very grateful for your help, of course, but I must endeavour to carry out my plan. I realise I would have been in great difficulty without your timely assistance but I still need to get to my grandfather.'

She turned to Lady Caroline. 'Please, ma'am, will you give me your help?'

'You may rely upon me to do whatever I can, my child,' said her ladyship, kindly. 'But it will take some time for the mail to reach your grandfather. You will remain in my care until then, of course, but—as I have just been telling Robert—we must concoct a story to explain your arrival. I have already put to him a suggestion that may serve...' She looked towards Sandford and he took up the conversation.

'My mother is concerned that you should suffer no harm to your reputation,' he explained. 'She will be sending to your grandfather, apprising him of your present situation and whereabouts. That, of course, will take several days. Therefore, her ladyship has suggested that, for the time being, it may be useful to engage yourself to me...'

Harriet jumped to her feet in consternation. 'No, no!' she cried, shaking her head in protest. 'I have not run away from one groom simply to have another thrust upon me!'

Biting her lip, she confronted her hosts. 'I am sorry—but I do not wish to marry anyone. I want to go to my grandfather. If you cannot help me, I must leave...' Her voice trembled.

'Please sit down!' Sandford's voice was curt. 'Perhaps you could do me the courtesy of hearing me out. You mistake the matter. I assure you that there is no question of marriage!'

Harriet looked at him in amazement. 'But you said...'

'He said "engaged", my dear,' her ladyship said gently, drawing Harriet down beside her once more.

'You see, it will save such a lot of talk if Robert is thought to have brought home his new fiancée. It would be quite unexceptional that you should accompany him after his father's accident. We can send notices to the local *Mercury* and to the *Lincoln Post*—for your mother's benefit—then no one will have cause to make unseemly comment. When we hear from your grandfather and know his intentions towards you, you can simply break off the agreement, saying that you found that you did not suit.'

'That, in any event, would be close to the truth,' muttered the viscount under his breath, as he poured himself another drink.

When, during Harriet's absence, Lady Caroline had proffered her suggestion of a mock 'engagement', Sandford was at first horrified and then laughingly dismissive, but slowly began to realise that the scheme would in fact solve a good many difficulties that were certain to arise while they awaited Douglas Ramsey's response to his mother's letter, not the least of which, from his own point of view, was the embarrassing situation in which he always seemed to find himself on his visits to his sister-in-law's house.

Since his return from the Continent he had been a frequent visitor to Westpark, offering brotherly advice and comfort to the young widow and getting reacquainted with his little nephew and niece, who had grown to regard him almost as a substitute for their beloved father, because of the viscount's uncanny likeness.

He, in his turn, found great delight in their company and had spent many happy hours with Christopher, engaging in those activities so beloved of small boys and grown men alike. Shy little Elspeth had, equally, won his heart with her huge brown eyes and appealing ways and Sandford would gladly have continued this happy association with Philip's family had it not been for Judith's mother, Lady Butler.

This cantankerous old lady had made her home with the young Hursts after her own husband's death three years previously when Judith, having been Sir Frederick's sole heir, had joined her property with Philip's own estates. Although Lady Butler had been left an excellent annuity, she had deemed it more convenient to move in with her daughter, thereby avoiding any of the household duties and attendant difficulties with which she would have been obliged to involve herself had she remained in her own home. She eschewed anything that interrupted the level tenor of her existence and, being an indolent and tediously complaining woman who considered that Life had dealt her a shabby hand, she regarded even the slightest inconvenience as a personal affront. She refused to involve herself in domestic affairs, yet happily criticised their organisation and, whilst she would never dream of offering her daughter any guiding advice on household management, she was always quick to point out where errors had been made. Easygoing Philip had merely laughed at his mother-in-law's eccentricities, even occasionally chaffing her, but Sandford found her both irritating and encroaching and had, in the past, always excused himself from her company at the first opportunity.

Recently, however, the viscount's necessary visits to Westpark had thrown him into Lady Butler's society more often and she had lately taken to pointing out how the children 'loved him so', and how 'dear Judith blossomed' in his company and, worse, 'how comfortably we all sit together'. With increasing dread, he saw clearly where her fancies were leading.

His continuing lack of a bride was being misconstrued by Lady Butler as a sure sign that he was still 'carrying the torch' for her daughter and a second marriage into the Hurst family would simply 'make all neat and tidy' from her point of view, as well as raising her a notch higher in the social scale, for she was very much concerned with her own consequence.

But Sandford was not about to indulge the old woman's fantasy that one brother could simply step into the other's shoes. Judith had made her choice years ago and, Sandford was certain, had never regretted it, so, with this scheme of his mother's, he now saw what seemed to him a perfect solution to his own difficulties. For this reason alone he had finally agreed to the charade.

He was, therefore, more than a little piqued at Harriet's reaction to the suggestion, for he could hardly help being aware that his rank and wealth inevitably classified him as a considerable 'catch' in the marriage mart. He found to his surprise that, although his mother's scheme was clearly meant to be merely a temporary arrangement, he had anticipated a more flatter-

ing and appreciative response from this chit of a girl
and, considering her present situation, a certain gratitude towards himself.

In his early days as a subaltern in a Rifle Brigade
he had found himself fighting alongside Major Sir Jonathan Cordell in several engagements of the Peninsular
campaign and had soon learned to respect the older
officer's judgement. Conditions were such, during that
time, that he had met Lady Cordell very infrequently
and her daughter, as far as he was aware, not at all.

Preferring to be in the thick of the action, he was
seldom to be found far from the front lines, this enthusiasm earning him rapid promotion, but inevitably he
had, during one engagement, received a splinter in the
thigh, which had necessitated him being carried off the
field and transported to what passed as the hospital
area. Here, amidst the sickening carnage and filth, he
had witnessed 'Mrs Major', as she was termed, working alongside the wives of the troopers and artillerymen
as though she were a mere camp-follower instead of
an officer's lady. He had seen that she spoke as gently
and compassionately to the roughest infantryman as
she did to those of rank and title and he had been
equally impressed by her firm efficiency as she tended
the most appalling wounds. His own injury had not
been severe and his conversations with her had been
few and he had soon been transferred to his own quarters but, on other fields and in other battles, he had
often recalled the sight of 'Mrs Major' walking quietly
amongst the rows of dead and dying, bending to offer
what little comfort she could.

Her daughter certainly seemed to have that same indomitable spirit, he now mused, as he watched Harriet deep in conversation with his mother. He had been quite taken aback at her entrance. True, he had not studied her very closely up until that moment, but the transformation from mud-urchin was astonishing.

The dirty, raggedly cropped hair was now a burning halo of soft curls framing a quite delightful face upon which was centred a neat straight nose, lightly dusted with some very unfashionable freckles. And that was a decidedly stubborn-looking chin, he conjectured in growing amusement. The generous rosy lips, unpainted, he would swear, were half open as they exclaimed at some words the countess had uttered, and the eyes—what colour? He could not immediately recall, but was answered as the owner turned her face in his direction. Green as moss and fringed, most unusually, with thick, dark lashes.

The result was breathtaking and, with a gleam in his eye, it suddenly occurred to him that being 'engaged' to this curious little creature could prove to be rather more than just an amusing diversion. Confident of his ability to charm her out of her unwarranted antagonism towards him, his spirits rose as he resolved to take her to visit his sister-in-law at the first opportunity.

Chapter Three

Harriet had suffered a restless night in her rose bed-chamber. Her head ached and parts of her body felt very sore as she tossed and turned in the big bed. She was glad that it was not a four-poster, as she had always hated them, slightly fearful that someone may be prowling around beyond the closed bedcurtains.

Having spent most of her youth in Spain and Portugal, she disliked being shut in, preferring open spaces and wide skies. She had discovered, to her surprise, that she loved the lush greenness of England and, even though she had also found that she was expected to conform to the rigid pattern of behaviour required of an English miss, she had eventually settled into her new life as a gentleman farmer's daughter quite contentedly.

However, although occasional digressions still occurred, her stubbornness still had to be held firmly in check, especially if she felt that her wishes were being unreasonably overridden, and her father had often had cause to wonder from whence this mulish streak had come. Her mother could only suppose that it must have been inherited from her Scottish forebears, once reminding her husband that her own father's cussedness had been legend in his lands and who, Harriet had been subsequently informed, had continued to earn this reputation over the succeeding years.

Harriet wondered if he would respond to Lady Caroline's missive. She had intended arriving, unannounced, on his doorstep, confident of her ability to win round the dear old gentleman she had supposed him to be but, after her conversation with the countess, she was no longer so sure of herself. In fact, he sounded a rather disagreeable sort of fellow, refusing to have anything to do with Mama just because she had wanted to marry darling Papa. He must be slightly touched in his upper quarters, she decided, pulling the quilt around her. Mama had seldom spoken about him and it was only after Papa's death that she had told her daughter that she believed him to be still alive, having read of some Highland clearance dispute with which he was involved. Hearing that he had taken a sympathetic view of the Highlanders' plight had been the main reason that Harriet had elected to seek out her grandfather. She could have succeeded too, she fulminated resentfully, had not that fool coachman knocked her down. Then, that arrogant Sandford! Carting her off like so much baggage! And in the opposite direction, too! And now, she had to pretend to be engaged to him! What a disappointment he had turned out to be! A small tear crept from her eye as she took stock of her situation and, sniffing, she realised forlornly that she would have to make the best of it until a better opportunity presented itself—the words her father had been wont to use if ever he heard her complaining about her lot. She drifted off to sleep, beset by dreams of marching columns, speeding coaches and Viscount Sandford, surrounded by hundreds of tartan sheep!

The following morning at breakfast, Sandford announced his intention of riding over to Westpark to introduce his 'betrothed' to the Hursts. He nodded briskly to Harriet, who glowered at him over the rim of her cup.

'If you could arrange to be ready in half an hour, I shall have the horses saddled.'

'Oh, I'm afraid I cannot accompany you,' she countered. 'I have no habit, although I dare say could wear my breeches, of course,' she offered pertly.

Lady Caroline frowned at her and shook her head. 'Don't be naughty, my child. You must not tease him. He has not yet got out of the way of giving orders.' She turned to her son and smiled. 'I have arranged for Madame Armande to bring her seamstresses to us this morning, my dear. If you could wait until Miss Cordell has some suitable garments I am sure she will be happy to accompany you. You will want her to make a good impression, I know—especially on Lady Butler.' Her eyes twinkled as she saw her words take effect.

'As you say, ma'am,' replied Sandford, rising. 'Then I shall go up to see how Father does and tend to other business instead. Your servant, ladies.' He bowed in Harriet's direction and left the room.

'He's very high-handed, isn't he?' Harriet said, in some surprise at his sudden departure, and strangely disappointed that he had refused to rise to her bait.

Her ladyship patted her hand. 'He has been used to making decisions, my dear,' she said. 'And, like yourself perhaps, he has been out of Society for so long that he forgets how it goes on. You must not mind him.'

Looking at the clock on the mantel-shelf, she rose to her feet. 'Come, now we must attend to Madame. She will be waiting in the sewing-room and we have a lot to get through.'

The next few hours were a test of stamina, with Harriet being pushed and pulled and pinned and measured until her head was in a whirl. Madame had brought several garments ready-made, which were to be altered to fit her at once, in addition to the many bolts of various fabrics that she offered for Lady Caroline's inspection.

At last, the countess took Harriet down for the cold luncheon that had been laid out for them in the dining-room. Sandford was nowhere to be seen. Harriet supposed him to be about his 'other business'. She, herself, was desperate to get out into the fresh air and was about to ask her ladyship's permission to take a walk on the terrace when March entered and announced a visitor.

'The Honourable Mrs Hurst, my lady,' he intoned grandly, and a tall, raven-haired beauty swept in past him.

'Judith, my dear!' The countess rose from her seat. 'I was not expecting you, surely? Not that you need an invitation, to be sure. Sit down, please—you will see we are still at lunch—such a busy morning we have had!'

Judith Hurst took a seat at the table, gracefully arranging the skirts of her black riding-habit and removing her gloves. Her soft brown eyes rested on Harriet with open curiosity as she spoke, her words almost tripping over themselves in her breathless haste.

'I confess to being all agog, Belle-Mere! Mother has sent me over to see how Lord William does and I have just this moment seen Madame Armande's equipage leaving Beldale. Forgive my vulgar curiosity, but I cannot contain myself as to what it is all about!'

Lady Caroline was forced into making an instant decision. Little as she cared to deceive her daughter-in-law, of whom she was very fond, she knew her to be somewhat feather-brained. One of the reasons dear Philip had loved her, the countess supposed but, nevertheless, she doubted Judith's ability to keep the bones of this secret to herself or, more especially, from her mother, which Lady Caroline knew was Sandford's main objective. Her mind worked quickly and she rose, moving to stand beside Harriet's chair and, placing her hand on the girl's shoulder, she announced, 'Allow me to introduce you to Robert's betrothed, my dear. This is Miss Harriet Cordell.'

Judith Hurst's eyes widened in amazement, then her face became wreathed in smiles as she clapped her hands together.

'Is it true, then? Is he engaged at last?' She, too, rose from her seat and came to Harriet's side. 'How truly delightful! I am so happy for you both. Do say we shall be friends, dear Miss Cordell.'

Harriet, by now full of embarrassment, was attempting to gather her wits in order to make some suitable reply when, to her relief, Sandford entered the room and, striding forward, held out his hands to his sister-in-law.

'How well you look, dear Judith,' he said, with a welcoming grin. 'Still the prettiest girl in the county, I see.'

There was a moment's awkward silence before Judith, laughing, pushed him away in mock dismay.

'Oh, Robert! You devil! Do not tease so!' she chided him. 'Why have you kept such a secret from me? I thought myself your dearest friend and have only just now been informed of your betrothal!'

Sandford shot a glance at his mother and quickly appraised the situation.

'I see I have been forestalled,' he said, with a rueful smile. 'I promise I intended to bring Miss Cordell to Westpark as soon as I was able. We were obliged to quit London in such haste that we had no time to pack our belongings—I believe Madame Armande is attending to some of your more pressing needs?' He cast what he felt to be a fond smile in Harriet's direction.

'I hope the morning's activities have not tired you out, *dearest*?' He continued, determined to play his part to perfection. 'I came to see if you would care to take a walk in the grounds—but perhaps you would prefer to stay and talk to Mrs Hurst? I'm sure she is *dying* to hear our story!'

Judith shook her head and laughed.

'Very true, my dear Robert—but I shall not play the gooseberry! And besides, I do want to know how Lord William does. You two lovebirds may run along now if you promise that you will tell me all later?'

Sandford bowed and, taking Harriet's hand on his arm, he led her out through the rear doors on to the terrace. He did not speak until they had descended the steps leading to the gardens.

'I should have foreseen that possibility,' he commented thoughtfully as soon as they were out of earshot. 'I trust that you were not too discomposed?'

'We were caught off our guard,' admitted Harriet, relieved to be out in the fresh air at last. 'Lady Caroline showed great presence of mind. However, it now appears that we have to concoct some sort of history for our sudden—romance.'

Her voice stumbled on the word and he looked down at her flushed cheeks in concern.

'It will not be for long,' he said soothingly. 'We must stick to the truth as far as possible—we could easily have known one another for years. I shall simply say that we met again in London and that I was overcome...'

He stopped, as Harriet came to an abrupt halt beside him.

'Oh, I would prefer that you do not say such a thing, my lord,' she exclaimed, hot with embarrassment. 'I must inform you that I feel sufficiently uncomfortable about this whole charade without having to fabricate even more deception.'

'Judith is no fool,' he informed her bluntly. 'She will expect ''love'' to be in it somewhere—and how else would you explain such a hasty betrothal?'

Harriet's chin came up and she flashed angry eyes at him.

'I take leave to remind you that it was not my idea, nor was I in favour of it!' she felt constrained to point out. 'Now it appears that we are to be embroiled in yet more deceit. I shudder to think what further complications lie in store!'

'Oh, come now! Surely it cannot be beyond your powers to engage in a little harmless play-acting—you seemed ready enough to dash about the countryside in questionable and, unless I'm mistaken, *stolen* garb only yesterday!'

Tongue in cheek, he was deliberately goading her and knew he had achieved a hit with this sally when he saw her fists clench.

'I did not steal them!' she replied hotly. 'I left a guinea—far more than they were worth!' Then she realised that he was set upon teasing her, which merely increased her anger.

'That, as you perfectly well know, was quite a different matter,' she threw at him, 'and, though I *tremble* to mention it, perhaps it will be your own lack of ability that will bring about the downfall of this ill-conceived plan—especially if you persist in referring to other young ladies as ''quite the prettiest''—even if they are,' she finished lamely, scowling as Sandford laughed outright.

'Clumsy of me,' he admitted cheerfully. 'On that I stand corrected! I promise to remember that you have that honour now and, if you will only play your part with a little more conviction, I'm sure we will hold out.'

He lifted her hand and firmly placed it once more on his arm.

'Shall we say twice around the fountain, my dear? And please endeavour to keep step. I do not wish to seem to be dragging you around the gardens!'

'Then stop striding along as though you were marching to war,' she protested. 'I cannot walk at such a pace and I refuse to run alongside you. Is everything always done to your bidding?' She swiftly withdrew her hand, as he halted once more.

'You really are the most infuriating young lady I have ever come across,' he said, no longer hiding his irritation. 'And this is fast becoming a bore! Surely you must prefer to be here at Beldale rather than under some hedgerow, or worse. After all your years in the Peninsula, I need not point out what might have happened to you had someone other than myself found you on that roadside…!'

'Yes, well—I do know that and I have repeatedly told you that I am very grateful to you, but that does not give you the right to be always ordering me about. Do you never allow anyone but yourself to have an opinion or a point of view? I am not one of your infantrymen, you know!'

Sandford, highly exasperated, glared down at her.

'I am well aware of that fact,' he said drily. 'In the field one seldom has time for philosophical debate when decisions have to be made. I have learnt to deal with tricky situations in a straightforward manner, without unnecessary roundaboutation or fuss. I fail to see why you should find that so unacceptable.'

'You may make your own decisions as much as you like,' countered Harriet, her eyes kindling, 'but please do not be forever making mine!'

With which remark she turned on her heel and walked quickly back to the house, leaving Sandford wondering, in baffled uncertainty, if this scheme of his mother's was going to be such a good idea, after all.

Sighing, he watched Harriet climb the terrace steps and disappear from his view. He hoped that Lady Caroline and Judith had, by now, left the dining-room, as the girl's singular return would certainly cause a raised eyebrow if witnessed. He hesitated, and then resignedly followed after her.

The room was, in fact, empty when Harriet entered and she stood undecided for a moment, having had time to give some thought to her hasty retreat, and was just about to retrace her steps when Sandford reappeared.

'If I have offended you,' he said, stiffly correct, 'I must apologise. It was certainly not my intention to override your wishes...'

'No, sir, if you please,' Harriet intervened in breathless haste. 'The fault is mine. I—often have—difficulty in curbing my—impetuosity. Father always warned it would lead me to disaster and he was right. It so often does. I beg your pardon, my lord. I shall try to behave as you suggest.'

She looked so much like a penitent child as she stood before him with her eyes cast down that Sandford felt a sudden urge to hold her in his arms. With an effort he turned away and walked to the doorway.

'Then let us consider the subject closed,' he shot over his shoulder as he went out. It appears that the little termagant has learnt her lesson, he thought, with a slightly bemused frown, 'Perhaps we should go and join the ladies?'

Arrogant beast, thought Harriet, immediately regretting her offer of apology but, since no other course of action was open to her, she gritted her teeth and, resolving to try to be on her best behaviour, she reluctantly followed him from the room.

In spite of this somewhat inauspicious start, it did not take Harriet long to find that she really enjoyed Judith Hurst's company, although the young widow was several years older than herself. She admired Judith for the stalwart way in which she had coped at the loss of her beloved husband, remembering sadly that her own mother had not done as well in her grief. Judith seemed truly happy at the news of Sandford's impending marriage and, eager to be involved in introducing Harriet to the local society, at once offered to hold a small party at Westpark House in honour of the engagement. Since Lady Caroline felt that the earl's frail condition must restrict any immediate gathering at Beldale, she readily agreed and, having already taken Harriet's wardrobe requirements into her stride, she was satisfied that her protégée would bring nothing but credit to the family.

Sandford himself had picked out a frisky mare for his betrothed, for he was quite sure that she would be a good horsewoman after her years in Spain, and the first time he tossed her up into the saddle he was gratified to see how capably her hands controlled the prancing bay.

Harriet's eyes had lit up with joy at the sight of the mare, for she was agog to explore the grounds, having waited impatiently for her riding habit to be delivered. Madame Armande had excelled herself in the swift execution of the brandy-coloured outfit, trimmed with military frogging of gold lace down the front of the jacket, along with a pert little shako complete with its own cockade of bronze feathers. Sandford was more than satisfied with Harriet's appearance as they set out on their first visit to Westpark.

They rode through a wooded spinney along the bridleway that joined the two properties and the viscount pointed out various landmarks, which would help her should Harriet choose to visit Judith on her own. When they reached the area where his father had been thrown from his horse, Sandford related the groom's description of the accident.

'I still cannot see why he should have fallen at this spot,' he said, shaking his head. 'He is fairly lucid now and continues to maintain that something caused his horse to go down, but I have scoured the area and can find nothing untoward. He does not recollect seeing an animal on the path or hearing anyone in the vicinity, but swears that Cobalt went down all of a sudden...'

'Perhaps he got a flint in his foot?' suggested Harriet. 'I have seen horses go down in that way. And you say that Cobalt was a veteran—did he suffer from a rheumatic condition which might have caused his legs to fold?'

Sandford considered. 'Smithers didn't mention it, but it is possible.' He studied her curiously. 'You seem to know a great deal about horses,' he said.

Harriet gave a wry smile. 'For a girl, you mean. You are forgetting that I practically grew up in the cavalry,' she replied. 'Being an infantryman, you had only your own string with which to concern yourself, but we had to be horse doctors as well as soldiers, you know.'

She pulled ahead of him as the path narrowed and he was obliged, for the moment, to ride behind her in silence which, as well as preventing him from uttering an indignant rebuttal, gave him ample opportunity both to admire her straight back and elegant posture and to think better of his intended remark.

The bridleway from Beldale opened out through a wide-barred gate into a clearing and Sandford indicated the Westpark gate on the other side of the meadow.

'This is the short cut that the two families use,' he said. 'Carriages have to go round by the lane, of course, which adds five miles to the trip.'

Harriet gauged the distance across the field. 'Race you,' she offered, and was off like an arrow before he had time to reply.

'Watch out for rabbit holes!' he shouted and was after her in a trice, but she had the advantage and reached the far side ahead of him. He reined in beside her, his face wreathed in smiles. Harriet's face was bright with the exhilaration of the gallop and her green eyes were sparkling with delight as she looked at him.

'She's a beauty! Thank you so much for letting me use her,' she said, as she patted the mare's neck fondly. 'Clipper! What a fitting name for her.'

'I'm glad you approve. You ride very well—and don't say ''for a girl'', for I'm sure I don't mean to minimise your ability. Only, next time, give me fair warning before you challenge me!'

'Oh, I'd hardly take on that boy of yours in fair play,' she laughed. 'I believe in the element of surprise, your lordship. I'm amazed you never encountered the strategy in your battles!'

'Oh, I encountered it, all right, Miss Cleverboots,' he laughed, leaning down to close the gate behind them. 'Now I shall be on my guard—just make sure that you are, also!'

They rode on, side by side, exchanging similar persiflage until they eventually turned into the stableyard at Westpark House, where their horses were handed to the grooms and they entered the house by the rear doors.

'We got into the habit of doing this,' said Sandford, as he ushered Harriet through the entrance. 'Lady Butler doesn't approve, of course, but Phil and I always found it more convenient...' He paused, then continued, '...this passage leads into the main hall. The staff will already have been notified of our arrival.'

He pushed open a green baize door and nodded to the waiting footman.

'Good morning, Finchley. Mrs Hurst is expecting us. Is she in the small parlour?'

The elderly manservant nodded disapprovingly. 'Yes, my lord,' he intoned gravely, as he led the way and showed them into a cheerful sitting-room where Judith was to be found playing spillikins with her two children while her mother was half-heartedly attending to the tapestry on her fulsome lap.

At the footman's announcement, Judith rose gracefully and came towards them, hands outstretched.

'Oh, you came! I'm so pleased. Look, Mother. Robert has brought Miss Cordell to visit us—and what a stunning outfit, I do declare. Do sit down, won't you? Shall I have Finchley bring in some tea—or would you prefer coffee?'

Sandford was already engaged in the game with his niece and nephew and declined refreshment. Harriet, having accepted a glass of lemonade, seated herself opposite the elderly Lady Butler and asked her politely how she did.

'I must not complain,' said her ladyship, pulling her copious shawls about her ample shoulders more snugly, although the day was warm and humid. 'One is beset by so many aches and pains. But I have learned to bear my discomforts with fortitude.'

She leaned forward, peering closely at Harriet. 'You are very young, to be sure. Just out of the schoolroom, I suppose. Do your parents allow you to travel about the countryside without a chaperon? In my day it would have been unheard of.'

Harriet laughed. 'I am not as young as I look, ma'am,' she said, 'and I disremember ever having been in a schoolroom. And as for a chaperon, you must agree that Sandford will serve?'

The old lady sniffed. 'I'm told you met Robert while he was off fighting—a camp-follower, or some such, I hear.'

Sandford stiffened and raised his startled eyes to meet Harriet's. She, however, smiled and nodded her head at Lady Butler.

'We certainly had to follow the camp, ma'am, but we were in excellent company. Several of their lordships' wives and daughters were with us, you know, and it was not fun and frolics quite all of the time!'

The viscount's eyes gleamed with amusement, then became more serious as he intervened.

'Hardly any of the time, actually,' he said, getting up from the floor, 'and as for camp-followers, ma'am, we would have been hard pressed, at times, to manage without their assistance. I must inform you, ma'am, that Miss Cordell's father was a courageous comrade of mine and her mother was well respected for her voluntary tending of the wounded.'

'Oh, do not start to discuss these unsavoury matters again, I beg you.' Lady Butler shuddered, reaching for her vinaigrette and breathing in some of its heady contents. 'Tell me instead of your father. First we are told he is at death's door and now he is quite recovered, I hear? I would that I were blessed with such stamina! What a pity Hurst did not have his father's constitution!'

Sandford winced as he answered, 'Beldale is getting stronger by the hour. Sir Basil hopes that he will be able to come downstairs in a few days but I am afraid that he will be unable to attend Judith's party next week. *We* are looking forward to it, of course,' he finished, gamely attempting a show of enthusiasm.

'Well, it will be a great deal of trouble to arrange, you know, at such short notice, but I am sure we shall try to put on a creditable show. Why it cannot have waited until Lady Caroline could see to it herself, I cannot imagine.'

She folded her untouched Berlin-work and rose to her feet.

'Now, if you will excuse me, I suppose I must see Mrs Walters about the menus.' She trod majestically across the room and left.

There was a moment's silence then Judith laughed, a little self-consciously.

'I hope she does not do such a thing! Mrs Walters would faint from astonishment! Take no notice, Robert, dear. You know how Mama is. I am sure that she means no harm.'

Sandford doubted this, but let it go. 'If this party affair is going to cause you a lot of trouble…' he said hopefully, but Judith looked shocked.

'Trouble? I'm looking forward to it. I have been in mourning for a whole year now, Robert, and this is the first time we will have had any sort of gathering at Westpark since Philip's—funeral—and you know he would not have wanted it so!'

Gathering up the skirts of her black bombazine gown, she began to pirouette around the room, much to little Elspeth's delight.

'Shall we have dancing, do you think? A few country reels, perhaps?' She stopped, flushed prettily and sat down once more beside Harriet. 'What shall you wear, Miss Cordell—oh! Do say I may call you Harriet! I have a gown I have never yet worn. I think it may be just the occasion to bring it out!'

Having only recently come out of mourning herself, Harriet could sympathise with the young widow's feelings and, happy to defer to her hostess's obvious knowledge of what was fashionable and what was not, she was quite amenable to hear Judith's suggestions. She could see that Sandford seemed perfectly content to be entertained by the two children. He pored over Christopher's snail-shell collection with apparent fascination and even helped his little niece to fasten a miniature cape around her beloved doll, with no sign of the self-conscious reticence she expected from most members of his sex when confronted with young children. She noticed, too, that Judith was viewing the scene with a certain fondness and wondered if, perhaps, her own unexpected appearance had interrupted a blossoming relationship between Sandford and his sister-in-law. Judith's words, however, dispelled that thought.

'He is so like Philip,' she said tremulously, bright tears shining in her eyes. 'They do miss him so. Robert has been absolutely marvellous with them and given them so much of his time.'

'I'm sure he loves them dearly.' Harriet laid her hand on Judith's. 'And who would not. They are such sweetly behaved children. Lady Caroline has said that they are a credit to both their parents. She dotes on Elspeth, as you must know.'

Judith nodded, composing herself. 'We were very happy together, Philip and I. I do so wish the same joy for you and Robert. I was afraid he would never meet anyone. He was always so involved with his regiment that it seemed to me that he had no sort of social life at all. You should have known him when he was a boy—he was quite the young tearaway!'

'Do I hear my character being demolished over there?' came Sandford's amused voice. 'I hope you are not about to apprise Miss Cordell of my youthful misdemeanours, Judith. I have worked very hard to gain her approbation, I assure you, and if you are set on ruining all my efforts...'

Both ladies burst out laughing and, seeing Sandford reach for his hat and gloves, Judith rose to see them to the door. Elspeth curtsied shyly to Harriet while Christopher begged his uncle to 'come again soon'. The viscount assured him that he would be over to take him riding the following day and the little boy was allowed to lead the visitors back to the rear exit.

'Grandmama says you shouldn't use this door,' he confided, as they walked out into the stableyard, 'but

Papa and I always did and, as I am now the man of this house, I give you both my permission.'

Sandford took his nephew's proffered hand and inclined his head. 'We are pleased to be so honoured, Christopher,' he said gravely.

Harriet nodded smilingly, adding, 'And thank you for including me.'

The little boy was puzzled. 'But you are to be one of the family now, aren't you? Mama said...' He looked from one to the other.

Sandford laughed and clapped him gently on the shoulder. 'Absolutely right, dear fellow!' he breezed. 'And do you approve of your new aunt? She's a cracking good rider, let me tell you!'

Christopher was suitably impressed. In his opinion girls couldn't really ride, having such stupid saddles to contend with but, if his Uncle Robert said his fiancée was good then, by golly, she must be and that made her fine by him. He watched as Sandford helped Harriet mount, then ran, waving farewell to them as they rode off.

'They are such lovely people—your brother's family,' commented Harriet, as they crossed the meadow to the Beldale estate. 'What a terrible tragedy that he will never see his children grow up. Judith has been so brave in her loss. Am I correct in thinking that Lady Butler cannot have been much help or comfort at the time?'

'None at all, I understand from my mother. She took to her bed with ''the vapours'', which caused poor Judith even more distress and then she had the gall to preside over the funeral reception wearing black veils and so on. We have very little affection for her, I fear, but she is Judith's mother and grandmother to Philip's children so one must endure her remarks. I have to congratulate you on your forbearance. Another of your famous strategies, I deduce?'

'Just ''getting over the heavy ground as lightly as possible'' as they used to say,' said Harriet, her face wreathed in smiles at his compliment.

'A veritable fund of manoeuvres! I can see I shall have to be careful not to join battle with you,' he chaffed laughingly.

Fencing companionably in this manner, they rode on for some minutes until a shout from the trees caused them to turn their heads. A horseman appeared on the track ahead of them and a cheerful voice called, 'Home then, Sandford? I'm very glad to see you back. And with a betrothal, I hear. Do I get an introduction?'

The rider was a comely, well-built man dressed in leather jerkin and riding breeches. Sandford greeted him with pleasure and presented him to Harriet as his cousin, Charles Ridgeway.

Ridgeway, as Harriet had already learned from her conversations with Lady Caroline, was estate manager of both Westpark House and Beldale. He lived with his mother, the earl's sister, in the Dower House of the Beldale estate, his own family residence having been sold off many years ago to meet his impecunious father's debts. Baron Ridgeway, having gambled away his wife's fortune, had finally taken his own life when his son was still a schoolboy, leaving them both penniless and, eventually, homeless had it not been for her brother's affection and generosity. The earl had given his sister, Lady Eugenie, lifetime tenancy of the Dower House, along with a generous annuity, as well as funding his nephew's remaining education. When Charles had expressed an interest in land management the earl had arranged for him to work alongside Baxter, his own elderly manager and, upon that worthy's retirement, had handed the office to his nephew. Philip Hurst had also trusted Ridgeway's judgement and had offered his cousin the same post at Westpark. The twins had grown up alongside Charles, of course, he being some six or seven years their senior. He had never married and, although both Sandford and his brother had frequently maintained that Judith Butler had always been the object of his youthful affection, he had never once, during all the years of his employment, treated her with anything but gentle courtesy and respect. After Philip's carriage accident Ridgeway had taken on without complaint the extra load his young master's death had inevitably caused and now, with the earl himself indisposed, his working days were longer still and he was not sorry to see Sandford home again.

'Your servant, ma'am,' he said, smiling as he bent over her hand. 'You will not regret your choice of husband. After his father, Sandford is the finest man I know.'

'Steady on, old chap!' Sandford protested. 'Not quite in the old man's league, I fear!'

'True,' acknowledged his cousin, laughing, 'but you are getting there. I have heard about some of your exploits in Spain, you know, in spite of your efforts to keep them secret. Jimmy Braithwaite's boys came home last month and were full of stories they had heard about you.'

'Mostly exaggerated and of no account, I assure you! These things tend to get blown up out of all proportion. I only did what other fellows were doing all around me.'

'And that was hardly of no account!' interjected Harriet hotly. 'His lordship's exploits were well known when I myself was out there, Mr Ridgeway, so allow me to vouch for the truth of the stories!'

Charles Ridgeway laughed. 'Well, Robert, it's clear that your young lady will defend your achievements for you, however much you care to deny them—which is just as it should be, of course.' He wheeled his horse round and turned to go. 'When you can spare an hour—I must talk to you about the bottom fences. They need replacing—oh!—and Potter's cottage caught fire last week. He's staying with his daughter at the moment, but we really need to discuss the whole row—when you're ready, of course.' He saluted them both with his crop and cantered back into the spinney.

Sandford waited until his cousin was out of sight before turning his head to Harriet.

'Whilst I recognise your need to defend our military exploits, Miss Cordell,' he said, as they continued along the bridleway, 'I feel I must point out to you that most of our countrymen have no real comprehension of what went on over there. I, myself, have increasingly found that is not a popular topic in polite society and you have already seen how eager certain people might be to place the wrong interpretation on your presence in the train. I would not want you to be embarrassed...'

'Oh, pooh to such people!' interrupted Harriet. 'You cannot think that I am ashamed to have been with the army! You, of all people! You know that most of the women were wives of the soldiers and spent their time cooking and foraging for their menfolk. The few others I saw were usually local girls and *very* choosy, so I'm told!'

Sandford raised his brows, stifling his laughter. 'You shouldn't have been told any such thing. I'm surprised your mother allowed such a conversation.'

'Oh, don't be so stuffy! When we were surrounded by death and injury! Some of the men behaved appallingly, it's true, but hadn't they good reason, at times? Papa never condoned their behaviour when they went to extremes, but he did understand the cause. Most of them will never come home,' she finished sadly.

'Nevertheless,' counselled the viscount, after a pause, 'none of this is deemed to be a fitting subject for polite conversation and I must recommend that you endeavour to steer clear of it, if at all possible.'

He had not enjoyed listening to Lady Butler's attempts at giving Harriet one of her infamous setdowns, especially as the girl had won the field on this occasion. From past experience he knew that the older woman would try to find new ways of discomfiting her because there were few things she enjoyed more. Judith's party would provide Lady Butler with an excellent opportunity, he reasoned, and was determined to do his best to safeguard Harriet against public calumny.

'As you wish, my lord,' said Harriet in a small voice, her shoulders drooping. What a pompous prig the hero had turned out to be, she thought in dismay, and wondered if, after all, some of the tales of his exploits had been embellished.

They rode in silence once more, each absorbed in private reflections and, upon entering the house, Sandford excused himself from Harriet, saying that he would go straight up to his father before changing.

Harriet went to her own room where Rose was waiting to help her undress. The girl had laid out one of the new dresses, which had been delivered during her mistress's absence, and Harriet was delighted with the pretty, soft green muslin, its short puffed sleeves just right for the warm afternoon. Rose tied the matching sash high above her young mistress's waist, as was the prevailing fashion, and adjusted the tiny frill that edged the low neckline.

'I hear tell that some of the young ladies do damp their dresses to make them cling to their bodies!' she marvelled, as she knelt to tie the strings on Harriet's slippers. 'And they don't always wear a petticoat either!'

'I don't think I should care for such a fashion.' Harriet assured her. 'This dress is very pretty as it is, don't you think? Is there an evening gown amongst the others? Madame said that it would be ready in time for Mrs Hurst's party.'

Rose showed her the rest of the deliveries, which did, indeed, include the gown for Judith's party. This was a simple but elegant tunic in a sea-green shot silk, which was to be worn over a white satin slip. Harriet's eyes shone with delight when she saw it, immediately taken with its clean-cut shaping, for she was not a girl who cared for too many frills and flounces in her clothes.

'There's slippers to match too, miss,' Rose indicated. ''Tis a pity that you had to leave your jewel-case behind, for a necklace would make all the difference.'

Harriet did not reply. She was beginning to feel somewhat concerned about her increasing indebtedness to her hosts and wondered when she would be in a position to repay them. She hoped that her grandfather would soon be in touch with instructions for her to be sent to him at once as she was still most uncomfortable about the role she had agreed to undertake. A lot of good people were being deceived, she reflected, and was sorry that Judith and her children should be amongst these for she felt that she could easily become very fond of them. Even Sandford's company was surprisingly bearable when he refrained from telling her what she could or could not do, she mused, and she was smiling at the memory of the cheerful raillery they had exchanged during their morning ride when there came a tap at the door.

'His lordship wishes to speak to Miss Cordell if she could spare him a moment.'

Harriet heard March deliver his message and rose at once to her feet. Now what had she done? she wondered, casting about in her mind for possible aberrations as she hurried downstairs to find the viscount waiting in the small salon.

'How very prompt,' he said, surprising her by turning with a smile as she entered. 'Father has expressed a desire to meet you—he knows your story, of course, and he also knew your grandparents in his youth. Do you feel up to it?' He looked at her anxiously.

'But, of course.' Harriet's eyes sparkled. 'I'd love to meet Lord William. Are you sure he is well enough for a visitor?'

'He maintains that he is well enough to look at a pretty face,' Sandford said cheerfully, as they made their way upstairs. 'He is keen to see if Mother's description of your likeness to your grandmother is justified.'

At Sandford's gentle scratch, Chegwin opened the door of the Earl's chamber and placed his finger against his lips to urge their silence.

'His lordship has fallen asleep again, sir,' he whispered, as he ushered them to his master's bedside. 'But he left instructions that you were to remain until he awakes—he drowses off on account of the medicine, but seems anxious to speak with you, my lord.'

His eyes were troubled as they fixed upon the earl's sleeping form. Harriet, too, stared concernedly at the pale and lined features of the white-haired old man in the bed.

Sandford led her to a chair by the bedside and seated himself opposite. Together they watched the shallow but steady rise and fall of the bedcovers at the earl's chest. Harriet felt unaccountable tears pricking her eye-lids as she studied the viscount's father. How alike they are, she thought in a flash; the same aristocratic bone structure, straight nose, high cheekbones, firm chin—even in repose. Were his eyes that same clear grey? she wondered, and almost jumped out of her skin when, as if in answer to her question, Beldale's eyes opened and were staring at her intently.

'Don't weep, girl, I'm not gone yet,' came a gruff voice and a hand crept out of the covers to take hers. She held it firmly between both her own and smiled, a gentle flush staining her cheeks.

'And very pleased I am to hear it, sir,' she replied softly. 'Did we disturb you?'

'No, my dear, I was waiting for you, but this infernal laudanum keeps dragging me off to sleep—do better without it.' He glared balefully at his manservant, who regarded him fondly in return.

'Bring a light, man. I want to see the girl properly!'

Although it was daylight the heavy curtains were drawn to keep out the sunshine, making the room quite dark. Chegwin lifted a branch from the dresser and held it aloft so that Harriet's face was bathed in its pool of candlelight. The old man contemplated her steadily for several minutes, his eyes faded but indubitably grey, and she felt no embarrassment at his scrutiny.

Sandford grinned, feeling a surge of respect at such composure. 'Well, sir? And do you approve?'

Beldale gently squeezed Harriet's hand. 'Very fetch-ing, my boy,' he said. 'Your mama was right—image of her grandmother—glad you found her, Sandford—

made her ladyship very happy.' His voice faded, then his eyes flashed wide open once more. 'Keep your guard up, Robert—just remembered—something—happened...' His head drooped back on to the pillows and Sandford started up in alarm, but Chegwin put his hand on the viscount's arm and steadied him.

'He's all right, sir,' he said. 'Keeps dropping off like that. Needs the stuff for the pain, you see. Leave him to me, if you please, sir—and ma'am.'

He bowed towards Harriet who, seeing Sandford's agitation, had immediately risen from her own chair but, at the sight of the tears in his eyes, had swiftly bent to tidy the covers over Beldale's recumbent form.

'I know you'll take good care of him, Chegwin.' Sandford's voice held a tremor but, straightening his shoulders, he held out his hand to Harriet and escorted her from the room.

Downstairs, Lady Caroline was waiting in the small dining-room as the dishes were being brought in. They took their places at the table and she signalled to Rothman to begin serving.

'His lordship seems so much better, don't you agree?' she applied hopefully to her son. 'Sir Basil thinks to reduce the medication tomorrow—it has been over a week since his fall.'

Sandford nodded. 'He will be relieved to be off the drug—he dislikes taking it, I know. It seems to make him ramble somewhat, too. I remember having to take it myself on one occasion and had the most awful hallucinations. I'm sure he will be better without it.'

The meal progressed through the various courses, during which Lady Caroline, eyes twinkling at her son, inquired as to the success of their visit to Westpark. Harriet, after describing Judith's plans for the forthcoming assembly, thanked the countess for the garments that had been delivered in their absence, expressing her particular delight with the green silk gown intended for the party and it was in a happy, friendly mood that they all repaired to the salon afterwards, with Sandford opting to take his brandy with the ladies and the evening being rounded off with some rousing games of piquet.

The following day the viscount rode over to Westpark, as he had promised, to take his nephew out riding. Harriet spent part of the morning with the earl, at his request. He was more lucid than he had been on her previous visit and had expressed a desire to hear her story first-hand. He, in turn, was able to tell her more of her family's history and Chegwin was very satisfied to hear, more than once, the sounds of stifled laughter issuing from his master's bedside.

When Harriet rose to leave, having judged that his lordship was beginning to tire, the manservant accompanied her to the door with a smile, saying, 'This has done him a deal of good, miss, if I may say so. He will sleep naturally this afternoon, I feel sure.'

Finding that Lady Caroline was engaged with the housekeeper, Harriet decided to take herself for a walk down to the lakeside, where she hoped that the air would be fresher. The day was warm and very humid and, having been cooped up in Lord William's darkened rooms for some time, she felt that she needed the exercise. She walked sedately across the sweeping stretches of the rear lawns until she was sure she was out of sight of the windows then, running and skipping with pleasure, she reached the waterside.

The lake had been sunk many years previously and its banks were quite steep in parts. Both willow and aspen straddled the water's edge and bulrushes grew in profusion. A small pavilion was situated on an island in the middle of the lake. This was reached, as far as Harriet could tell, by the rowing-boat that she could see tied up outside a boathouse on the far side of the lake and she began to make her way towards it along the path, which meandered around the lake.

Now shaded from the sun by the leafy branches of the trees on both sides of the path, she felt much cooler. Smiling at the sight of the mallard duck leading her almost-grown brood in stately procession across the water, she frequently strayed to investigate the various splashings and rustlings of other small water creatures exploring their habitat. These delays caused her to take much longer than she had intended but, when she eventually arrived at the boathouse, she was still determined to take just a little peek at the pavilion, judging that it would not take her many minutes to row the short distance to the island. She checked that the oars were in place and was beginning to untie the mooring-rope when she heard a cry. Startled, she looked around, fearing that she had, once more, broken some unwritten rule. The cry was repeated, this time louder and she realised that it was a cry of distress.

Someone was calling for help. Her eyes scoured the water and the banks, trying to identify the place from which the sound had come. Then she saw. A small boy, up to his waist in the water, was clinging to the roots of a willow tree that grew at the water's edge. Picking up her skirts, she ran quickly along the path to the spot. She could see that the bank sloped steeply down into the murky water, which was thick with weeds. She could not tell how deep the water was at that point, but did not stop to consider it. Crawling on her knees, she edged her way downwards, stretching out a hand towards the grimy lad.

'Reach forward,' she said. 'See if you can take my hand.'

'Oh, miss—miss—I can't do it,' came the wailing reply. 'I'm stuck fast in the mud.'

Harriet slithered further down, her hands on the roots of the tree and grabbed at the boy's wrist. He suddenly jerked back and pulled himself away and, to her horror, disappeared beneath the surface. Scrabbling to regain her balance, she felt her body sliding sideways down the bank and, although she managed to keep hold of the tree root, she found herself up to her knees in the mud. Frantically, she looked about her for the child, who was nowhere to be seen, but a sudden sound from the water's edge some distance to her right alerted her to the astonishing sight of a small, bedraggled figure climbing out of the lake and disappearing into the bushes.

'What on earth...!' Harriet exclaimed in rage, as she struggled to free herself, but, upon finding that her feeble attempts had merely caused her to lose one of her slippers, she held still and tried to apply her mind to her situation. Her feet were on firm enough ground as far as she could tell, but she could see nothing within her reach that would help her to extricate her legs from the mud's tenacious grasp. She was eyeing the thin root she had managed to keep hold of, weighing up its ability to take any strain, when to her dismay she heard the sound of approaching hooves and then the unwelcome sight of the rider, Sandford himself, appeared on the path. He could not fail to observe her.

'Good God!' he exclaimed, reining in and leaping from his mount. 'How has this happened? Here, take my hand...' and, leaning his weight against the boll of the tree, he effortlessly hoisted Harriet to firm ground. She ignored the glimmer of laughter in his eyes as she tried, ineffectually, to sweep away the thick black mud from her clinging skirt.

'You just can't stay out of mischief, can you?' he said, his grin widening.

'This was not my doing,' she said crossly. 'Someone pulled me in. There was a young boy—I thought he was in trouble—but I slipped and he—he swam off and left me.'

Sandford regarded her with unconcealed amazement. 'A boy? What boy?' he said, looking about him.

Harriet stamped her unshod and mud-encrusted foot. 'How dare you disbelieve me!' she stormed. 'I am not in the habit of telling lies! There *was* a boy, I tell you!'

Tears of fury began to prick her eyes, but she blinked them away and struck out at him with her muddied fists. He backed away quickly before she could touch him.

'Whoa! Steady, there!' He looked at her uncertainly. 'We'd better get you back to the house before anyone sees you like that. Are you cold?'

Harriet shook her head, wearily controlling herself. 'No, thank you. I will soon dry in the sun but—I have lost a slipper and it is a long walk back.'

'I'm sure Pagan can cope,' Sandford rejoined. Pulling a rolled-up blanket from his pannier, he wrapped it around her muddied skirts and proceeded to lift her effortlessly on to his saddle.

How tiny her waist is, he marvelled, holding her steadily as she attempted to find her balance. His senses quickened as he felt the vibrant warmth of her body through the thin muslin fabric. Warning signs immediately flashed in his brain. Abruptly, he withdrew his hold.

'All set?' he asked, with apparent cheerful unconcern. 'See if you can steady yourself against the pommel. Hang on to Pagan's mane.'

Harriet complied with his instructions in silence. Assuming that the viscount would climb up behind her, a mounting sensation of breathless confusion gripped her at the thought of the necessarily close physical contact.

Sandford had intended to ride with her but, for some unfathomable reason, now found that he was unable to trust himself with her tantalising nearness. He hesitated momentarily, then gathered the horse's reins in his hands. 'I'll lead him in,' he said, still feeling somewhat shaken. With a slight frown on his face he started back towards the house.

Harriet registered his hesitation and her heart seemed to shrivel, overwhelmed by feelings of humiliation and rejection. With difficulty she repressed these emotions as she tried to apply her concentration to keeping her seat and her replies to Sandford's searching questions became curt and, for the most part, monosyllabic.

Sandford led his horse into the stableyard and Tiptree came running at the sound of his master's voice. His eyebrows shot up at the sight of the dishevelled figure being helped down from Sandford's mount, but he said nothing as he took the reins and the mud-stained blanket from the viscount.

'Don't put him away,' Sandford instructed. 'I shall need him again. Get Thunder saddled for yourself. I'll be back presently.' He escorted Harriet through the rear of the house to the foot of the staff staircase.

'Come up this way,' he said. 'The kitchen staff will be at lunch. I'll head off anyone who appears.'

Harriet reached her room unobserved and, as soon as she had closed the door behind her, she slumped down on to the nearest chair, regardless of the mess she was making, for she was utterly chagrined. What else could go wrong? she wondered. The morning had started so well and she had enjoyed her time with Beldale. The lakeside walk had been so pleasant until that incident. A puzzled frown creased her forehead. What was the meaning of it? It was no accident, of that she was convinced, but could see no point in what had occurred. Just a malicious prank? But, to what purpose? And, more infuriating, why had Sandford dismissed her story out of hand? Oh, if only her grandfather would reply to Lady Caroline's letter! Harriet felt that she could no longer remain at Beldale under such a cloud and wondered if she could confide her troubles to Judith Hurst. In spite of Sandford's instructions she was tempted to ask her new friend's advice should a suitable opportunity arise.

During the next few days Harriet did her utmost to avoid Sandford's company. She spent much of her time with the earl, who enjoyed her pretty attentions and was making steady progress towards a full recovery. She managed to take one or two rides about the park and to visit Judith, but only when she was sure that Sandford was elsewhere. She was obliged to take her meals with him, of course, but made sure she had a fund of Lord William's stories to relate to the countess so that it became unnecessary to hold a separate conversation with the viscount. Sandford himself appeared not to notice her evasive behaviour and, in any event, always seemed deeply preoccupied with estate business. To Harriet's relief, he made no further reference to the lake incident. Harriet had decided not to tell her hostess the full story of her misadventure, merely saying that she had slipped on the bank whilst trying to untie the boat. Lady Caroline had, at first, been rather shocked that Harriet had not asked a manservant to row her to the pavilion, then she had laughed and said, 'You modern young ladies! You have so much more free-

dom than we did in my day. I envy you, I do truly!'
And the matter was forgotten.

At last the letter for which Harriet had been praying
arrived. Rothman delivered it to her ladyship at the
breakfast-table and the countess broke open the seal
eagerly.

'How quickly he has replied,' she said, as she
scanned the contents. 'Yes, he says he has written at
once—you are to remain with us—he is actually coming to fetch you himself! He says he is overjoyed—
and forever in our debt—what nonsense—but how
sweet! Oh, my dear! Your troubles will soon be over!'
She placed the missive into Harriet's trembling hand.
'There, my child. You may read it for yourself. Your
grandfather will be with us in no time at all if all goes
well with his travel arrangements,' and, turning to
Sandford, she said, 'Isn't this happy news, Robert?
Ramsey will surely come to his granddaughter's rescue
now that he knows her whereabouts, don't you think?'

Sandford nodded, but did not reply. He felt a sudden
lowering of spirit for which he could not account and
stared moodily across the table at Harriet, but she was
still deeply engrossed in her grandfather's words. Ex-
cusing himself, he quickly finished his coffee and left
the room.

'We must go and tell Beldale the good news,' said
the countess. 'He will be so happy for you—and glad
to see Ramsey again, I dare say—if only to compare
the wrinkles!'

Harriet laughed joyfully. She was feeling euphoric, hardly believing that her dream was finally about to become a reality. How long would it take her grandfather to travel to Beldale? Two weeks, perhaps. She could surely hold out until then, now that she knew he was actually coming. Then she was struck by a sudden thought.

'But—Judith's party?' she inquired of the Countess. 'We must inform her before it is too late to cancel. It will not be necessary to pretend an engagement now, surely?'

Lady Caroline hesitated on the stairway, considering the problem.

'On balance, my dear,' she said at last, 'I think it would be wiser to wait until your grandfather arrives— supposing he were delayed? Remember that we conjured up the plan in order to prevent unsavoury gossip. It is still the best protection we can offer you until he comes. Judith's guests will have seen the notice in the *Mercury* and it will not do to start up a hive of speculation so soon after the announcement. Don't worry, dear child. It's only a small local party, after all.'

And with this she continued up the stairs.

Harriet was perturbed, but did not mention the subject again. She knew that the countess had gone to considerable trouble to keep other members of the family away from Beldale House, using Lord William's indisposition as an excuse even to her own two daughters, who had been besieging her with requests to visit their father. Harriet had been relieved to learn that she was not expected to come under Sandford's sisters' scrutiny, as she doubted that her acting ability would pass muster under such close inspection. Casual observation by a few local families at a small houseparty would be much less of a trial, she decided. She determined to put away her fears and do her best to look forward to the forthcoming assembly, reasoning that Sandford was unlikely to accord her anything other than the devoted attentions of the newly engaged man he was supposed to be, especially since the plan seemed to have been concocted with his approval. After that, as far as she was concerned, he could please himself!

Chapter Four

Sandford stood at the entrance to the Dower House with a frown on his face. He was not looking forward to confronting his aunt with his discovery and, on being shown into Lady Eugenie's morning room, he saw that his cousin Ridgeway was also present and resigned himself to an uncomfortable few moments.

Ridgeway saluted him from his seat at the desk and Lady Eugenie smiled at him in welcome.

'Why, Robert,' she said, holding out her hand for his kiss. 'This is indeed a pleasant surprise—but your father—' her voice grew anxious '—he has not taken a turn for the worse?'

The tiny, birdlike Lady Eugenie was a sweet and gentle soul who had suffered a very unhappy marriage to a man who had married her only for her considerable dowry and name. He had treated her monstrously, flaunting both debts and mistresses with total disregard for her sensitivities. When he had finally taken his life she had felt nothing but relief and had dedicated the succeeding thirty years to charitable works. Her brother's pensioner, she had no money of her own, but gave her time unstintingly to any deserving organisation that approached her, from orphans' relief to support for fallen women. The meagre staff she employed at the Dower House consisted entirely of waifs and outcasts rescued from disaster by her ladyship. Ridgeway jokingly predicted that they would one day be found murdered in their beds but, secretly, he was immensely proud of his mother's achievements and her entire household was devoted to both the baroness and her son.

Sandford, having assured his aunt of the earl's continued improvement, stood undecided momentarily, abstractedly tapping his crop against his boot.

Ridgeway, attending to some paperwork, raised his head at the sound and looked at Sandford curiously.

'Problem, coz?' he asked cheerfully.

The viscount nodded. 'Rather tricky, Charles, actually.'

Ridgeway's face grew serious and he rose at once to his feet. 'Let's have it then, Robert—and for goodness sake, sit down. If it's not Uncle Will, what's the trouble?'

Sandford cleared his throat and turned to his aunt with a troubled look. 'It's one of your boys, Aunt Eugenie—he seems to have been up to mischief.'

Ridgeway laughed and his mother's pensive frown vanished immediately.

'The young scamps are always up to something, Robert,' said his cousin. 'Stealing apples, I suppose? You'd think we didn't feed them...' He stopped as Sandford shook his head.

'Fact is, Charles,' he said brusquely, 'two days ago one of them pulled Miss Cordell into the lake and swam off!'

His aunt gasped and put her hand to her throat while Ridgeway started in disbelief.

'You can't mean it, man! Let's have the whole, if you please!'

Sandford related Harriet's tale briefly, then went on to describe how he and Tiptree had scoured the lake area for the culprit, without success. He had then extended his search into the village where every boy of relevant age had been questioned thoroughly.

'I admit I was at point non plus,' he confessed wryly, 'until Tip brought me word that old Mrs Jennings remembered having seen one of your young imps scrambling through our hedge with his clothes soaking wet. She supposed he had been messing about in the lake and thought no more about it. I'm sorry, Aunt Eugenie,' he finished awkwardly, 'but I'm afraid I'll have to follow it up.'

His aunt looked helplessly towards her son, who nodded briskly at Sandford.

'Right, man,' he said. 'Let's get at it.'

Turning to his mother as they left the room, he said, 'Don't worry, Ma. I'll sort it out. It'll be one of Sukey Tatler's young 'uns—you mark my words.'

He led Sandford down the back stairs to the kitchens where a group of Lady Eugenie's reclaimed streetwalkers were to be found chattering merrily as they went about their work. They immediately fell silent at the sight of the two intruders to their domain.

Ridgeway sought out the young woman he had named and beckoned her to the doorway. 'Come outside, Sukey, his lordship wants a word with you.'

Eyes full of foreboding, the young woman complied, while the rest of the group stood looking at one another in consternation. Grateful to have been rescued from the awful poverty and degradation of their former existence, they still lived with the constant fear of being rejected and returned to their old haunts. They idolised their benefactress with unalloyed reverence for her part in their salvation, but were generally resigned to the fact that life had a habit of delivering the most crushing blows when one least suspected them.

Ridgeway ushered the scullery-maid out into the yard.

'Do you know where Billy is?' he asked her gently. 'His lordship needs to speak to him.'

Sukey shook her head.

'Don't never know where 'e is, guv,' she said tremulously. 'But 'e'll be 'ome for supper, that's fer sure. What's 'e done this time, guv?'

'Something very serious, I'm afraid, Sukey,' said Ridgeway.

The woman's face was filled with fear.

'You ain't gonna send us back, guv?' she pleaded. 'I'll skelp 'is 'ide, I swear to God!'

'I hope it won't come to that,' Sandford intervened. 'I have a feeling that he isn't entirely to blame. Do you know who his friends are?'

Getting no further help from the boy's mother, they sent her back to the kitchen where she was at once surrounded by her peers demanding to know whether they were all about to lose their places.

'I'll send one of the men to look for him,' offered Ridgeway. 'If he comes back and hears you were after him, he'll make himself scarce. We need to find out why he did it. Someone must have put him up to it—it makes no sense.'

Sandford agreed with his cousin and reluctantly left the matter in his hands for the time being, but insisted on being notified as soon as the boy was found. He asked Ridgeway to give his regards to Lady Eugenie and took his leave.

Riding back across the fields to Beldale he attempted, for the umpteenth time, to analyse his own turbulent emotions in what he hoped was an objective manner. It had now reached the point where he found himself increasingly reluctant to venture into any of the rooms in his own home for fear of encountering Harriet's stony expression! He was beginning to find it almost impossible to deal with her continued indifference towards him. He had pretended not to notice, of course, and had done his best to stay out of her way while trying to clear up the matter of the missing boy. He was furious with himself for having, apparently, given her the impression that he thought she had been lying, for no such consideration had entered his mind. He had simply been utterly taken aback that such a thing could happen on Beldale lands and had, subsequently, left no stone unturned in his efforts to find the culprit. His constant spur had been the thought of restoring that winsome smile to Harriet's face, but he was still no nearer to any solution and the prospect of another long and wretched evening loomed before him.

He entered the hallway just as the countess was ushering Harriet into the estate office and, as he made for the stairs, he breathed a sigh of relief that at least he would not be called upon to suffer that cool, disdainful gaze in the immediate future.

'Harriet has visitors, my dear,' said his mother, over her shoulder. 'Are you going up to your father? I will join you when I have finished here.'

Sandford frowned as he climbed the stairs, curious as to the identity of Harriet's visitors and wondering why they should be ensconced in the office, which was normally reserved for estate matters. His throat tightened as he considered the prospect of her leaving Beldale sooner than anticipated.

Harriet was also in some apprehension as to who her visitors could possibly be but the initial look of puzzlement was wiped from her face in a flash as she beheld the stocky figure before her and, rushing forward in delight, she threw herself at him crying, 'Ozzy! Oh, Ozzy!—how on earth did you find me?'

Ex-Sergeant Jeremiah Osborne, late of the 67th Cavalry and her father's one-time batman, took her hands in his and shook his head at her behaviour.

'Now then, Miss Harry, a little more conduct, if you please! What would my Martha say—let alone your mama? Did they teach you to be a hoyden, I wonder?'

He grinned as he spoke and her eyes sparkled in return as she took the seat that Lady Caroline had motioned her into. Standing proudly erect in military manner, the old soldier looked to Harriet exactly as he had done on that day, two years previously when, hard upon her family's disembarkation, he and his wife had decided to part company with them to start a new life of their own.

Harriet turned from Osborne to the countess, who had been smiling at the interchange.

'I don't understand, ma'am,' she said carefully. 'I thought you said a messenger from my mama...?'

Lady Caroline patted her hand and waved Osborne to a chair as she herself sat down at the desk.

'Perhaps we should allow Mr Osborne to relate his own tale, my dear,' she said gently and, nodding to Osborne, 'Please be so good as to begin.'

'Well, my lady, as I was telling you earlier—' Osborne leaned forward, clasping his hands together between his knees '—after we left the family at Dover, Martha—my wife—and I went on to Hampshire, where we'd heard of a little inn we might fancy—you know we'd been keen to try it, Miss Harry...?'

He wagged his bushy head at her and she nodded, hardly able to contain her impatience as he continued with his tale. The inn, it seemed, had been a success and Ozzy and Martha were in a fair way to being quite prosperous and had lately decided to take a much-deserved break, having promised themselves a visit to their old master and mistress as soon as they could manage it.

'We wanted to give you a surprise, you see, but—it was us that got the surprise—or, shock, more like. We only got as far as the Partridge—the village inn, my lady—and the tongues were wagging fit to drop off. Miss Harriet was gone and worse, as far as I was concerned, the Major was dead and Lady Cordell had up and married her next-door neighbour.'

He brushed his hand across his eyes to conceal his emotions, cleared his throat and resumed. 'But I had to go up to the house to see for myself—and what a change I did find in the mistress—her once so brave and feisty! I never knew anything to faze her the whole time we was out there, Miss Harry.'

Tears had started in Harriet's own eyes as she answered him.

'I know, Ozzy. It was Papa dying, you see. It threw her right off balance and it seemed that she couldn't cope with anything at all. That's how she came to marry Sir Chester—for he somehow seemed to take over, dealing with the funeral arrangements, and Mama allowed him to ferret through our papers and all sorts of things. Afterwards, it was very easy for him to persuade her into marrying him. She was just so unhappy and lacked interest in everything. It wasn't until he had moved us up to the Hall that all became clear. He had enormous debts and he was absolutely furious when he found that I would inherit and not Mama. He accused her of trickery, would you believe? Then he started on this plan for marrying me off to his odious son—Mama wouldn't have it, of course, but he made her life unbearable as a result and I could tell he was beginning to wear her down. Then, when I overheard him talking to the ghastly Gilbert—and it appeared that they were planning some sort of abduction—they intended to trap me into marriage—I left a note for Mama telling her I was going to find my grandfather—then—I just left!'

There was a moment's silence. Osborne shook his head and sighed as the countess gave Harriet a little smile of sympathy.

'Don't fret yourself, my dear,' she said gently. 'You will come about, believe me. Lord Ramsey will take care of everything, I feel sure.'

'I am hoping so, ma'am,' Harriet said dispiritedly. 'If only he could come more quickly. You have been very good, your ladyship, but I wish that I, myself, could do something more useful on my own behalf.'

Turning to Osborne, she asked anxiously. 'And you did not see Mama at all?'

'Oh, yes, my pretty, I did that. I crept round to the gardens and gave her the shock of her life, I can tell you! But she was real glad to see me and wanting to hear all my news. We even had some laughs over old times but, as you've said, she wasn't herself although she did tell me much of the tale. Apparently Middleton got hold of your note and had the stagecoach lists checked at both the Lincoln and Grantham offices and your mama was mighty worried until she saw the announcement of your betrothal in the *Post* because she knew then that you were quite safe—and, although it was no easy matter for her to write a letter for me to deliver—here I am, at your service, as you might say. And I also have to tell you that my Martha is a-waiting in your housekeeper's room—fretting herself to bits, no doubt!'

Lady Caroline stood up and motioned to Harriet to remain seated.

'I must go and acquaint his lordship with this news. Robert is with him and I can as easily tell both together. You will want to have more conversation with your old comrades-in-arms. You may use the small parlour—I will instruct Rothman to have some luncheon sent up. Now, pray, excuse me.'

She swept out of the room with a smile for Harriet and a kindly nod to the old soldier.

'A real lady, that one, Miss Harry,' said Osborne in approving admiration after the countess had departed.

As a mere innkeeper and one-time soldier, he was well aware of his status in this sort of Society. Nevertheless, he had a justifiable pride in himself and his achievements. He had served with Harriet's father from the beginning, having been the young Sir Jonathan's groom and then his batman throughout the action in Iberia and he had seen Harriet grow from babyhood into girlhood. He had taught her to ride her first pony, had rescued her from many a childhood scrape and, along with her constant attendant, Martha, had contributed more than a little to Harriet's life and happiness during her unusual upbringing. When his part in the fighting was over he had finally persuaded the worthy Martha to marry him and try for a more settled way of life in their later years.

Harriet understood him well and took his meaning perfectly.

'A real lady, indeed. She has been so extremely kind to me. I wonder if Mama realises that the earl and countess were very well acquainted with her parents and that her ladyship would likely have been Mama's godmother if my grandmother had lived?'

She rose from her seat and, despite his protests, hugged him again. 'You have no idea how glad I am to see you again, Ozzy,' she said, unable to hide the tremor in her voice. 'Now we must go and fetch Martha and then we can all get comfortable—oh, Heavens! I have not yet read the note you brought me!' and, having peeled off the wafer, she began to peruse the missive, alternately shaking her head and frowning in consternation at the hastily scribbled contents.

'I clearly cannot reply,' she sighed, 'for it is unlikely that Mama would ever receive my letter and you will not want to be forever posting up and down the country as a messenger. I hope that Sir Chester has not discovered where I am—but it is a problem what to do. I cannot remain here much longer and there is no knowing how long it will take my grandfather to get here! I have no funds and I do so dislike being a charge on her ladyship.'

She folded the note and placed it in her reticule and, lifting her eyes to Osborne's while forcing a smile, she said, with as much cheerfulness as she could muster, 'Come, let us find Martha.'

Later, as they sat together in the small salon, she related the misadventures that had brought her to Beldale and confessed the deception in which she had become involved. Martha expressed concern and disapproval that Harriet should have become so embroiled in such subterfuge, although she commended the underlying reasons for the duplicity, saying that 'Miss Harry should think herself lucky that it was such a gentleman who had rescued her!'

Privately, Harriet was becoming rather weary of being told how lucky she was and she quickly went on to describe the incident at the lake, which curious event caused both of her old comrades to eye one another in dismay.

Osborne rose to his feet and started pacing the floor.

'Can't have that, miss,' he said, shaking his head. 'That's downright suspicious, if you ask me. Maybe that Middleton has already discovered your whereabouts—and you say his lordship didn't believe your story?'

He stopped suddenly and turned to face his wife. 'What about taking Miss Harriet back with us, Martha? We wouldn't allow anybody to go pushing her into lakes in Ringwood, that's for sure.'

Harriet jumped up and clapped her hands as Martha nodded her agreement.

'Oh, would you? That would be the very thing! Then I needn't pretend to be engaged to Sandford any longer! You can't know what a joy it would be to be able to tell him that!'

She spun round guiltily as the door opened behind her and the viscount entered, his face impassive. Flushing, she wondered if he had heard her remarks but, if so, he gave no indication, merely striding forward to grip Osborne by the hand.

'Good to see you again, Sergeant,' he said. 'Glad to hear of your success. Tiptree will be wanting to swap yarns with you. You'll be staying at the *Fox,* I imagine? He'll be down to join you later, I'll be bound.'

Taking up his stance at the fireplace, he smiled at Martha in cheerful recognition and cautiously allowed his eyes to travel to Harriet's bright cheeks. Although he hadn't actually caught her remarks it was fairly obvious to him that he had been the subject of them. He sighed inwardly.

'My lord?' Osborne was addressing him nervously. 'Mrs Osborne and I were thinking that maybe it would be best if Miss Harry—Harriet—was to return to Ringwood with us, sir—seeing as how she knows us so well and she'd be quite safe...'

He stopped as the viscount put up his hand and shook his head emphatically.

'Oh, I think not, old chap,' he said, experiencing a fleeting moment of self-reproach as he witnessed Harriet's look of stunned incredulity. 'I'm sure Sir Jonathan would have preferred that Miss Cordell remain at Beldale. It's very good of you—and Mrs Osborne, of course—' he bowed to Martha '—but I really feel that it will be more suitable for her to stay here, at least until her grandfather arrives.'

It was not in Osborne's nature to give up without a fight. 'Miss Harriet has had a fright, your lordship,' he said stoutly. 'And it's not right for you to go doubting her word.'

'Miss Harry couldn't lie to save her life!' cut in Martha bravely, determined to say her piece.

Sandford held up both hands to silence them.

'I am aware of that,' he said calmly. 'The matter is being dealt with, I assure you.' He turned to Osborne. 'Tiptree will fill you in on the details if you care to consult him. Miss Cordell is perfectly safe here, you have my personal guarantee. Now, if you will excuse me.' Without another word he turned on his heel and left the room.

Martha looked anxiously at her husband.

'I hope he hasn't taken offence, Jerry,' she said. 'Maybe we shouldn't have tried to interfere?'

Harriet's brain was in a turmoil of conflicting emotions. She was convinced that Sandford had heard her shameful outburst. He had dismissed Ozzy's suggestion just to punish her, she decided indignantly and yet—it appeared that he had believed her after all and had actually been trying to clear up the mystery all this time while she—she had been treating him with such disdain! What must he think of her? All of a sudden she felt deeply ashamed and looked up to find both Osborne and Martha regarding her with frowning disapproval.

Osborne cleared his throat. 'Seems as if you've done his lordship a disservice, Miss Harry. I'd say he was doing his best for you and, from what I know about him, I'd have been surprised at anything else!'

'And, if you ask me,' Martha scolded, 'it's time you grew out of that impetuous behaviour of yours, miss. I sometimes wonder if we didn't all spoil and pet you too much when you were a little lass. However, you must try to remember that you're a young English lady now and act accordingly!'

'Oh, Martha, please don't be cross with me,' gulped Harriet. 'Everything is so mixed up. I hate living this beastly lie. Lady Caroline has been so kind to me and the earl and I deal extremely well together. It's just Sandford—he seems to be set on finding fault with everything I do and I did admire him so when I was a girl!'

She choked back a sob and Martha, relenting, folded her arms around her one-time charge and held her to her ample bosom.

'There, there, my precious,' she crooned. 'It won't be for long now. Your grandpapa will come and carry you back to his Scottish castle and, no doubt, you will meet some handsome young laird who will sweep you off your feet and you'll all live happy ever after!'

Harriet sniffed and shook her head with vehemence.

'No, I am determined I shall never marry,' she said sorrowfully. 'I shall devote my life to my grandfather's comfort. I intend to be his constant companion and the indispensable helpmeet in the evening of his life.'

'Oh, deary me, Miss Harry!' laughed Martha. 'Then I trust he has a strong constitution.' And gathering up her belongings at a signal from her husband, she said bracingly, 'Now we must be off, so give me a kiss and promise to be a good girl!'

Waving her handkerchief frantically until their hired post-chaise was out of sight, Harriet wondered glumly whether she would ever see these two staunch allies again.

Chapter Five

Sandford, meanwhile, had returned to the Dower House in the pursuance of his earlier inquiries. He found that his cousin had, in fact, made some useful progress during his absence.

Ridgeway had eventually tracked down the boy, Billy Tatler who, along with several of his disreputable friends, was discovered attempting to ride some ewes bareback. The terrified sheep had been herded into a corner of a field and Billy was issuing orders to his cronies as to the best way to mount these animals. Needless to say, their efforts were meeting with little success and, at the sight of their master's angry countenance, the urchins scattered and endeavoured to make themselves scarce.

Ridgeway, leaping nimbly from his horse, had managed to grab Billy by the seat of his breeches as the boy tried to scramble through the hedge and, hauling him upright, he had frogmarched him to a nearby barn to question him.

This cross-examination, accompanied by dire threats of the awful punishments and penalties that would be incurred if any lies or omissions were discovered, took both time and patience but, eventually, Ridgeway had managed to extract what he took to be the bones of a very odd tale.

It transpired that Billy and his friend Nick often spent their days larking around the Beldale lake, hopeful of catching a trout or two and, on the day in question, had been splashing about in the water by the boathouse when 'this cove' had appeared and collared them both before they could escape. He had, firstly, threatened to haul them up to the 'big house' then, at their pleas for mercy, he had persuaded them to play a 'little trick' on the young lady who was presently making her way around the lake path. Billy was to pretend he had fallen into the water and, when the young lady leaned forward to help him out, Nick was instructed to give her a sharp push from behind. This was, apparently, to teach the young lady a lesson for some 'bad thing' she had done to 'Lady 'Genie'. Both boys knew that the water was quite shallow on this side of the lake and Billy, when tickling trout, had often knelt upon a large flat stone just below the surface a few yards away from where they had been standing. The 'cove' had then directed Nick to conceal himself in the bushes and Billy had slithered to his place on the stone. They were told they would be being watched by the 'geezer' from behind the boathouse and that he, of course, would go to the young lady's assistance if she got into any real difficulties and, if they carried out the 'job' to his satisfaction, he had promised them a shilling each!

'In the event, Nick got cold feet and scarpered, leaving Billy to do the deed on his own and when he climbed out of the lake and saw Miss Cordell standing up in the water, he didn't think much harm had been done and, when he saw you riding along the path, he made off before the "cove" could grab him again!'

'But did he say who this "geezer" was?' Sandford demanded of his cousin, at the end of the recital. 'You asked him, surely?'

'Naturally.' Ridgeway was indignant. 'He said he'd never seen him before but thought he must have come from the House. "Tall, thin and dark" was all he could say.'

'Young or old?' asked Sandford impatiently.

'Well, he said "old" but to a child of his age, that could be anyone from twenty upwards,' Ridgeway pointed out. 'Sorry, old chap, back to square one, almost.'

'Not quite,' said Sandford, frowning. 'We know how it happened, but as to why? Miss Cordell has not yet met your mother, so where does she fit into the conundrum?'

'Oh, I figured that one out,' said Ridgeway. 'If the little varmints have any loyalty at all it's to "Lady 'Genie". Billy actually thought he was doing it on Ma's behalf and this chap, whoever he is, must have known that!' He looked squarely at Sandford. 'You want me to lay them off—send them back to London?'

Sandford flushed. 'I hope you know me better than that, Charles,' he said shortly, getting ready to mount his horse. 'Sounds as if you've put the fear of Lucifer into the brats already. The real villain has still to be discovered!'

He wheeled his horse out of the Dower House stableyard and, raising his crop in salute, he galloped back down the lane to Beldale.

Upon his entry into the hall he encountered Harriet sitting on a chair, reading. To his surprise she jumped up and came forward to meet him.

'Lord Sandford,' she said, clearly in some agitation. 'Could I speak with you, if you please?'

Puzzled, he led her into the salon and, closing the door behind them, he turned to face her.

'How may I help you?' he asked, feeling his heart contract at the sight of her downcast face. He steeled himself for whatever battle of wits he was sure must be about to follow.

'I—I—want to apologise, my lord,' she said in a small voice. 'I fear I have misjudged you. I...'

Discomfited, he put up his hand to stop her.

'Please, Miss Cordell, no more!' he protested. 'It is I who am at fault if I gave you the impression that I disbelieved your story. Believe me, it was never my intention...'

'But you have found the culprit?' she interrupted eagerly. 'You have solved the mystery?'

'Alas! Not entirely,' admitted Sandford, vexed at having to disappoint her. 'Sit down please, Miss Cordell. Let me tell you what I have ascertained.'

Briefly, he related his own investigations and his cousin's discoveries, deeply conscious of Harriet's eyes on his own the whole time he was speaking and sick at heart that he was unable to bring a smile to her face.

'But these boys,' she said, anxiously gripping her hands together. 'Surely they are in some danger now? The man must be aware that they could expose him. Who can he be and what do you suppose it all means?'

Sandford shook his head and laid his hand on hers, to still the trembling.

'I confess I am at a stand,' he said reluctantly. 'Unless you know of anyone who would wish you harm? These Middletons...?'

Harriet shook her head. 'They could not have known of my whereabouts last week,' she said. 'Even Mama did not, until the—engagement—notice was in the paper.'

Sandford regarded her silently for a moment then, rising purposefully to his feet, he became his normal efficient self again. 'Then we must assume that the whole thing was some unfortunate mistake,' he said decisively. 'For the present, however, I must insist that you refrain from wandering off on your own again and that you always tell one of the household where you may be found...'

He stopped, at her look of astonishment.

'Must you persist in treating me like a child?' she asked in disgust. 'Perhaps you could look out some leading-strings for me?'

He sighed, all at once too weary to engage in the inevitable bout of verbal fisticuffs he had come to expect from their interchanges.

'My concern is merely to ensure your safety until your grandfather arrives to remove you,' he said stiffly. 'I would be obliged if you would comply with my request during the remainder of your stay here. I have wasted far too much time on this wild-goose chase already.'

Wrenching open the door, he left the room, conscious of an overwhelming desire to give Harriet a good shaking or, perhaps, just hold her tightly in his arms. Cursing under his breath, he crossed the hall and climbed the stairs to his chamber, where he curtly dismissed Kimble and attended to his own toilette, much to his valet's chagrin.

Harriet, still angry, paced the floor of the salon for some minutes after the viscount had gone, mulling over both his revelations and his subsequent chastisement. Aware that she had little choice but to heed his instructions, she contemplated the possibility of dashing down to the village the following morning in order to catch the Osbornes before they left for Hampshire. Rejecting this idea as impractical and, ruefully sensible of the fact that Martha would simply return her to Beldale, she wondered once more whether she could confess her situation to Judith Hurst but, oddly, the closer her friendship with Judith grew, the less that idea appealed to her. Reluctant to expose herself to her friend's possible disapprobation, she realised that she had no alternative but to sit tight until her grandfather arrived, however long that might be. She resigned herself to remaining inside the four walls of Beldale House for the foreseeable future, since there was absolutely no way she was going to stroll about the grounds with a footman at her heels and, as for riding with Sandford, she would see him damned first!

Once more an uneasy truce attended their meetings, which Sandford confined to the barest minimum, unwittingly causing his mother deep misgivings, for she could sense his unhappiness and concluded that he was regretting his decision to return to Beldale permanently.

The earl continued to make good progress and no longer seemed to have a compulsion to dwell on his accident. Harriet spent a good deal of her time with him, playing chess and piquet and reading scurrilous articles from the newspapers to him, which latter usually developed into heated debates between the two of them, culminating in paroxysms of laughter.

Sandford entered his father's room on one such occasion and, although the sight brought a smile to his lips, his eyes remained bleak and he indicated to Chegwin that he would return later.

Lord William, however, noticed his son's retreat and speculated upon the cause of it, but was reluctant to broach such a delicate subject with Sandford. Instead, he elected to quiz Harriet during one of their games of Hazard.

'I shall miss you when you are gone, my dear,' he said gently. 'I'm sure you must know how attached I have grown to you—we all have. Her ladyship calls you her breath of fresh air!'

'Sandford would probably say "whirlwind",' she said, smiling ruefully as she took her turn at the dice. 'He seems to take such exception to everything I do.'

'You dislike him?' he shot at her, regarding her intently.

Startled, she raised her green eyes to his faded grey ones and sighed. 'There are times when I really do, I'm afraid,' she admitted. 'He can sometimes be so overbearing, you know, and then, just when I could happily murder him—he does something so—so—unexpected.'

Beldale gave a snort of laughter. 'Well, you are honest, I'll give you that—not that I'd expect anything less of you, of course,' he said, looking at her fondly. 'Care to tell me about it?'

'Well, it seems that no matter how hard I try to conduct myself with the dignity and propriety he expects of me,' said Harriet with a grin, 'I find myself involved in some sort of scrape. Papa always used to say it was lucky I wasn't a cat—although I do have the eyes for one—for I must easily have lost all nine lives before now!'

'Curiosity is regarded by some philosophers as a prime virtue,' observed his lordship thoughtfully. 'How else could we acquire knowledge? My throw, I believe.'

Harriet passed him the dice-box and studied her scoresheet. 'That makes about fifty thousand guineas I owe you, my lord,' she laughingly informed him. 'I will have to ask for time to pay, or shall you have me cast into Bridewell?'

'Bridewell? Hmm—that might just be the answer.' The earl answered absentmindedly, as he shook the box.

Harriet looked up puzzled. His lordship seemed abstracted.

'Oh, I have tired you out,' she exclaimed, jumping up in concern and beckoned to Chegwin to clear away the bed-table.

Lord William smiled at her agitation and took her hand in his. 'Perhaps I shall take a nap, my dear,' he said. 'It's Judith's assembly this evening, is it not? Be sure to come and see me before you leave.'

Harriet, bending to kiss him on the forehead, promised that she would.

As soon as the valet had closed the door on her departure, Beldale hauled himself up on his pillows and issued several succinct orders and a request for Lady Caroline's immediate attendance.

That evening, as she stood submitting herself to Rose's final administrations, Harriet felt a pang of regret that she would shortly be losing the cheerful young maid and wondered if her grandfather would allow her to offer the girl a position in his household.

'Don't frown so, miss,' admonished Rose, as she buttoned her mistress's glove. 'You'll get lines on your forehead soon enough, believe me! There, now—a real picture you look!'

Harriet studied her reflection in the pier-glass. Her soft, copper-gold hair had adapted happily to its new shape, its curling tendrils framing her elfin face, whilst her deep green eyes mirrored the colour in the shot silk of the over-tunic. The neckline of the white satin underslip was low but decorous, without ruffle or frill, accentuating the creamy curves of her bosom. The tunic, which was sleeveless, fastened around the waist with a narrow sash decorated in a gold-threaded Greek-key design and Rose, still bemoaning her mistress's lack of jewellery, had fashioned a similar ribbon to weave through her curls.

Feeling enormously pleased with the whole effect, Harriet took the fan and reticule Rose was holding and thanked the smiling girl for all the effort she had made on her behalf, determined that she would find some way of rewarding her for her loyalty before she left.

'You're to go and see the master,' Rose reminded her, as she handed Harriet a dark green velvet cloak. 'He'll be wanting to see you in your finery, I expect.'

Both Lady Caroline and Sandford were waiting in the earl's room when Harriet arrived. The old man's eyes lit up when he saw her and he beckoned her to him.

'Just like a little sea-nymph,' he chortled, beaming with pleasure and nodding at his wife. 'See, my dear? I was right. Hand me the box, please.'

The countess, smiling, passed him a flat leather case from which he lifted a glittering necklace of tiny emeralds strung on a gold chain. Harriet gasped as Beldale passed the necklace to Sandford and bade him fasten it round her neck.

The viscount, whose senses had been considerably affected by Harriet's appearance, found his fingers trembling as he battled with the clasp.

'Oh, Lord William!,' breathed Harriet, as she leaned over to kiss the earl's cheek. 'I promise I shall take the greatest care of it! I shall return it to you personally first thing in the morning.'

'It is not a loan, my dear.' His lordship patted her hand. 'It is but a small token of thanks for the many hours you have devoted to my recovery.'

'But I cannot possibly accept such a gift,' she protested. 'And you know perfectly well that I, too, have enjoyed our tête-à-têtes.'

'Which is why you cannot possibly refuse my gift, I think,' said his lordship gently. He looked at his son. 'Isn't there something else, my boy?'

Sandford cleared his throat. 'Father was concerned that Judith's guests would be sure to mark the absence of an engagement ring,' he said, reaching for the small box which he had previously selected from the assortment on the side table.

'These jewels are all part of the Beldale collection, my dear,' said Lady Caroline conversationally, as Harriet removed her glove. 'They belonged to Lord William's grandmother, the third countess. She was very fond of emeralds, we are told. I myself prefer the sapphire and our girls have always regarded the green stone as unlucky...' She hesitated. 'Oh dear, I trust you have no such qualms, my child?' She looked anxiously at Harriet, who let out a ripple of delighted laughter.

'Not at all, ma'am—it is, in fact, my birthstone so I believe that to me it must be lucky...' She stopped, as the box Sandford was holding fell from his grasp and bounced across the floor. Chegwin bent to retrieve it and handed it back to the viscount, who was looking at Harriet with an incomprehensible glint in his eyes.

'Perhaps you would do us the honour of wearing this tonight,' he said, executing a stiff bow and handing her the box. 'Certain people are sure to comment—will it suffice?'

Harriet opened the lid and beheld a flawless square-cut emerald, surrounded by diamonds and mounted on a gold ring. Her lips trembled as she slid the jewel on to her finger and, holding up her hand for all to see, 'It fits perfectly,' she observed, in shaky surprise.

'I hoped that it might,' murmured Sandford impassively as, somewhat shaken himself, he picked up the box and returned it to the pile.

'And just one more,' interposed the countess, holding out a bracelet she had selected. 'This matches the necklace, I believe—now you will do us proud.' She clasped the bracelet around Harriet's wrist and stood back to admire the result. 'Your grandmother would have loved you so—I can hardly wait to see the effect you have on Ramsey!'

'I shall be sorry to miss seeing the effect she has on Judith's male guests,' chuckled Lord William, bringing a deep blush to Harriet's cheeks. 'I shall expect to hear all about it tomorrow, so don't disappoint me.'

She threw her arms around his neck and kissed him again. 'Oh, I shan't, I promise—and thank you so much—all of you. I swear I have never looked so grand!'

Sandford's lips twisted in a wry smile as he turned to pick up his cloak. 'A vast improvement on certain of your outfits, I am bound to agree,' he said, failing to register either Harriet's crestfallen expression or the look that passed between his parents. 'Shall we depart, ladies?'

Chapter Six

The August evening was warm and still. Judith had thrown open the doors of her largest drawing-room to allow her guests to walk on the rear terrace, should they desire to take the air. She had also arranged for the carpets to be taken up, determined to encourage 'a little dancing' in spite of Lady Butler's sighing disapproval.

Groups were already assembling around the room when the Beldale party was announced. Conversation ceased as all heads turned to scrutinise Sandford's betrothed and more than one hopeful mother of unwed daughters heaved a sigh of regret at the charming picture that Harriet presented.

About a dozen families had accepted Judith's invitation and Harriet was quickly presented to the most senior of these, amongst whom were the local vicar, the Reverend John Taylor, with his very pleasant wife and two daughters, and Squire Bevans accompanied by his prodigious family. Also present were the earl's family physician, Sir Basil Lambert, along with his wife Patricia and their son Cedric. This youngster considered himself a very bang-up, dashing man-about-town and lost no time in claiming Harriet for one of the sets, which started a minor flurry as other young men jostled to be included in her favours, and Sandford found himself having to take a back seat during these proceedings.

'Making quite a mark, dear coz,' came Ridgeway's amused voice next to him. 'Trust you to win such a prize. Every man in the room is full of envy.'

Sandford forced a smile. He had been studying Harriet's bright and animated expression and wondered how it was that he always seemed to manage to quench her natural liveliness. Other young ladies of his acquaintance had always conducted themselves with elegant composure and dignity, but this one seemed to have little respect for convention—even laughed at it—and yet everyone was drawn to her. His father was obviously entranced and his mother adored her and yet he, himself, constantly found fault with her and could not explain the sometimes violent irritation she aroused within him—especially at this moment, surrounded as she was by laughing admirers.

Harriet lifted her eyes and caught his frown and her eager expression vanished as she excused herself from her court and came at once to his side, acknowledging Ridgeway with a polite and conventional smile while Sandford inwardly cursed himself.

'Oh, I see Eugenie is here,' said Lady Caroline, taking Harriet's arm. 'Do come and meet her, my dear. Charles, do your duty.'

Ridgeway bowed to his aunt and presented Harriet to his mother. Again that lively look of real interest appeared on Harriet's face and in no time at all she was deep in friendly conversation with the earl's sister as the countess brought Lady Eugenie up to date with Beldale's progress. Harriet had been as fascinated by Sandford's aunt's history as Lady Eugenie quickly became with hers and they were soon immersed in a cheerful debate concerning some charitable organisation or other with which Lady Eugenie was involved.

Sandford, all at once discovering a growing hatred of himself, interrupted their laughing exchanges to point out to Harriet that he supposed the company might expect them to dance together at least once. She handed him her card and invited him to take his pick.

'Not a lot of choice, I see,' he said, scribbling his initials in the few blanks that remained. He desperately wanted to tell her how lovely she looked and to compliment her on her success but, realising that he had missed the moment, could think of nothing that sounded neither flippant nor contrived. 'I shall take you in to supper, of course.'

'Of course, my lord,' she replied, without enthusiasm.

He hesitated and was about to begin his speech when one of her young admirers arrived to claim her for the reel that was presently assembling.

Harriet threw herself into the dance with relief, skipping around the circle, changing partners as the movement required and clapping her hands in time to the sprightly tune being executed on the piano by Lady

Eugenie, who had been happily persuaded to perform that task.

Judith, looking radiant in her ruby silk gown, mingled gracefully with her guests, ensuring that no one was ignored or left without a partner for a set. She was sad that Philip was not with her to enjoy the success of his brother's betrothal party, but equally determined that she would not shun society because she had been widowed. She had the children's future to consider and knew that Philip would want her to see that they grew up with the same standards and expectations that he would have given them. He himself had not been fond of high-society occasions but had always entered wholeheartedly into the many country dances and musical evenings which had been held at Westpark and Judith was delighted to find that she had not lost her touch.

His vigilant sister-in-law had paired Sandford off with one of the vicar's daughters, still in the schoolroom, and it required all of his social skills to put the girl at her ease and to rescue her from her many foot-faults. When he was finally able to return her to her parents, having brushed away her stumbling apologies with a melting smile, he looked about the room for Harriet and, as he could not immediately locate her, he strolled outside along the terrace, fearful of being collared once more by his zealous hostess.

Couples were forming for the next set and Harriet had promised this to Charles Ridgeway but, finding herself slightly out of breath from the Circassian Circle she had just thrown herself into, she begged him to take her outside for some air instead. Laughing, he admitted that he was not the most practised of dancers and would be glad of the respite himself.

Lady Caroline, holding court beside the doors, waved to them as they went through and Harriet was embarrassed to overhear her own virtues being extolled at some length as Ridgeway led her down the terrace steps into the garden.

'—even won Cook over by begging to be taught to make almond tartlets and three hours later I discovered her sitting on the table regaling the entire kitchen staff with her tales!' This was received with peals of delighted laughter from most of her ladyship's listeners, but one or two ladies raised their eyebrows at one another.

Harriet glanced up at Ridgeway. 'I suppose I shouldn't have done that?' she said mournfully.

Charles laughed. 'Why not? You are something of an original, to be sure. Robert must be delighted that you have everyone's admiration.'

His own eyes travelled across the room to where Judith Hurst was standing. 'Not that he would care if they took you in deep dislike, I'll be bound,' he continued, absentmindedly.

'Does she know that you're in love with her?' Harriet asked bluntly.

With a shocked expression, Ridgeway swung to face her. 'What are you saying?' he said, as a dull flush crept up his cheeks.

'Well, it is pretty obvious,' said Harriet cheerfully, motioning him to the seat at the foot of the steps. 'You never take your eyes off her. She speaks very highly of you, you know.'

'As her estate manager,' Charles said bitterly. 'What could I possibly offer her? She even pays my salary!' Involuntarily his eyes homed in to their target once more and his shoulders slumped. 'I should leave,' he said. 'I have tried, but I cannot.'

Harriet put her hand on his sleeve. She was desperately sorry for him, realising how keenly he felt the hopelessness of his situation.

'Judith is still young and so beautiful,' she said awkwardly, 'but she is also very lonely and she still has a lot of love to give—someone. Why should it not be you? Do you mean to stand by and watch her turn into an embittered old harpy like—well, you know...' She bit her lip and looked around anxiously.

Ridgeway burst out laughing and his eyes suddenly gleamed with a newfound confidence as he stared at Harriet curiously. 'How did one so young come to be so astute?' he asked.

'Well, I've hardly had the conventional sheltered upbringing,' Harriet answered dismissively. 'I've mixed with people from many different walks of life, which I believe has helped me to appreciate other points of view. I have always been interested in people and—well—travel is supposed to broaden the mind,' she laughed. 'Isn't that why young men were sent on the Grand Tour?'

Ridgeway's eyes crinkled appreciatively. 'I missed that myself, as a matter of fact,' he said. 'So I suppose you must consider my mind to be on the narrow side, since London and the Lake District are the furthest reaches of my travels!'

Harriet flicked his hand with her fan. 'You know perfectly well that is not what I meant and just for that I shall oblige you to stand up with me for the next dance. So, kindly do your duty, sir, and lead me to my place.'

Laughing together, they re-entered the room and joined the set that was presently forming, Ridgeway carefully ensuring that he positioned them as close as possible to Judith and her partner, young Cedric Lambert, and, as Lady Eugenie struck the first chord, Sandford arrived back just in time to see his betrothed swing into the steps of the dance which he had selected as his.

A hot anger filled his throat as he watched Harriet's laughing interchanges with the other members of her set and, turning away, his fury was such that he was obliged to sit down to control his breathing. Unfortunately, he chose the seat next to Lady Butler's.

'Without a partner, my lord? Your little miss is quite the little honey-pot, I see.' Her voice held its customary disapproval. 'She is no doubt used to being the apple of all the men's eyes.'

Sandford's eyes glittered in distaste. 'What makes you think that?' he asked carefully.

'Oh, I see how she tosses her head at them all—it is but a come-on—I was used to do it myself, of course, as a girl—I was much admired. She will have had plenty of practice with the military, I'll be bound, and without such chaperonage as is considered *de rigueur* in our own society. Certain young women nowadays do seem to have the most perfidious disregard for convention, as I am sure you have found. However, I must admit to a certain surprise that you allowed your own betrothed to disappear into the garden with one of her recent conquests—and for so long!'

Sandford rose to his feet and bowed stiffly. 'I cannot say that I have much experience of young *women*'s ways, ma'am,' he ground out between clenched teeth. 'And, since it appears we are about to go in for supper, I am sure you will excuse me if I now make a push to collect my own young *lady* before she bestows that singular honour on one of her many conquests!'

'Your loyalty does you credit and is most touching, I'm sure,' sniffed Lady Butler, also rising heavily to her feet. 'I suppose I must see to my own repast, as usual.'

She waited expectantly for Sandford to offer his arm but he, still seething with indignation, ignored both her remark and her person and turned swiftly away from her just in time to see a smiling Ridgeway leading Harriet towards him.

'Apologies, Sandford,' said his cousin cheerfully. 'I appear to have stolen your dance—Miss Cordell seems to have misread her card—not going to call me out, I trust?'

Sandford swallowed. He had been about to take Harriet to task, but had no quarrel with Charles. He doubted that Harriet had misread her dance-card, for she had made it perfectly clear that she did not care to dance with him. He gave Ridgeway a mock punch in the arm and said, with forced gaiety, 'Pistols at dawn, I should think—I trust you're as much out of practice as I am?'

Ridgeway returned the punch and laughed. 'Quite right, coz. Guard her with your life—she's a pearl beyond price!' He smiled down at Harriet. 'Thank you, dear lady—I think I know what to do now.'

Sandford frowned as he watched his cousin walk away. 'What was that supposed to mean?' he asked suspiciously.

'Oh, nothing,' countered Harriet quickly, not wishing to divulge Ridgeway's confidences. 'I'm truly sorry about the dance mix-up—shall we go in to supper? I see Lady Caroline beckoning us.'

The viscount led her to his mother's table, where the countess and Lady Eugenie were exchanging reminiscences.

'Harriet, my dear. Do join us.' Lady Caroline patted the seat next to her. 'Robert and Charles will fetch us our supper.'

She smiled at her son, who battled his way through the crowd to find Ridgeway already at the supper table collecting a plateful of sweetmeats and comfits.

Charles glanced at his cousin and grimaced. 'Can't stand these things meself,' he said. 'No substance to any of 'em.'

Sandford laughed, nodding. 'A good beef sandwich would suit me—and a tankard of decent ale.' He looked around. 'I suppose it's Madeira or Portuguese for us, as usual?'

Ridgeway pointed to the decanters. 'Brandy too, I see. I wonder how Judith managed to slip that past her ladyship?' Laughing, he made his way back through the throng to his table.

Sandford tossed back one large glass of brandy and indicated to the footman to pour him another. Thus fortified, he collected his glasses of lemonade and delivered them to the ladies who were still discussing the dances.

'Not nearly so graceful as the minuets,' Lady Caroline was saying, 'but a good deal more lively. The young ones look so merry. We always had to be so serious, for the steps were quite intricate, you know.'

'The country tunes are so cheerful, too,' agreed Lady Eugenie. 'Mrs Brewster brought me some new ones from London—and some German waltzes, too. I have been practising all week for this evening.'

Sandford's eyes lit up at her words. 'You play the waltz, Aunt Eugenie?' he asked, the germ of an idea stirring in his mind.

Lady Eugenie nodded, and then shook her head doubtfully. 'Judith's mother will never allow it,' she said. 'I understand it is still considered rather risqué.'

Sandford, now in a very mellow mood, laughed. 'Not at a private party, surely?' he asked. 'And with such doughty chaperons present? I shall speak to Judith myself—come along, Charles, let us petition her together.'

Ridgeway glanced at his cousin curiously as they sought out their hostess. 'What are you up to, Sandford?' he asked. 'Lady Butler won't be at all amused, you know.'

Sandford stopped and whirled round to face him, his face flushed and his eyes bright. 'Dammit, man!' he said angrily. 'This is Judith's house, and she will decide. What's more—if I want to waltz with my fiancée, I defy anyone to stop me!'

Charles put his hand on Sandford's arm. 'Steady on, dear boy,' he said quietly. 'Surely you cannot be foxed? Judith will not appreciate your making a scene, you know.'

Sandford hesitated. It was true that the strong spirit might have somewhat impaired his judgement, but it had been the exhilarating thought of whirling Harriet around the room that was responsible for the sudden rush of blood to his head. He took a deep breath and flashed a conspiratorial grin at his cousin.

'Ne'er a bit, Charles,' he said. 'Just thought to liven things up a touch. Wouldn't you like to waltz with Judith?'

Ridgeway reddened and looked away. 'Not sure I'd know how,' he said diffidently. 'Not been much of a one for dancing.'

'This one is different. Your feet will soon tell you, once the music starts, I promise you. Come on, let's ask the lady.'

They found their hostess collecting couples for the first after-supper dance and soon discovered that, after all, she needed little persuasion. Her party was an assured success and, as the guests consisted entirely of family and friends, she felt sure that it was highly unlikely anyone would take exception to this little divertissement.

'Apart from your mother, of course,' pointed out Sandford basely.

Judith pulled a face at him. 'You need not remind me, dear brother,' she said. 'However, Mama will not make a fuss until everyone has left, so do let's—it will be the perfect finish to our assembly!'

Since this had been his lordship's intention, he merely grinned and nudged his cousin who, catching some of Judith's excitement, had grasped her by the hand.

'Will you do me the honour, Judith?' he said breathlessly. 'I can't promise expertise, but I will do my best.'

Judith looked up at him in surprised delight and found herself blushing. 'Thank you, Charles,' she said almost shyly. 'It will be my pleasure.'

As soon as the last chord of the eightsome reel had died away, Judith clapped her hands to gain everyone's attention. She then announced that the very last dance of the evening was to be a waltz and that anyone who wished to try out this new dance was very welcome to take the floor. There was a gasp of excitement from the younger members of the local gentry, most of whom had undergone tortuous instruction from Monsieur Lavette, the local dancing master, but few of whom had ever expected to put their dubious skills into action quite so soon. There was a feverish rush of brothers seeking out the sisters who had been their usual partners when Monsieur had attended them for their weekly lessons and a hasty consultation with parents by those without convenient siblings.

The reels and sets that followed Judith's announcement were danced with an undercurrent of anticipation. Few of the older guests had actually seen the waltz performed but they were, for the most part, level-headed country folk who liked to make up their own minds about such things and who felt that there were enough chaperons amongst them to curb any excessive behaviour that their offspring might exhibit.

Sandford found that the sets he had secured with Harriet were rather unsatisfactory, insofar as conversation was concerned, and the 'grand chaining' that formed part of the movements meant that he was forever having to change partners. No wonder no one else had initialled them, he thought savagely, as he led yet another schoolgirl under the arches of raised arms.

Eventually he had his moment as they stood together once again waiting their turn to 'strip the willow' and, looking down at her bright and laughing face he said in a low voice, 'You will waltz with me, Miss Cordell.'

'Oh, no! I don't think so, thank you, my lord,' she said, flushing momentarily.

'You misunderstand,' he said shortly. 'You *will* waltz with me!'

Startled, Harriet looked up at him in dismay, but was swung away down the set by her new partner before she could formulate a reply. She completed the rest of the movements in a stunned rage, causing at least one of her young admirers to wonder in what way he had offended her that she should look so crossly at him.

At last the floor was cleared and Lady Eugenie struck a new chord. The first notes of the stirring music were played and there were a few suppressed giggles as the floor remained empty while the local blades dug their friends in the ribs to spur them into action. Their movements were stilled as Sandford led his new betrothed into the middle of the floor.

Placing his right hand firmly on her waist, he pulled her towards him and clasped her hand in his. Holding her breath, she raised her free hand to his shoulder, trembling as she felt herself propelled backwards. Moving together as one, they swung across the floor in time to the compelling beat of the music and all eyes were upon them as Sandford neatly executed a reverse turn at the corner of the room. There came a ripple of applause and Dick Bevans, the squire's youngest son, grabbed his sister by the hand and dragged her on to the floor, to the accompanying cheers of his friends, who quickly found their own partners and joined them.

As the floor became more crowded, Sandford skilfully guided Harriet around the less-practised pairs. So smooth were his steps and the pressure of his hands was so confidently in command of her body that she began to feel quite heady, as though she were skimming across a frozen lake. She had waltzed several times before, at the winter headquarters in Lisbon, but never with such an expert. She glanced up at his face, which was curiously expressionless, his eyes carefully anticipating unexpected manoeuvres from all sides. Like a general going into battle, she thought suddenly and choked back her laughter in a hiccough.

He looked down at her in concern and almost missed his step. The laughter brimmed into her eyes as her lips curved in a wide smile.

'You don't seem to be enjoying this much, my lord,' she challenged him. 'In fact, onlookers might suppose that you were undergoing some sort of penance.'

The viscount studied her animated face and sighed. 'My apologies,' he said wryly. 'I suppose I was trying to impress you.'

He swept her round another untutored pair as he spoke and she marvelled once more at his ability.

'Oh, but I am,' she said. 'Impressed, I mean. You've obviously done this before.'

Sandford laughed and his spirits began to rise. 'A fair bit. It was all the rage in Vienna last year.'

He sidestepped nimbly to avoid a young couple in danger of imminent disaster and, in doing so, drew Harriet more closely to him. This is more like it, he thought with a surge of satisfaction.

'More pleasant than our continual jousting, wouldn't you say?' He tightened his hold around her waist. 'A much better way of ''getting to grips'' with one's enemy.'

Harriet looked up at him in consternation as he swung her around once more. 'I do not consider you to be an enemy, my lord,' she protested, 'and I trust you do not think of me in that way.'

Sandford smiled down into her eyes. 'Better if I don't tell you how I do think of you, perhaps?'

Harriet, flustered, drew her eyes away from his and missed her step. Swiftly, he corrected his to hers and they were once more in time with the music.

Struggling to keep her eyes away from his outrageous gleam, Harriet attempted to devote her attention to her footwork. She refused to look up, but had the strangest sensation that the viscount was laughing at her. She caught sight of Charles Ridgeway quite competently shepherding Judith around the room and both were looking extremely pleased with themselves. All at once her reticence evaporated and, tossing her head back, she relaxed into the haven of Sandford's embrace and abandoned herself to the compulsive rhythm of the dance.

Sandford's cup was full. Holding her in his arms at last made him feel as though he had won a great victory. He wished that the music could go on forever, taking them both into a land where there would be no more bickering, no stand-offs, no contention, just pure unadulterated bliss. Oblivious to all else around them, together they swayed and moved as one, whirling and twirling in perfect harmony. Inevitably, the spell was broken as Lady Eugenie played her last triumphant chord and the roomful of laughing, breathless couples swung finally to a halt.

There was a burst of spontaneous applause from both dancers and audience alike and the younger ones crowded around Judith, begging for just one encore but, shaking her head, she smilingly pointed at the clock, for it was almost midnight and, as she reminded them, the following day was Sunday.

*   *   *

In the darkened carriage Sandford leaned back against the velvet squabs with his eyes closed, only half-listening to his mother's approving comments regarding the success of the evening. He had to strain to catch Harriet's soft replies to the countess's questions, but found himself quite content just to hear the rippling sound of her voice. He was acutely conscious of the sensation of being at the threshold of some lofty precipice where a single false step would send him hurtling into an uncharted ravine. Tomorrow, he thought, tomorrow I shall tread lightly and with great care.

Chapter Seven

'There's a letter for you, Miss Cordell,' said Rose, as she helped her mistress remove her pelisse on her return from the morning service.

'A letter?' exclaimed Harriet, examining the sealed missive curiously. 'Who can have written to me—I saw everyone I know at church this morning!'

'Ned sent it up from the gate lodge, miss,' said Rose, hanging up the outdoor garments. 'Said it had been pushed under the door.'

Harriet unfolded the paper and read the contents with a frown. *Dearest—meet me tomorrow in our own special place—C.*

Puzzled, she turned the note over to check the direction and saw her name clearly written there.

'Well, it can't be meant for me—who do I know with that initial? Charles Ridgeway, to be sure, but I am certain it is not he—and young Lambert, last evening—oh! I see!'

Smiling broadly, she sat down and removed her bonnet. 'It's some sort of boyish prank, I suspect—a wager with one of his friends, I suppose—although I don't quite see—still, it's of no importance.' And she tossed the note aside and allowed Rose to tidy her hair before going to the earl's chamber to keep her promise of giving him a full account of the previous evening's entertainment.

She found his lordship sitting in a large armchair by the window and clapped her hands in delight. 'You are out of bed!' she exclaimed, as she bent to kiss the top of his head.

He held out his hand and motioned her to a footstool at his feet.

'So you've come to tell me of your great success.' He smiled. 'I fear you have been forestalled. Sandford has already been here singing your praises. I hear he had to fight his way through the mêlée to dance with you!'

Harriet blushed guiltily as she recalled the embarrassment she had caused the viscount over her mix-up with the dances, although it would appear from the earl's words that she had been forgiven for her lapse.

'Not quite, my lord,' she said. 'But it was all very great fun and Judith looked delightful. She came out of mourning especially—you do not mind?' She looked at him anxiously, conscious of the knowledge that Philip had been his son.

The earl shook his head and sighed. 'No, poor child. It is time. She has a life of her own to live.' He patted her hand. 'Now, what about this daring exhibition you gave with Sandford?'

Harriet beamed. 'Oh, he must take all the credit for that, my lord. I was completely innocent and taken totally off guard, I assure you! But he does dance divinely, you know!' At her vivid recollection of that episode her heart seemed to skip several beats.

'Takes after his sire, of course,' chortled the earl.

Quickly marshalling her thoughts, Harriet took hold of his hand and replied with an impish grin, 'Then I insist on being privy to these remarkable skills! So you must make haste to get back on to both feet.'

Beldale studied her animated face. 'I doubt I shall be on my feet before you leave, child,' he said, his voice gentle.

Harriet flinched and her vivid eyes clouded over.

'I keep forgetting,' she said tremulously. 'When I am here with you I keep forgetting!'

She bent her head to brush away a tear and the earl laid his hand on her burnished locks and smiled a strange, quiet smile to himself.

'Now, now, no tears today, if you please,' he commanded briskly. 'I demand to be amused. Tell me more of Judith's party.'

Harriet dismissed her melancholia and set about entertaining Beldale in her usual appealing manner and soon they were both laughing at her anecdotes of the previous evening.

'And the oddest thing,' she finished, wiping her eyes. 'One of the young daredevils has actually sent me a *billet-doux* but neglected to sign his name, so I fear I shall never know who my reluctant admirer is!'

'Then he must take his chances with the rest of us,' chaffed Lord William. 'I have no doubt you will now be so inundated with invitations from our neighbours that I shall have to make an appointment.'

Harriet shook her head vigorously. 'Not so, my lord,' she responded, with great seriousness. 'Your requirements would always take precedence. I have come to regard you as—almost—as a—father. Is that very presumptuous of me? I do miss him so.'

The earl was silent for a moment and Harriet was afraid that she had offended him with her impetuous remark until he took her hands in his and said, warmly, 'Harriet, my dear child, you have paid me the greatest compliment. I am well aware of the deep bond that existed between your father and yourself. When you have been with me I have often found myself regretting that I did not spend as much time with my own daughters as I might have done—although I must confess that I do not recall them having quite as lively a nature...'

His eyes twinkled at the blush that appeared as he patted her cheek. 'Do not be so eager to extinguish it completely, dear girl. I am already filled with envy that your grandfather is soon to be the fortunate recipient of your infectious chuckle.'

'I pray that I find such favour with him,' said Harriet fervently.

'I cannot think that you will fail to do so,' his lordship vociferated, 'unless he is blind or deaf or the greatest curmudgeon ever and we know that he cannot be any of these, for he is presently braving the tribulations of long-distance travel to come to your rescue!'

Harriet nodded and rose to her feet, seeing Chegwin approaching with the earl's medication. 'That's true,' she said. 'And my consolation is that the longer he takes the more time I can spend with you!'

'Away with you, shameless hussy,' laughed Beldale. Then a thought struck him. 'Go and practise your beguiling charms on Sandford—I'll warrant he is not so easily moved!'

Harriet smilingly wagged her finger at him and left the room, with every intention of keeping as far away from the viscount as good manners allowed, for she was perplexed to find that his very presence suddenly seemed capable of exercising the strangest effect upon her composure. At the morning service, for instance, he had elected to stand next to her in the family pew and his fingers had (quite accidentally, she was sure) brushed against hers as she had leaned forward to pick up her prayer book. This, for some reason that she could not fathom, had prevented her from finding her place and he had taken her book from her and had handed her his own, open at the correct page. She was not even sure that she had given her responses correctly, so aware had she been of Sandford's own resonant, articulate returns. Worst of all, she was sure that she had detected an undercurrent of suppressed laughter in his voice and a swift sideways glance at him had revealed his amused scrutiny of her discomposure. His eyes had held that same disconcerting gleam, which she had done her best to ignore on the previous evening. When he had helped her into and out of the carriage his hand had seemed to linger on her arm a fraction too long and she had, once more, been conscious of the unrelenting intensity of his gaze as he sat opposite Lady Caroline and herself during the ride home from church.

Mentally shaking herself, Harriet hesitated outside the earl's door, unable to decide whether to return to the safety of her own room and stay out of harm's way or to venture downstairs. The events of the last few days were clearly affecting her brain, she concluded, and turned resolutely to the head of the stairway, only to perceive the object of her reverie emerging from his own chambers nearby.

'Ah, Miss Cordell!'

Sandford registered Harriet's violent start at his appearance but made no comment. He had, in fact, been listening somewhat impatiently for the click of his father's door-latch to signal her emergence; therefore his presence was no accident.

'You have been regaling his lordship with a fuller and more entertaining account of last evening's delights than that with which I was able to furnish him, I imagine?'

He seemed to Harriet to be in possession of some private and amusing intelligence and this added to her sense of confusion.

'Oh, well—yes—that is—I did my best to do so,' she answered, in breathless agitation, at the same time attempting a decorous retreat to her own quarters, but he put out his hand to stay her movements.

'Would you care to join me in a carriage ride?' His voice suddenly seemed almost boyish in its eagerness. 'It is such a lovely afternoon and I have to inspect some cottages. I would be honoured if you would accompany me.'

Harriet's eyes widened in surprise. 'That is very good of you, my lord,' she said cautiously. 'I confess I should be glad to get out into the air. If I may just collect my bonnet...?'

Sandford, watching her disappear into her room, had a sudden insane urge to leap on to the banisters he was holding and slide down them, just as he and Philip had done in their youth. Instead, to March's grinning amazement, he bounded down the stairs two at a time and ordered up the carriage.

Sitting on his box behind the driving-seat, Tiptree wondered dismally if he was witnessing his colonel's last stand. Having been privy to most of the 'guvnor's' intermittent campaigns into 'petticoat territory', he had to admit that he couldn't recall anything quite like this one. There had been that stunning blonde in Vienna, he mused, until Lord Sandford had discovered that the lady was a damned sight more interested in his money than in his manners and a certain contessa in Salamanca had seemed to be streaking to the winning post except for her unfortunate tendency to gamble heavily—not one of his lordship's favourite pastimes, Tiptree knew, considering the anguish such profligacy had brought to certain close members of the family. Other beauties had been guilty of having either no conversation at all or far too much and one memorable dazzler had kept dogs! Tiptree shuddered at the recollection of trying to keep three dribbling lapdogs under control in his lordship's open carriage whilst his master accompanied her ladyship into a milliner's salon. Those boots had never recovered, he thought, scowling at the back of Harriet's chip-straw bonnet, as though she were to blame. So, what was special about this one? he wondered. Her dad had been a real good goer, he allowed, and her ma—well she had been a proper trooper in her time. He'd never heard anything either good or bad about the daughter. She was certainly no beauty, not to his taste, anyway, with her ginger hair and cat's eyes, although she was quite a taking little thing—plucky, too and with a laugh that 'fetched the sun out', so he'd heard Smithers say, not that there was much sign of it at the moment, he observed.

Harriet was doing her best to remember Martha's teachings. Her back was straight, her feet were together and her gloved hands were clasped neatly in her lap. Her eyes she kept firmly to the front, on the road ahead. She had exhausted her entire fund of polite conversation, wondering glumly if the English gentlewoman's lot in life were always this dreary and almost wishing that she had stayed at Beldale. Sandford, on the other hand, seemed to be enjoying himself hugely. Out of the corner of her eye she had caught sight of a wide grin on his face, his beaver hat was tipped rakishly to the back of his head and his whole bearing seemed to be one of carefree relaxation, while she herself felt foolishly stiff and uncomfortable.

'How about the hedges?' His voice was brimming with suppressed laughter.

'I beg your pardon?' She half-turned towards him, and then quickly recovered.

'Well now, let's see,' he continued. 'We've had the weather—yes, it is extraordinarily warm for the time of year! And it is fortunate that the rain is keeping off for the haymaking and, yes, the orchards are full of fruit and, yes, I do consider thatching to be the most skilful of crafts!'

Harriet could feel a chuckle starting in her chest and struggled to suppress its unruly behaviour.

'Wh-what about the hedges?' she asked, holding her breath, but refusing to look at him.

'Let's think,' he said, his head on one side, considering. 'Do they need trimming, I wonder, or shall I have them pulled up, burnt down or simply consign them all to the Devil!'

Harriet put her hands up to her mouth in an effort to maintain her composure, but it was to no avail. Her lips curved into a smile, her eyes began to sparkle and the wayward chuckle burst into a peal of laughter.

A delighted Sandford reined his horses in to a halt and motioned to the widely grinning Tiptree to jump down and hold their heads. Taking out his handkerchief, the gleeful viscount then proceeded to mop up the tears of merriment that were spilling down Harriet's cheeks.

'Not fair—not fair,' she gasped, pushing him away. Her lips still quivering, she attempted to straighten her bonnet, which had somehow cast itself adrift, and regarded Sandford disapprovingly from beneath her wet lashes.

'Ah, but don't they say "all's fair..."?' he said, reaching out to take her hand and leaning towards her but, just at that precise moment, there came the sound of horses' hooves on the lane and Tiptree's low warning, ''Ware "parkers", guv.'

Harriet looked on with undisguised interest as Tiptree vaulted back on to his seat and the viscount spurred his team once more into action.

The occupants of the oncoming chaise saluted Sandford as the two vehicles passed one another and his lordship, although smilingly lifting his whip in reply, wished them in Hell.

Truth to tell, he was feeling slightly abashed at his conduct. He knew perfectly well that he would have tried to kiss Harriet had it not been for the interruption, but knew equally well that their relationship was far too tenuous to survive such precipitant action. Glancing down at her, he wondered if his rash behaviour had indeed set his cause back still further. He immediately resolved to make up any lost ground without further ado, but found himself forestalled.

'I do believe you were setting up a flirtation, my lord,' said Harriet cheerfully, rearranging her skirts.

Sandford, totally unprepared for this challenge, reddened and could only stammer, 'Not at all—you are mistaken—I must apologise...'

'Oh, come now, sir,' Harriet apostrophised. 'I am not a schoolgirl—you surely do not think that you are the first gentleman who has tried to kiss me? Although, upon reflection, I must confess that I have never before been ravished on the public highway!'

'Ravished, madam!' Sandford was appalled. 'I have never ravished anyone in my entire life—I'll have you know...' He stopped, having caught sight of her laughing countenance, and grinned ruefully. '*Touché*—your hit.'

He drove on in sheepish silence for some minutes until a thought occurred to him.

'Where did gentlemen try to kiss you, may I ask? Not since you have been under my protection, I trust?'

'Certainly not, my lord,' replied Harriet, demurely peeping up at him from beneath the brim of her bonnet. 'There was a very dashing subaltern in Lisbon, I recall—two, as a matter of fact.'

'And did they succeed?' asked Sandford, all agog for her reply.

'Succeed? Oh, I see.' Harriet laughed in delight at his masculine phraseology. 'Well, one did—kiss me, that is—but then the other discovered us in the alcove and offered to ''darken his daylights''—I believe that was the expression...?'

Sandford's lips twitched. 'Sounds about right,' he said carefully. 'What happened then?'

'Well, my first gallant appeared to doubt the other's ability to do any such thing and responded with a similar offer of his own—something about ''drawing his cork'' and ''spilling his claret''—as I recollect.' Harriet said mischievously.

'Your memory serves you well,' said Sandford, grinning as he pictured the scene. 'And then?'

Harriet sighed deeply. 'They then seemed to be more intent on having a mill than making love to me,' she said, in rueful reminiscence. 'So I returned myself to the party!'

The viscount gave a shout of laughter and lightly flicked his whip at the horses' heads, his good humour having suddenly returned.

'I wish I had known you in those far-off days,' he said, recalling some of the headier moments of his own time in Portugal.

'We were introduced on one occasion, my lord,' she offered. 'I doubt you will remember—I was only sixteen at the time—a mere child curtseying to your exalted personage. I fancy that your thoughts were more occupied with the very colourful *señora* two paces to my left...' She dimpled at his look of shocked recollection. 'I see that you recall the lady—a capitano's wife, I believe?'

'Yes—well, perhaps the least said about that particular incident, the better,' Sandford interposed hurriedly, ignoring his passenger's laughing eyes. 'And that was the only time we met?'

Harriet considered. 'My friends and I used to run to watch you ride past at the head of your company—you were something of a hero to us,' she said, her lips curving in memory. Then she collected herself and laughed a little self-consciously. 'We were only children, of course—I doubt if you noticed us.'

'I never thought of myself as a hero, certainly,' protested Sandford, remembering many such scenes. 'But I am sorry that I was not better acquainted with you— I wish I might have doffed my hat to you all as we rode out of town!'

'And what ecstasies we would have fallen into then, my lord,' replied Harriet gravely, although her mouth twitched at the corners.

Sandford's eyes gleamed with amusement.

'If you are trying to provoke me, Miss Cordell,' he said, his enjoyment mounting, 'you would do well to remember that you are no longer a child—and must therefore be prepared to accept the consequences of such fulsome encouragement.'

Harriet laughed out loud and shook her head at him. 'I withdraw all such comments, my lord,' she chuckled. 'And you may be assured that I had outgrown all such adulation well before my teens had ended.'

'Now that is a pity,' Sandford groaned, in mock despair. 'I was quite prepared to accept just a modicum of adulation.'

'Oh, no, sir,' replied Harriet, mirthfully aware that she had won the round. 'You have persuaded me that I must seize every opportunity to discourage such vanity!'

'Hoist by my own petard, dammit!' he laughed, pulling in the reins.

The curricle had reached a fork in the lane and Sandford had slowed the horses to negotiate the narrower of the two ways. This smaller track led down to a row of ramshackle dwellings, the furthest of which had obviously been destroyed by fire.

'Mr Potter's cottage, I collect?' said Harriet, looking about her with interest as, with Sandford's assistance, she descended from the carriage.

He nodded, surprised but gratified that she had remembered Ridgeway's tale.

'We'd been trying to persuade him to move out for months,' he said, walking over to the ruin. 'The rest of the tenants were rehoused last year in the new cottages by Top Meadow...' He gesticulated back towards the fork in the lane. 'Old Josh refused to go—said he'd lived here since he was first married and he intended to die here.'

'Pretty near did, too, by all accounts,' interjected Tiptree, who, having tethered the horses, had joined them. 'Set fire to his bed with his pipe, so I hear. Lucky for him Jack Rawlings was driving his cart along the top lane and got him out.'

'Was he hurt?' Harriet asked, her sympathy for the old tenant immediately aroused.

'Not really, so I'm told,' replied the viscount, 'superficial burns to his hands and legs. Meggy—his daughter—soon sorted him out, according to Charles, but she's had the Devil's own job trying to keep him away from here.' Sandford indicated the blackened roof timbers. 'Going to fall in any minute, I should say. We'd better get a gang on to it right away. The whole row should be pulled down and rebuilt.'

'Poor old man,' said Harriet, her eyes pricking with involuntary tears as she surveyed the pitiful ruins of Josh Potter's belongings. She bent down and picked up part of the charred remains of an ancient book.

'Oh, look!' She showed it to Sandford. 'It's his family bible—how awful! His whole history written off in a single stroke.'

She placed what was left of the ruined volume reverently on the stone windowsill and, as she did so, a withered blossom fluttered from between its leaves. Harriet caught the faded, almost transparent pressing in the palm of her hand and stared down at it bleakly.

Sandford could see the tears trickling down her cheeks and stepped hastily towards her.

'Please don't distress yourself,' he said, holding out his hands. 'I should not have brought you here—I hadn't realised it would be so—you are recalling parallels, I imagine?'

Harriet nodded. 'As you say, my lord.' There was a catch in her throat and she smiled tremulously at him as he once again applied his handkerchief to her face. 'What a watering-pot you must think me!'

'You never allow me to tell you what I think of you,' brusquely returned his lordship, resignedly pocketing his damp accessory. 'What have you got there?' He pointed to her hand.

She showed him the pressed flower, then looked at him in sudden inspiration. 'Do you have a card-case with you, my lord?'

Sandford frowned and nodded. 'Of course,' he said, patting his breast pocket. 'Why do you ask—you surely do not require me to leave a calling-card here?'

'Don't be ridiculous,' sighed Harriet patiently, as though to a child. 'I need to keep this memento safe for Mr Potter. You can slip it carefully between your cards until we return to Beldale—then I shall think of something.'

'Yes, I'm sure you will,' said Sandford, eyeing the relic in distaste, but he handed over his card-case as requested and watched in amused silence as Harriet gently placed the ancient favour between its folds and tucked it into her reticule.

The return journey to Beldale was accomplished without incident. The interchanges between them were friendly and relaxed and when Harriet mentioned that she would be riding with Judith early the following morning Sandford, anxious to avoid damaging the fragile tenure of their newly forged relationship, forbore from insisting that she should take a groom.

Chapter Eight

The two horses cantered side by side to the top of the hill and their riders reined in together, laughing. Judith dismounted gracefully on to a stone block set there for just that purpose and moved away to allow Harriet to do likewise. Tethering their mounts to a nearby sapling, they seated themselves on a fallen tree trunk and surveyed the magnificent view below them.

Harriet breathed in deeply, savouring the fresh morning air. 'This is such a glorious country, Judith,' she said. 'At first I wasn't sure if I could get used to it—after the heat and the mountains, you know, but now I think I shall never want to leave. I do hope I shall like Scotland as much.'

Judith looked at her curiously. 'Are you to visit Scotland? You have not mentioned it.'

Harriet recollected herself with a start. She had grown to be so at ease in Judith's company that she had quite forgotten that there were still things not to be shared with her new friend.

'I believe I am to visit my grandfather,' she said carefully. 'He has an estate near Edinburgh and he has expressed a desire to—to meet—my betrothed,' she finished, on a sudden inspiration. She pleated the folds of her habit between her fingers, unhappy at having to lie in this way to someone of whom she had grown so fond, but Judith appeared not to notice her discomfort.

'That sounds delightful,' she said, nodding absently and, rising to her feet, she strolled across the grass and sat down under a spreading beech tree and began to pluck the daisies, which grew in profusion around her. Harriet watched her in amusement. Already she was beginning to judge her friend's moods to a nicety and had been waiting for Judith to speak first but now, she realised, it was up to her to venture the subject.

'Did Charles enjoy the evening?' she asked suddenly.

Startled, Judith dropped her miniature bouquet and, flushing, bowed her head as she bent to retrieve the scattered flowers.

'Y-yes—I believe so—at least—I don't really—I haven't...'

She gave up, looking ruefully at Harriet, who grinned encouragingly at her.

'I suppose Lady Butler gave you the expected scold,' said Harriet. 'You haven't committed any great sin, you know, and it was an amazing party!'

Judith nodded, her eyes brightening. 'Yes, everyone has said so. I'm so pleased that it was a success and you were so popular—that is very important, you know, for you will be Countess of Beldale one day and to be well liked by the locals is a feather in your cap.'

Harriet blanched at the thought and quickly changed the subject. 'Will you ever marry again, do you think, Judith?'

'I have no need to,' replied Judith, in a low voice. 'Philip left me very well provided for—we have no financial worries and, of course, it is my—my duty to see that Christopher inherits his father's estates in good order and...'

'And Charles no doubt regards it as his duty to do the same,' interrupted Harriet. 'What a pair you are— you do like him, don't you, Judith?'

'I have known him all my life,' laughed Judith, self-consciously straightening her stock. 'The twins always chaffed me about him—he used to bring me wild strawberries on a dock leaf when I was a little girl—I never thought of him in—you know—that way—I never loved anyone but Philip—but I get so lonely sometimes that everything suddenly becomes very hard to bear.'

She stared bleakly at the horizon, watching the early morning sun slowly ascending the cloudless blue sky.

'Well, you must have seen that he's absolutely dotty about you,' said Harriet bluntly. 'He'll never say so, of course, because of convention and protocol and— oh, Judith, don't waste the rest of your life! Surely Philip wouldn't want you to be sad forever?'

Judith smiled briefly. 'No, but then we didn't exactly discuss the possibility of one of us remarrying—we were too busy being happy, I suppose.'

She looked down at her entwined fingers and then faced her friend. 'Mother always expected me to marry

Robert, you know,' she said, in a rush. 'They were both forever in and out of Staines—my home—and Mother always thought it would be Robert who would offer for me, but I chose Philip. Father liked both Hurst boys and was perfectly happy with my choice, which was why he made over half of our farmland to Philip on our marriage. The earl settled Beldale's western boundaries on Philip and we built Westpark House. My parents remained at Staines until Papa died and then Mother let the house out to tenants and moved in with us, lock, stock and barrel, as they say—she even brought most of the old staff with her and expected Philip to find them positions. He did his best, of course, and organised pensions for those whom we couldn't accommodate. Mother has always held a grudge about that, even though she doesn't concern herself in the least about servants—she just took it as a personal slight.'

She glanced at Harriet. 'I'm being fearfully disloyal telling you all this, aren't I?'

Harriet shook her head. 'No, it explains a lot,' she said. 'I couldn't understand why she took me in such dislike—obviously she hoped that his lordship would come back from the wars and snap you up—I'm only amazed that he didn't!' She burst out laughing at her friend's look of astonishment and Judith found herself laughing in return.

'Well,' she said, in relief, 'it doesn't really matter. I couldn't possibly have married Robert. That would have seemed quite immoral somehow—I love him as a brother. Charles is different altogether but ..it will be terribly difficult...' she paused wistfully '—he is such a proud man.'

'That's true.' Harriet nodded. 'So it is up to you to show him how much you depend upon him—how you can't manage without him, in fact. Gracious me, but aren't you lucky to have all these fellows crazy in love with you—it makes me positively green with envy!'

She got to her feet and began brushing the bits of grass from her habit, thereby failing to see Judith's look of puzzlement at her final remark.

'Now we really must get back,' she said, leading Clipper to the mounting block. 'I told them I would return for breakfast.'

'Oh, dear,' said Judith, scrambling to her feet. 'I promised Mother I would bring you back to have breakfast with the children.'

Harriet paused for a moment to consider this invitation.

'Well, I dare say I could stay just for the veriest minute—it is still very early and I could do with a drink, couldn't you? All this heart-searching is very thirst-making!'

Laughing together, they made their way back down the hill and on to the lane that led back to Westpark.

The two children were waiting with their grandmother on the rear terrace of the house and jumped up excitedly when they saw their mother bringing Harriet through the archway which led from the stables. Lady Butler frowned her disapproval as Christopher bounded down the steps to take his new aunt's hand and sharply instructed her granddaughter to remain in her seat.

'Aunt Harriet, Aunt Harriet,' the boy squealed breathlessly. 'Uncle Robert has bought me a new pony—a real goer, he says, and he's having jumps set up in Top Meadow—and he's going to teach me himself!'

His eyes shone with the wonder of it all and Harriet was enchanted with him once more. She allowed him to lead her up the terrace steps into the conservatory where she could see a small table laid for a nursery breakfast.

'You won't mind the informality, Harriet, I know,' said Judith, removing her gloves. 'The children and I often have our breakfast out here in the summertime and Mother was keen to join us today—as you were to be our guest.'

She handed a little silver bell to Elspeth and bade the little girl ring for Jemima. Harriet watched in delight as the child crossed to the house door and, with great dignity, solemnly and carefully shook the tinkling instrument. Almost immediately the smiling housemaid appeared, carrying her tray of glasses and milk jugs. It was clear that the sound of the bell could not have brought her so swiftly, but that Elspeth believed it had was evident by the stately pride with which she marched back to her seat and took her place at the head of the table.

Judith smiled at Harriet, without apology.

'It is we who are taking breakfast with the children, you see,' she explained. 'Philip and I liked to think that this was the best way to teach them.'

'Piffling nonsense, in my opinion,' sniffed Lady Butler. 'The place for children's meals is in the nursery with Nanny.'

'Oh, no! It's charming,' breathed Harriet, ready to enter into the spirit of the idea. Passing her cup to Elspeth, she requested her small hostess to pour her a cup of milk and graciously accepted a slice of buttered sponge from young Master Christopher. Judith thanked her wordlessly with her eyes and, once more, Harriet felt deep pangs of regret at the deception in which she had become entangled.

After the meal, during which Harriet had managed to smile her way through several biscuit and cake offerings, she was persuaded to pay a visit to Polly, the new pony, to discuss the best tactics of taking fences. The pleasant minutes slipped swiftly by until she suddenly recalled her promise to return to Beldale for breakfast! Hurriedly making her farewells to her hostesses on the terrace and fairly scooting back to the stables to collect her mount, it was not until she turned for a final gay wave to the two children that she found, to her annoyance, that she had mislaid her gloves. No time to go back for them now, she decided, spurring Clipper into a gallop across the meadow to the Beldale bridleway. Luckily, no one would see her on this private path, but she laughed out loud as she visualised Martha's shocked expression had that stickler for propriety been privileged to see her in such a state of undress!

As the dew-fresh scents of the morning rose about her Harriet breathed deeply in appreciation. She would be almost sorry to leave this glorious place, she mused, as she leaned down to secure the gate behind her and started along the ride back. She wondered if Sandford would be joining Lady Caroline and herself for breakfast. Until yesterday morning, he had usually sought to quit the room before her arrival, thereby avoiding the strained atmosphere that had prevailed at the dinner table during the previous week. Since yesterday afternoon's eventful ride, however, he had been all attention and she had to admit that she was looking forward with an inexplicable eagerness to their next encounter. Why, the very thought of it was making her feel quite giddy, she laughed to herself, and endeavoured to turn her mind to more sober topics.

The thickets of trees on either side of the path shaded both horse and rider from the heat of the rising sun and, almost drowsily, Harriet slowed to a gentle trot, allowing her mount to make its own pace along what had by now become a well-recognised route. They had not proceeded far in this leisurely manner when, to her irritation, she noticed that the dappling of the sun through the trees on one side of the path seemed to be causing her some sort of problem with her vision and she attempted to pull her hat down to lessen the effect. As she did so she became aware of an insistent thrumming in her ears that grew louder and louder as she desperately tried to maintain her balance. Clipper, ever sensitive to her mistress's touch, tossed her head as the reins loosened and at that sudden movement Harriet lost her grip and felt herself sliding from her mount. She seemed to have no control over her limbs and her head was filled with a swirling mist as she felt her body collapsing into someone's hands! Somewhere in the mist she could hear the mare whinnying and a man's voice, which seemed to came from far-away, was saying: 'Whoa, girl! Well, get her foot out of the stirrup, ninny! Come on! We haven't got all day!'

In a trance-like state Harriet felt herself being half-dragged, half-carried deep into the copse between clumps of briar and gorse. She could offer no resistance owing to the waves of nausea and blackness that were drowning her senses. She was aware of being pushed into a shallow depression in the ground and felt her skirts being bundled about her as branches were heaped upon her body, but her voice could make no protest. As she felt herself falling deeper into the roaring abyss of unconsciousness she heard the man's voice once more.

'The ring! Cripes, man! We forgot the ring—where's her hand?'

With a supreme effort Harriet eased the emerald ring from her finger and feeling for her boot, she pushed the jewel under the front fastenings. Then she passed out.

The cold, dank smell of the earth pervaded her senses. For some moments she remained still, trying to break through the cloying mists of her brain. Her temples were pounding and her mouth was dry and foul-tasting. Cautiously she sat up, pushing aside the mound of twigs and branches that covered her and, after peering carefully about, she saw that she was quite alone. Steadying herself against the tree trunk, she managed to stand. Her assailants had gone and Clipper was nowhere to be seen! Surely she had not been the victim of horse-theft? Apart from some rough handling she had not been hurt and she had nothing of value…!

Gasping, she thrust her hand down into her boot and felt the hard ridge of the precious stone against her fingers and almost wept with relief. That was what they were after! They were just common foot-pads after all—but what were they doing on Beldale property? Gradually, it began to come back to her—they must have been waiting for her—but had they actually pulled her from her horse—what had caused her sudden dizziness? Her head ached so, she was covered in bracken and mud and her hat and cravat were both missing!

As she shaded her eyes against the piercing glare of the summer sun she was suddenly transfixed as she registered its position in the sky. It must be past noon! She had been in the copse for hours! Casting about her for a sign that might help to guide her back to the path, she was eventually able to locate the trail of flattened grass along which she had been dragged and, still very unsteady, she slowly and painfully managed to make her way back to the bridleway. Scrambling in sobbing relief through the final clump of gorse, she fell straight into Sandford's arms.

He thrust her roughly aside and she was shocked at the look of naked fury on his face.

'Where the Devil have you been?' he demanded. 'We have been searching for hours. How dared you go off in such a way. Are you totally without shame? Look at yourself—just look at yourself!' His voice was filled with disgust.

Harriet staggered back. 'What are you saying? I was attacked...'

Sandford's lip curled. 'Again?' he said coldly. 'You do seem to make a habit of that, don't you?'

Ignoring her protests, he turned on his heel and strode up the path to where his horse was tethered. Harriet, grabbing up her skirts, stumbled after him, convinced that she must still be in the grip of some dreadful nightmare and her eyes widened in amazement at the unexpected sight of Clipper grazing peacefully on the verge ahead.

'You found her!' she panted, as Sandford came to a standstill beside the horses. 'I was afraid...'

'Much you cared!' Sandford spun round to face her. 'You left her tied up at the gate while you cavorted with your—your what?' He raised his crop as though to strike her.

Harriet flinched, dumbfounded. 'I don't understand,' she said, her head still pounding. 'What are you accusing me of? I was riding with Judith—I told you yesterday...'

'Spare me the details. I've seen the note—you carelessly left it on your dressing table. Rose brought it to my mother when you failed to return from Westpark.'

'Note? What note? Oh—yes, I see—but that was not intended...'

He turned away from her, his shoulders suddenly slumped and he leaned his head wearily against Pagan's neck.

'It doesn't matter,' he said bleakly. 'I am tired of your tricks. Hopefully, you will soon be gone. I wish to God that I had left you in the ditch—my life has been in turmoil since that day!'

'Oh, please,' exhorted Harriet, laying her hand on his arm. 'Please tell me what you think I have done? I beg of you...' She winced as he gripped her wrist, his eyes suffused with anger as he regarded her unadorned fingers.

'You witch!' he choked. 'Where is it? If you have given it...'

'Stop it! Stop it!' Harriet tried to pull away from him and, finding that she could not escape, she raised her free hand and slapped him hard across his cheek. For an interminable moment he stared down at her, almost unseeingly, then with a groan he crushed her to his chest and buried his face in her hair.

'Oh, dear God! What have I done!' he breathed, but Harriet hardly heard him. She dragged herself away from his grasp and glared at him in rage.

'How dare you! Have you gone mad! I hate you! I cannot wait to get away from this place!' She thrust her hand into her boot. 'See! Here is your precious ring! And to think that I went to the trouble of saving it! I pity whoever has the misfortune to become your wife!'

Casting the jewel at his feet, she burst into tears and swept regally past him. It was more than a mile back to the house, she knew, but she had no intention of asking for Sandford's assistance to mount her horse. She trudged resentfully along the path, clutching up the muddied skirts of her riding habit as best she could, fulminating at the unfairness of life. She had been at this beastly place barely two weeks and already she had been dragged into a lake and set upon by brigands, which was more than had ever befallen her in all her years with the military! What else could happen? She couldn't expect her grandfather to arrive for at least another week, at the earliest. If only she had insisted on leaving with Ozzy and Martha! What right did Sandford have to dismiss their suggestion? Hadn't she just heard him admit that he would be glad when she had gone? He had left her in no doubt as to his opinion of her—calling her a witch—and a trickster!

She came to a sudden standstill on the path, trying to remember the exact words he had used. He had behaved as though he had been the victim, when it was she who had been attacked and tricked not once but three times, she realised, if one counted the puzzle of the note! Walking on, she deliberated upon that particular enigma. Sandford had referred to it with an anger she considered totally uncalled for. It must have been perfectly obvious that the note was not intended for her. Who on earth did he suppose she would arrange to meet in secret? And why? Then an incredible notion entered her head as she recalled his words—he had supposed that! He had been accusing her of having a clandestine tryst!

For a moment or two Harriet felt quite sick as a cold clamminess swept over her body and she had to press her shaking hands over her lips to control their trembling as she struggled to digest the implication of his words.

While Sandford and his men had been supposedly scouring the park she had been concealed inside a bush practically under their noses and then, far from giving her a chance to explain her absence, he had been so convinced of her guilt that he had refused even to listen to her. Worse, he had accused her of having spent hours in some furtive and underhand assignation!

Something else occurred to her. Sandford had said that Clipper had been found tied to the gate, but the only gate was at the end of the Beldale bridleway that, as far as she could judge, was more than a mile from the spot where she had fallen from her horse! Someone must have taken Clipper back to the gate and tied her there! But, in God's name, why?

As she neared the house Harriet's indignation was replaced with apprehension. Who else had been furnished with this untruth? Had Lord William and Lady Caroline also come to the same conclusion as the viscount? What other interpretation would they put on her long absence?

The sound of horse's hooves alerted her to the sight of Tiptree riding up behind her, leading her mare. He dismounted and cupped his hands.

'Up you get, miss,' he said dispassionately. 'His lordship wants you to ride in.'

Harriet allowed the groom to raise her into the saddle. She knew that this would be far better than being seen arriving at the stables without her horse but was still at a loss as to how she would begin to explain her disappearance.

The two horses walked into the yard and were immediately surrounded by the grooms and stable-lads, all expressing delight at 'Missy's' return and clamouring for information. Tiptree waved them aside as he swung down from his mount.

'Miss Cordell got lost in the woods,' he said, in brief explanation. 'She's very tired. Make way, lads. Let's have a bit of space. His lordship is calling in the others.'

Smithers helped Harriet down and took Clipper's reins.

'Glad to see you safe back, miss,' he ventured. 'We was all worried you'd hurt yourself. Don't need no more accidents, you know.'

Harriet took heart from his remark and gave him a shaky smile. Turning to go into the house, she found Tiptree at her side.

'Beg pardon, miss,' he said quietly, 'but his lordship says you dropped this.' He held out the emerald ring. 'He says to tell you ''not to worry''.'

Harriet looked inquiringly at him but his face was expressionless. She slipped the ring on to her finger once more and took a deep breath as she entered the hallway.

'Harriet, my dearest child!' Lady Caroline swept forward to throw her arms around her protégée. 'Oh, thank goodness you are safe! His lordship has been in such a torment!'

Harriet didn't inquire as to which 'lordship' the countess was referring. Kissing her ladyship on the cheek, she assured her that she was, indeed, unhurt and merely in need of a wash and a very long drink.

Lady Caroline indicated her requirements to March and tenderly led Harriet into the salon.

'Sit down, dearest, do,' she said, pressing the shivering Harriet down on to a sofa and offering her a rug to put over her knees.

Harriet, eyes brimming, shook her head and smilingly refused the cover.

'Please, ma'am, you must not wait upon me,' she protested. 'I promise you I have suffered no great harm—but I would like to see Lord William, if I may—if he has been concerned about me I must put his mind at rest—and there is something I need to ask him, if he is not too tired?'

'About that mysterious note?' the countess nodded. 'Yes, he told me. Sandford had rushed off in search of you before we could tell him that it was some sort of joke—although I cannot believe he took it seriously...'

'I'm afraid he did, ma'am,' said Harriet miserably. 'He seems to believe I was involved in some secret—tryst—with someone I met at Judith's party!'

Lady Caroline was indignant. 'But that is preposterous! Why should he think such a thing? His father will give him such a trimming when he returns! Come, my dear, finish your drink and, if you feel up to it, we will go straight to his lordship this instant.'

The earl had been furnished with the news of Harriet's return on the moment of her arrival at the stables and was waiting impatiently for her entrance. Running to his chair she cast herself into his arms and burst into tears. He stroked her hair gently, murmuring comforting endearments, at the same time raising his eyebrows questioningly at his wife, who shook her head in response.

After allowing Harriet to cry herself out, Lord William took the handkerchief the countess was offering and set about repairing the damage to her face, tut-tutting as he did so.

'Now, now, my child,' he said softly. 'This will not do. I will not have these pretty eyelids swollen. This redness simply does not go well with that glorious shade of green—and I fear I shall come down with the croup if my dressing-gown gets any damper!'

Harriet, smiling weakly, sat back on his footstool and twisted the sodden kerchief between her fingers.

'I'm so sorry,' she said tremulously. 'It isn't usual in me to give in so easily. But I find myself at such a loss!'

The earl and countess exchanged glances and Beldale motioned to Chegwin to fetch a chair for his mistress. This done, at his lordship's gesture the valet quietly left the room and Lord William took Harriet's hands in his.

'I think you had better tell us what is troubling you and together perhaps we shall make some sense out of your problems.'

'But you have been so ill,' said Harriet, in an anguished tone, 'and I wanted to avoid bringing you more worry!'

Beldale sighed. 'I have a broken foot, my girl,' he said briskly. 'There is nothing wrong with my brain—whatever that fool Lambert thinks!'

And so, tentatively at first, Harriet told her hosts the full story of her lake misadventure and, with increasing confidence, she breathlessly related this morning's extraordinary events.

Lady Caroline's eyes grew round with horror at Harriet's description of her woodland tomb.

'But this is quite dreadful,' she exclaimed in dismay. 'On Beldale lands—how can this be happening?' and she turned at once to her husband to await his conclusions.

The earl was silent for some little while, conscious of both ladies' eyes upon him at they awaited some erudite explanation that he feared he did not have. Eventually, he spoke.

'It is clear that someone has wished you harm from the moment of your arrival,' he said to Harriet. 'That person—or persons—seem to be privy to a good deal of information about your movements. On the other hand, a fair amount of coincidence seems to be involved. For instance, at the lake, where you might not have chosen to walk on that particular morning and today—you say you had left Westpark much later than you intended—and who could possibly have foreseen your fainting attack? The emerald ring that they failed to find—thanks to your swift action—has only been in your possession since Saturday evening and advertised only at Judith's party and yet, it seems to have been the particular object of the attack—I would not have thought it to be of such singular value.' He shook his head. 'I confess, my dears, I am at as much of a loss as you are, but one thing is very clear—one of this household is involved in passing information outside. How else could Harriet's movements be so well observed?'

He looked at his wife, concerned at her obvious distress.

'This has been a great shock for you, my love,' he said, tenderly squeezing her fingers. 'Most of our staff has been with us for so long, it does not bear thinking about.'

'I cannot bring myself to suspect any of them,' said Lady Caroline unhappily. 'We have hardly any recent additions—Robert's valet and his man Tiptree, of course, and Rose Watts—but she was parlourmaid here long before Harriet's arrival...'

'Nothing of this sort happened before my arrival!' Harriet pointed out despondently. 'It is clear that it is my presence which is causing someone great annoyance!'

'But everyone adores you!' her ladyship protested.

'Apparently not everyone, ma'am,' said Harriet, rising from the footstool and straightening her skirts. And I can think of at least one person who positively dislikes me, she thought, at the same time sadly recalling the previous day's easy companionship between herself and that very individual.

'There is just one thing I must ask of you, Harriet,' said his lordship with a very serious expression on his face.

'Anything you wish, sir,' she replied, uncomfortably aware of what his request was likely to be.

'Please do not leave the house without a manservant—one that Lady Caroline has chosen personally. I do not wish to curtail your movements, but you must know that your safety is our prime concern. Quite apart from the fact that we have all grown to love you dearly, you must not forget that we have undertaken to deliver you to your grandfather undamaged!'

Harriet nodded glumly, unable to dismiss from her mind the irritating thought that had she obeyed Sandford's identical request she would not have found herself in this unenviable position.

Chapter Nine

Young Rothman waited outside Meggy Watts's cottage, immensely proud that he had been chosen to accompany Miss Harriet on the visit. Being only third footman in the Beldale hierarchy, he knew that this was a singular gesture on his employer's part and due entirely to the fact of his being the butler's son.

The elder Rothman had served the Hurst family since his youth and had worked his way up from under-footman to the full prestigious office of butler. He had married one of the ladies' maids and produced three sons, the older two of whom had secured positions in other large houses elsewhere. The strapping young Davy had elected to remain at Beldale, thus gaining the benefit of his father's expert tuition.

He was aware that there was some sort of mystery surrounding Miss Harriet and had heard that she had somehow got herself lost in the copse the other day. Since then he had been appointed to attend her on all of her outings from Beldale, including those from which he derived the greatest pleasure, riding behind her just like a groom! The stable lads had been properly miffed at that, he thought cheerfully, but then her ladyship had wanted someone who could be presentable in both occupations and stable lads just weren't cut out to be footmen.

He peered through the small window, satisfying himself that his charge had not been spirited away, and seated himself once more on the bench outside the cottage, casually wondering as to the purpose of Miss Harriet's visit to the villager's cottage.

Harriet herself was seated on the best chair in the little used parlour, Meggy having dashed around in a flurry after the young lady had requested a few words with her father, flinging open curtains and removing dust-covers from her few precious pieces. The cottager had dismissed Harriet's request to remain in the kitchen, seldom having had such an opportunity to hold court in her own little palace. She had brought her unexpected visitor tea in a china cup and now sat gazing fondly at the sight of Harriet in deep conversation with her father.

Harriet had brought old Potter a gift. In the form of a small, opening booklet, such as was used for needles and pins, it held within its covers the withered rose petal she had rescued from the ruin of his old home. Protected from further ravages by the transparent veil of fine gauze she had stitched over it, the relic was bordered by intricate stitchery that proclaimed the legend 'Joshua and Millicent, 10th August 1769'. On the front cover, depicted in delicate watercolours, was as faithful a representation of number 7, Bottom Meadow Cottages, as Harriet had been able to conjure up from her visits to the site and her further consultations with Rose, the old man's granddaughter.

Josh held the little case reverently in the palms of his calloused and blistered hands and stared down at it with tears in his rheumy old eyes.

'How did 'ee find it, lass?' he whispered, with a catch in his throat. 'I never thought to see it again. I went up there the once but her...' he jerked his head towards his daughter '...her wouldn't let me back.'

Meggy Watts came and stood by her father and lovingly stroked his shaggy head.

'It were dangerous up there, Dad,' she said. 'The roof timbers is falling all along the row and some of them kitchen flagstones have dropped right down into the cellars. You've had one very lucky escape—we don't want no more such accidents, now do we?'

She was studying Harriet's workmanship with admiration.

'It's such a true likeness. But how did you know all this, Miss Cordell?'

'Reverend Taylor furnished me with the details of your parents' wedding day from his parish records,' said Harriet, enormously gratified that her efforts had been awarded such a reception. 'And your own daughter Rose corrected some errors I had made in the painting.'

Turning to Joshua, she laid her hand on his arm. 'I know what it's like to lose treasured possessions, Mr Potter,' she told him. 'My family travelled across Spain in the war years and we had to leave our chattels behind on many occasions—and other times they were destroyed almost in front of our eyes. Your sweetest memories—the ones you keep inside your heart—will never die, I am certain, but sometimes a more tangible memento is needed and I hope that this little token might, in some small way, help you to recover from your dreadful loss.'

'You couldn't have brought me anything in the world that would have pleased me more, miss,' said Josh, slipping the little case into the breast pocket of his shabby old jacket and patting it gently. 'It'll be like having my own dear Milly with me again and I can take it out and look at it whenever I choose! 'Twere part of her bridal nosegay, you see.'

His faded blue eyes twinkled at Harriet from under his bushy brows and he patted the hand that was still holding his own.

'You'm going to make a fine countess when your time comes, miss,' he said, nodding his head at her. 'We should've known that when his lordship finally made his choice his lady would be worth the wait— and, begging your pardon, miss, we all think he's struck gold!'

'Dad! Really!' Meggy was shocked. 'Excuse him, Miss Cordell—he goes too far, sometimes. Honestly, Dad—what will the lady think of us all!'

Shaking her head, Harriet rose to her feet.

'It's to be hoped that a good many years pass before that day dawns, sir,' she said, picking up her reticule. 'And if I could grow to be only half as good as Lady Caroline I should think myself perfect!'

Meggy showed her to the door and Davy Rothman sprang to attention at their appearance, fingering the neck of his smart, new livery nervously.

'Well, hello, Davy,' Meggy greeted him cheerfully. 'My, aren't you the swell, these days?'

Davy inclined his head gravely towards her, feeling slightly awkward at having to address Rose's mother in such a formal way but, at the same time, anxious to impress Miss Harriet with his impeccable manners.

Meggy, too, knew her place and expected no more from him. She bobbed respectfully to Harriet and, on behalf of her father, thanked her once again for her generosity and time.

Walking through the village, with Davy the requisite two steps behind her, Harriet found, to her great discomfort, that she was having to acknowledge bobs and curtsies from all sides as she passed. This entire charade is getting completely out of hand, she thought crossly, but managed to smile as yet another tradesman tipped his hat to her. All of these good people actually thought that she would, one day, be their 'Lady of the Manor' and it was all terribly embarrassing and, she had to admit, inexplicably quite painful to her.

She had spent most of the past week in her room, pleading exhaustion, and the countess, sympathetic as to her real reasons, had not pressed for Harriet's attendance at the dining table and had generously arranged for her to take her meals in her room. Harriet had forced herself to venture out on two previous occasions, in the furtherance of her project, both times escorted by the stalwart Davy, and was deeply conscious of the interest her appearance always aroused. She admitted, but only to herself, that she was now quite afraid that there might be another attempt to harm her in some way and the greatest fear of all was that she had no way of knowing who her enemy could be.

She had not spoken to Sandford at all since the episode in the copse and had seen him only once when, about to come out of her room later that same day, she had caught sight of him leaving his father's chambers. She had stepped swiftly back into the shadows as he appeared and she was certain he had not observed her, but she had been shocked at his demeanour. He had stood for a moment outside the earl's door, shoulders sagging, his face white and drawn and then, as if in a trance, he had walked slowly to his own doorway and entered his room. Harriet had been intending to visit Lord William herself but, after some deliberation, she had decided that it would be unwise to do so and had subsequently returned to her own chamber.

Judith Hurst had ridden over to Beldale that same afternoon, but Lady Caroline had managed to curb her daughter-in-law's curiosity. Westpark House had been Sandford's first objective when Harriet had failed to return to Beldale and Judith had naturally been frantically worried over her friend's disappearance and had demanded to be kept informed as to any developments, sending Ridgeway to assist his cousin in the search.

She failed to comprehend how anyone as level-headed as Harriet could have wandered off the bridleway and become confused in the copse, until the countess explained that Harriet had felt unwell, possibly suffering from a touch of the sun. It had been particularly warm that morning, as she was sure Judith would recall.

Judith did indeed recall that it was she who had been responsible for Harriet's hasty departure and, at once, felt guilty at having persuaded her friend to stay so long at Westpark, surmising that Harriet's headlong dash had been the cause of her fainting fit.

Lady Butler's contribution upon receiving her daughter's account of Harriet's misadventure was to the effect that 'persons who disport themselves all over the Continent with troops of soldiers could hardly be expected to behave with anything resembling acceptable decorum when they returned to civilised society' and Judith found herself heaving a sigh of relief that Sandford was not present when these uncharitable remarks were uttered.

Both Sandford and Ridgeway had been behaving very oddly since Harriet's mishap, she thought. Neither one of them seemed to have time for anything other than estate business and they were usually to be found with their heads together. When Sandford had, almost grudgingly it seemed, eventually found time to give his little nephew some attention in the paddock, he had appeared distracted and disinclined to linger. Judith found Ridgeway's behaviour strange, too. She had thought that he was beginning to let down his guard a little in her favour, for they had exchanged some very promising conversations since their dance together. Then all of a sudden, his interest in her seemed to have vanished overnight and he had no time for anything apart from riding around the park and hanging about in the stables or disappearing off to Beldale with Sandford.

At the end of the week an impatient Judith paid her second visit to Beldale. She had heard that Harriet was apparently well enough to go walking to the village and was hurt that her young friend had not come to visit her. Leaving her horse with her attendant groom, she deliberately forsook her normal practice and entered the house from the rear. In doing so, she almost collided with Harriet as she was crossing the hall. Both girls started back in surprise but it was Harriet who was the first to lower her eyes. Judith quickly noticed this puzzling reticence and impulsively put out her hand.

'Harriet, my dear,' she said, in rising concern. 'Please tell me what is wrong. I know that something dreadful must have happened to upset you so. Won't you confide in me? I thought we were friends!'

Harriet was sick at heart. She wanted to tell Judith the whole story from the beginning but, by now, the tale had become so convoluted that she felt that it would sound quite absurd. In fact, she suddenly decided, it really was absurd and she reached forward and grasped Judith's extended hands in her own.

'Oh, Judith,' she cried. 'I'm so pleased to see you. You can't think how much I have missed you.'

Judith at once put her arms around the younger girl and hugged her. As she did so she spotted Sandford in the act of opening the door of the nearby estate office.

To her amazement, he took one look at her and quickly closed the door again.

'What is going on here?' she said, thrusting Harriet away from her and, still holding her shoulders, gave her friend a firm shake. 'Have you fallen out with Sandford? Is that what this is all about?'

The office door re-opened immediately and Sandford stepped out, eyes averted, with a set of papers in his hand.

'Ah, hello, Judith,' he said, in a poor attempt at heartiness.

Judith registered both the tremor in his voice and the sight of Harriet's flushed face at the same time. She took a deep breath.

'Robert,' she said resolutely, 'you look awful. And Harriet looks awful, too. I can only conclude that the reason for such joint awfulness is that you have had a lover's tiff—and I simply will not have it!' And she stamped her elegant foot. 'Mark carefully what I am doing, Robert!'

'Not now, Judith!' Sandford walked towards his sister-in-law with a warning frown, but Judith put up her crop and prodded it into his chest.

'You don't frighten me, Robert Hurst!' she said defiantly. 'I'm the one who tipped a bottle of ink over your head—remember?'

'I remember, Judith,' said Sandford drily, pushing aside the crop, 'but this is not a bottle-of-ink sort of problem.'

Harriet found her lips curving into an involuntary smile.

'What sort of a problem is a bottle-of-ink problem?' she asked, with an interested glimmer in her eye.

Sandford, with a swift intake of breath, took a step towards her, but Judith moved quickly to stand in front of the girl.

'Leave my friend alone, Robert Hurst!'

Sandford lips twitched and he said, 'But you don't have a bottle of ink, dearest Judith—stand aside!'

'Will someone please tell me what ink has to do with all of this?' Harriet asked, now looking from one to the other in amused exasperation.

Judith gave her friend a quick, appraising glance.

'Harriet,' she said sweetly. 'Would you be so kind as to go into the office and fetch me a bottle of ink? A large one, if you please!'

'Judith!' warned Sandford, but his eyes were now alight with laughter. He backed sideways towards the office door as Harriet, not sure of the point but perfectly willing to give her friend whatever assistance she required, moved swiftly in the same direction.

They collided in the doorway and Sandford, automatically thrusting out his hands to prevent Harriet from stumbling, found himself with his arms around her and it seemed to him, in that second, that the earth rocked.

Harriet had put up her own hands to save herself and now found herself pressed against him with her hands on his chest. An extraordinary sensation was sweeping through her body and she was acutely aware of Sandford's laboured breathing. If I look up I am lost, she

thought weakly and forced herself to maintain a steadfast interest in his waistcoat buttons.

'Well, then?' came Judith's voice. 'Surely this is
where you kiss and make up?'

Harriet and Sandford sprang apart instantly. Harriet
felt herself blushing to the tips of her toes, but did not
fail to register that the viscount had refused to relinquish his hold on her hand and she herself, it seemed,
had neither the strength nor desire to pull away.

'Pretty dismal exhibition, I'd say,' said Judith, with
a wide smile. 'I've still a good mind to...' and her eyes
swept around the office as though in search of something.

Sandford, still holding Harriet's hand tightly, leaned
over the desk and kissed his sister-in-law on the cheek.

'Pax, Judith,' he said quietly. 'No need now, I promise. You win.'

'No, Robert, this time you win,' said Judith firmly,
beaming at Harriet, and Sandford smilingly nodded his
agreement.

'I wish someone would tell me what the joke is,'
came Harriet's plaintive voice. 'It's like being in some
foreign country where one doesn't understand the language.'

'Well, it used to be a private joke, sweetheart,' said
Sandford, reaching out for her other hand and smiling
into her eyes. 'But we shall tell you!'

Sweetheart! Harriet couldn't believe her ears. Sandford had called hcr *sweetheart*! Now what game was
he playing at? She had to force herself to concentrate
very carefully on his next words.

'Well now,' he began grandly, ducking away from Judith's hand, 'there was once a very spoilt little girl who had no playmates—*ouch! That hurt!*—for she always wanted—and usually got—her own way so no one would play with her. Her father—who was a very wise man...' At this point Judith nodded her head vigorously and Sandford, his grin widening, continued '—arranged for his unpopular little daughter to take her lessons with two charmingly behaved—*pax! I said Pax!*—fairly well-behaved young gentlemen. Well, the sweet child tried her tricks out with these lads and discovered that they were totally immune to her foot-stamping and tears until, one memorable day, she threatened the older boy with a bottle of ink...'

'Why?' asked Harriet, at last beginning to comprehend. 'What had you—he refused to do?'

'He had refused to get off his brother's head!' broke in Judith, laughing. 'The two of them were scrapping—as usual—if I may say so—and Mr Penrose—our tutor—had left the room. Our instructions were to fill in some cities in our map-books and I had persuaded...'

'Huh! Persuaded!' Sandford chimed in. 'Philip, who for some queer reason, was becoming increasingly besotted with this creature, had been doing her geography for weeks—she apparently being unable to distinguish north from south—and probably still can't for all I know—*missed!* Anyway, he was patiently filling in her book as well as his own and I accidentally flicked ink over hers. Philip jumped me, I sat on his head and, well—the rest is history!'

'Judith poured ink over your head?' breathed Harriet in awe, unable to believe that her elegant, well-behaved friend could ever have acted in such a totally undisciplined manner.

'Absolutely! Down my collar—over my hair, face, eyes—whole bottle—the lot!'

'What did your tutor do?'

'Thrashed us both—Phil and me,' Sandford answered dismissively, appearing to be deeply interested in counting her fingers.

'But what about Judith?' frowned Harriet, vainly attempting to extract her hands from his grasp.

'That's the point, you see,' said Judith gently. 'Both boys took the blame and said that I had been working the whole time—I was actually given a box of sugar plums—but I couldn't eat them. I was so ashamed! I never had another such tantrum as long as I lived.'

'Well, hardly ever,' put in Sandford. 'Jolly good sugar plums, too, as I recall.'

'You gave them to the boys?' Harriet smiled at Judith, who looked back at her fondly and nodded.

'And you wouldn't actually have poured ink on Sandford today, would you?'

Judith and the viscount looked at each other and both burst out laughing.

'Well, the thing is, darling girl,' said Sandford, raising Harriet's unresisting fingers to his lips, 'neither of us really knows that, for sure!'

He was watching her closely, desperately trying to gauge her reaction. She, for her part, found that she was unable to meet his eyes, afraid of what she might see. Surely he was still play-acting? At that thought a tiny ache crept into her heart and she knew that she was close to tears.

At that moment Judith bent to retrieve the papers that had fallen from her brother-in-law's hands during the scuffle, frowning as she happened to catch sight of her butler's name on one of the sheets.

'What are these lists, Robert?' she inquired, beginning to peruse them more carefully.

Sandford dropped Harriet's hands and leapt to his feet in consternation, plucking the papers from Judith's hands and thrusting them into a drawer.

'Really, Judith,' he chided, raising an eyebrow. 'Reading other people's private correspondence. What would your mother say!'

Judith flushed.

'Don't be a beast, Robert,' she said. 'That was a list of Westpark staff, as well you know. That is my business, surely?'

The viscount shrugged his shoulders carelessly.

'It's just something that Charles and I are working on,' he said, searching desperately for a brainwave. 'Er—fact is, we're trying to cut back a bit!'

'Cut back!' Judith was astounded, then her eyes grew anxious. 'We're not in any trouble, are we, Robert? I thought Charles had been managing rather well...'

'Nothing for you to worry about,' said Sandford, mentally crossing himself. 'We thought we might try to cut out some duplication, that's all—too many people doing the same job, it seems to me.'

'But you can't be thinking of putting people off?'

'No, no—just moving some of 'em around, perhaps. It's not a problem, honestly, Judith. Please forget about it.'

Only partly convinced, Judith dropped the subject and set about extracting a promise from Sandford to bring Harriet to Westpark for dinner the following evening. Having got the nod from that bemused young lady, the viscount agreed and Judith, kissing each of them in turn, forbade them to quarrel and left the room to seek out her mother-in-law.

Harriet turned at once to follow, but Sandford put out his hand to detain her.

'And where are you off to in such a hurry?' he demanded softly, the dangerous gleam once more in his eyes.

Harriet looked at him gravely.

'You don't have to keep up the pretence any longer, my lord,' she said calmly. 'Judith cannot hear you. But I must commend you on your excellent performance.'

'What the—what absurd fancy has got into your head now?' he groaned, clutching his brow.

'Thanks to your clever subterfuge, my lord,' said Harriet, ignoring Sandford's incredulous expression, 'Judith has returned home in a happier frame of mind than that with which she arrived. Your part was so well enacted that it prevented her from asking any awkward questions about my—mishap—and for that I am deeply grateful, for I find that I cannot lie to her any longer— whatever your opinion of my talents in that direction!' Her voice trembled at this point and she looked away.

Sandford sat on the edge of the desk, carefully contemplating Harriet's averted gaze. Tentatively, he reached out and, taking both her hands in his own, he drew her gently towards him, holding his breath as he felt her initial resistance slip away.

'Look at me, Harriet,' he pleaded.

In trepidation, Harriet obeyed and, raising her eyes to meet his, was confused to behold, not the confident gleam of amusement she had expected, but a very shamefaced expression.

'I don't know where to start,' he said, his voice low and hesitant. 'You said you hated me—I don't blame you—I hate myself. Please don't punish me any further!'

'You called me a witch!' she said tremulously.

'Oh, but you are a witch!' Half-smiling, he lifted one hand and traced his fingers down her cheek. 'You have bewitched me.'

Harriet dashed his hand away in vexation. 'You didn't believe me,' she cried. 'Twice—no, three times—you didn't believe me!'

'I am a contemptible swine,' he said, his throat tightening at the memory.

'You accused me of—of—dreadful things!' Harriet found that she couldn't bear the look of anguish in his eyes.

'I know I deserve to be horsewhipped,' he choked, his confidence on the verge of destruction.

'Horses shouldn't be whipped,' she whispered, her lips trembling.

'But I should?' A flicker of hope had crept into his voice.

'I didn't say that, my lord.'

'Robert,' he said fiercely.

Startled, she tried to move away from him, but he still held one hand tightly in his grasp and seemed intent upon recapturing the other.

'Lord Sandford,' she protested, weakly, 'please release me. This is most improper!'

'Call me Robert,' he cajoled her, the fire back in his eyes. 'Then maybe I shall let you go.'

'Maybe! That's very poor odds!' Harriet replied spiritedly.

He put his head on one side as though considering this point, then nodded. 'True. Call me Robert and I promise not to kiss you. How's that?'

Scandalised, Harriet struggled to free herself. 'You wouldn't dare—you told me that you were no ravisher!'

'There's a first time for everything,' he said coolly. 'Call me Robert.'

Harriet stopped struggling and regarded him balefully. 'Well, if it means so much to you—*Robert*,' she said, through clenched teeth. 'Now let me go.'

'Say it again—nicely!'

'Oh, Robert! Robert! *Robert!* Damn you!' she exclaimed, without thought for the consequences.

'Harriet, my love, you are truly magnificent!' Sandford stood up, swept her towards him and wrapped his arms around her, ignoring her squeal of dismay.

'Stop struggling—otherwise I shall forget myself—that's better. Now, listen to me, Harriet—please.'

For a moment he stood very quietly, simply holding her against him and, as her eyes crept up to his face, she could see that he had become very serious once more. She didn't move, somehow content to remain within the circle of his arms, listening to the rapid beating of his heart. At last he spoke.

'I know that nothing I can say will undo the hurt that I've caused you...' He hesitated, choosing his words with meticulous care. 'And it is probably of very little interest to you to know that, far from play-acting, I truly believe that I love you.' She quivered and his arms tightened. 'Yes, I do. I had begun to hope that you might learn to hold me in similar regard—I admit that I was mad with jealousy and so desperately afraid, my darling, I think I was about to lose my reason. I was ready to commit murder—I know that now. You brought me to my senses when you struck me and I knew instantly that I had been wrong—that the whole thing was clearly a well-executed plot...'

He stopped as Harriet pulled away from him.

'Why were you so ready to think the worst of me?' she cried. 'You refused even to listen to me!'

Sandford grimaced, finding the memory of that episode of his behaviour particularly repugnant.

'I had found certain items in a clearing near the gate,' he said, clearing his throat.

'What items?' Harriet demanded. 'And how did they concern me?'

Sandford flushed and shamefacedly fingered his cravat, as though it were suddenly too tight.

'Your hat and a glove—I recognised them both, of course...'

'And?' said Harriet stiffly, aware that something worse was to follow.

'A gentleman's pocket flask—it had contained brandy,' choked the viscount, unwilling to meet her shocked gaze. 'And a crumpled cravat.'

'Also a gentleman's, I take it?' Harriet's eyes glittered.

Sandford nodded in dumb resignation.

'All the signs of a sordid tête-à-tête, in fact?' Harriet inquired in a deceptively sweet voice. 'No wonder you didn't want to listen to me!'

'You had the smell of brandy on your breath!' exclaimed Sandford hotly, in his own defence.

'So that's what that funny taste was,' mused Harriet. 'They must have given it to me after I passed out.'

Chagrined, Sandford reached out for her once more, but she neatly sidestepped him and opened the office door. Swiftly he strode towards it, attempting to block her exit, but she was out into the hallway in a trice.

'No doubt your parents—who have proved themselves my true friends—have by now provided you with the correct version of that morning's events,' she said in a low voice, not wishing to attract March's attention. 'And your only excuse for your appalling behaviour is to tell me that you think you love me—well, we obviously have a very different understanding of the meaning of the word ''love'', my lord. The man to whom I give my heart will *never* doubt my word, *never* assume my guilt—even if confronted with the *blackest* of evidence—but, most of all, he will be prepared to lay down his life to protect my name and my person and—' here her voice broke '—I shall do likewise for him. You, my lord, are not and will never be that man!'

She turned to leave, but Sandford caught her arm. His face was rigid, his eyes unfathomable.

'I wish you well in your search for this paragon,' he grated, 'although such a pattern of perfection is unlikely to choose you as his mate...' He stopped, aghast. My God, what am I saying, he thought, horrified at his own words. He let go of Harriet's arm and bowed stiffly. 'My apologies, ma'am,' he said and re-entered the office, closing the door behind him.

For a moment Harriet stood frozen with shock. His damning words, which continued to echo in her ears, had shaken her to the core, for she was obliged to acknowledge that he was right. In spite of her high-flown speech, she was painfully aware that it had been mostly her own impetuous and foolhardy behaviour that had brought her to this stand. From the time she had left her home in Lincolnshire, right up to this very moment, she had insisted upon going her own headstrong way, ignoring advice from all sides, interfering in other people's lives—people she hardly knew, she realised, her face suddenly scarlet at some of the memories—and presumptuously assuming that she knew what was best for everyone. No gentleman on earth could be expected to regard such conduct with anything but the deepest abhorrence. What might be considered charming in a wayward child was not acceptable in a full-grown female. Would she never learn? she pondered in despair. Time and time again she had disregarded the warnings and now, it seemed, she had reaped the whirlwind and those rash and arrogant words she had so haughtily vaunted would surely return to torment her.

Hot tears welled up into her eyes as she made her way to the foot of the staircase and the sudden blurring of her vision caused her to stumble on the first step. She was aware of a firm hand on her elbow and an anxious March at her side.

'Miss Harriet?' His voice was gentle. 'Are you unwell? Shall I call Rose? Come and sit down for a moment until you recover.'

He led her to a nearby chair and stood uncertainly by, not wishing to exceed his duties but angry that something or someone had upset his little favourite. Ever since that first evening when she had tiptoed nervously down the stairs in her borrowed finery he had felt that she was something special. Always a smile and a kind word for the servants, quick with her thanks for their services and he, for one, had never heard a single complaint pass her lips. He had watched her change from that laughing-eyed, bright-haired angel into a silent shadow of her former self, all in the space of three weeks. One hardly ever heard her spontaneous and infectious laugh these days, he thought morosely, and if that's what being engaged does for a girl he was damned if he was going to offer for Maudie Hiller. He watched closely, wearing his usual impassive expression, as Harriet composed herself, dabbing at her eyes with the ridiculous piece of lace the ladies called a handkerchief, longing to offer her his own pristine equivalent but knowing that it would be quite over-stepping the mark to do so.

'Thank you, March,' said Harriet tremulously, rising to her feet. 'I fear I must be coming down with a cold. I will go up to my room now—if you would be so good as to send Rose to me?'

'At once, Miss Harriet,' said the loyal footman. 'And perhaps a glass of wine—a well-known restorative, so I'm told?'

'Thank you, I would be glad of that.' Harriet nod-ded, avoiding his eyes.

He watched her walk unsteadily up the stairs and had the most disrespectful urge to 'pop' his lordship 'one on the beak'. Blinking, he moved smartly to the green baize door that led to the lower stairs and deliv-ered his instructions to Rose.

Sandford, meanwhile, had been staring blindly at the sheets of paper in front of him on the desk, unable to believe that he had uttered those unforgivable words.

Any minute now I shall wake up, he thought, pray-ing that he must be in the throes of some dreadful nightmare but, raising his eyes to the window and per-ceiving the peaceful summer scene beyond, he knew beyond doubt that the whole episode had been only too real.

With a shaking hand he reached for the decanter on the side table and cursed when he saw that it was empty. Damned servants! What did they think they were employed for? He tugged angrily at the bell-rope and waited impatiently for March to appear. Pointing curtly towards the tray, he raised his brows imperiously.

March bowed his head in acquiescence. The fact that the room had been occupied for some considerable time, preventing the carrying out of certain domestic tasks, was no excuse for such laxity, as well he knew and offered no plea in his own defence. He picked up the salver and walked swiftly to the door.

'Your lordship's pardon,' he said, exiting at the double. 'I shall attend to it at once.'

Sandford eyed the closed door sourly. The whole damned house seemed to be going mad, he thought, quite certain he had sensed hostility in young March's demeanour. It's her fault, he concluded savagely, sweeping the papers to one side. She has everybody under her spell, from the lowest boot-boy right up to...

'Me, confound it!' he shouted, leaping from his chair. 'But I won't have it! I shall leave! I shall go back to London—Paris—anywhere! Put it down, man, and, for God's sake, get out!'

This last was to March, who had returned with the full decanters. The footman stared at the viscount in open-mouthed astonishment, unable to believe his eyes and ears. Never before had he been spoken to in this manner, not in this house! He carefully set the silver tray down into its appointed place and bowing, with ill-disguised contempt, he left the room once more.

Sandford was astounded. The man was nothing short of insolent, he decided. He'd have him out of here before he could say...! Suddenly, he checked, took a deep breath and gripped the edge of the desk to steady himself, grimacing with shame at this inconceivable lapse. Collapsing limply into his chair, he buried his head in his hands and shuddered in despair.

'Oh, God, Harriet! Forgive me!' he whispered brokenly. 'What am I going to do? The whole world is falling apart and I'm powerless to prevent it!'

He remained, for some time, slumped at the desk until the sound of the hall clock chiming the hour infiltrated his brain. Straightening up, his eyes fell on the papers he had been attempting to examine earlier. With very little enthusiasm he pulled them towards him and began to peruse the top sheet.

Chapter Ten

Charles Ridgeway sat pensively on his horse, survey-
ing the landscape below him. To the far right he could
just make out the chimneys and parapets of the Beldale
mansion, bathed in the late evening sunshine and protected by the mass of woodland and fields that surrounded it. At the foot of the hill up which he had just
ridden, on the very edge of the Beldale estate, nestled
his own home, the Dower House, with its neat gardens
and home farm. To his left lay the more modern structure of Westpark House, close to its own boundary with
the larger estate and, still further left, the slate rooftop
of Staines, the old Butler property, with only the ter-
raced gardens remaining within its demesne. Beyond
the distant village and as far as the eye could see, all
Hurst owned, in one way or another. A man without
property is surely an insignificant creature, he concluded, once more ruefully censuring his late and far
from lamented sire for his weak and prodigal lifestyle.
Then, not being a vindictive man, Ridgeway sighed and
bent his mind to the more pressing problem that was
troubling him as he turned his mount towards Beldale.

It is like looking for a needle in a haystack, he thought. Over a hundred men on the list and more than half of them could be described as 'tall, thin and dark'! Putting faces to the names had taken them all week, Sandford having refused to allow anyone, apart from his man Tiptree, to assist in the covert search. In addition, he had demanded that no one was actually questioned, pointing out that this would immediately put any villains on their guard, reminding his cousin that neither Billy Tatler nor his chum Nick had recognised the man at the boathouse and, therefore, this particular check was being carried out only for the purpose of eliminating the obviously innocent. Their objective, he had said, was to whittle down the total number to just a few men whom he could present to the young lads in the hope that they would be able to identify their tormentor.

'We're looking for a recent arrival or someone who doesn't go about in the village much,' he now said to Ridgeway, having arranged to meet his cousin in the paddock between the two estates, where he knew that their conversation would not be overheard.

'Or a casual worker, who has come and gone,' offered Ridgeway, exasperated that his hands had been so tied. 'Or a passing tinker, tramp—oh, lord, Sandford—any number of itinerants come through the village!'

'He won't be an itinerant,' returned Sandford firmly. 'Billy told you he thought he was from the Big House—that indicates his manner of dress and, probably, speech as well. He would have said, if he had thought him to be a vagrant. No, Charles, I'm convinced that this ''cove'' has to have some sort of status or position within one of the households.'

'Well, I hope to God you're wrong in that! And why should anyone have developed such animosity towards Miss Cordell in so short a time?' asked his cousin. 'As far as I can judge, from my discreet conversations around the village…' He caught Sandford's frowning expression '—very discreet, I promise you, old man— she is well liked, one could say almost revered in certain places. I, for one, can't imagine anyone taking her in dislike. She appears to have no faults, as I'm sure you agree.'

Sandford had turned away, a painful lump in his throat, the memory of the previous day's events still haunting him.

'She can be rather impetuous at times,' he said, struggling to keep his voice level.

Charles regarded him curiously. 'But that is her chief virtue, wouldn't you say, neck-or-nothing—that's your lady, Sandford. No half-measures about her. They're all saying she'll make you a grand viscountess, man, she has a rare understanding of people's feelings—not just their needs, as most of us have. You're damned lucky that she chose you—I wish that I were as fortunate!'

He turned his horse's head towards the Dower House and raised his brows questioningly. 'Coming over for a spot of grub? I'm famished, I can tell you—and Tiptree here is feeling mighty peckish, too, I'll be bound. We've been at it since the early hours without a break—although I dare say you'll be wanting to get back to your sweetheart?'

Sandford, wincing at Ridgeway's unintended irony, accepted his cousin's invitation with alacrity. Having encountered Harriet entering the breakfast room just as he was about to depart, he had stiffly reminded her of their joint promise to attend Westpark that evening and, until the appointed hour, he intended to stay well clear of her frosty gaze. She had informed him that she would, of course, be ready at whatever time suited him and had stonily agreed to his request that they should endeavour to keep up their charade for what would probably be only a few days more, until her grandfather arrived.

While the viscount was doing his utmost to flush out her assailants, Harriet was engaged in a verbal tussle with Lord William. She had spent part of the morning trying to calculate the extent of her financial indebtedness to the Hursts and had made the mistake of mentioning this matter to his lordship.

'Little girls shouldn't worry their pretty little heads about such things,' he said soothingly. 'I am happy to stand your banker.'

'Yes, but...' Harriet was not at all satisfied at this arrangement.

The earl wagged his finger at her. 'I refuse to discuss the matter with you, Harriet. It concerns only your grandfather and myself—at least, for the moment,' he finished, somewhat enigmatically.

Harriet, loath to cause him any distress, changed the subject. Aware that Lady Caroline, Chegwin, and even Sir Basil himself, had attributed much of the earl's speedy recovery to her earlier cheerful visits and, apart from that single lapse into tears which had occurred after the incident in the woods, she had endeavoured to behave in the usual sparkling and light-hearted manner he had come to expect of her. Lately, however, she was finding it a great effort to keep up the merry repartee that so delighted him and, although she was always quickly diverted by Beldale's own wicked sense of humour, she had occasionally experienced the odd sensation that his lordship was working equally hard to keep up her spirits.

'We are to dine at Westpark this evening,' she now told him. 'No doubt I shall have a fund of ''Butlapses'' to bring you tomorrow.'

'Butlapses' was an expression the earl had coined early in his acquaintance with Judith's mother and he had often used it during his conversations with Harriet after he had discovered that they shared the same sense of the ridiculous.

'I vow she seems to get worse as she gets older,' he chortled. 'Even as a young woman she was prone to making unfortunate remarks but, having apparently devoted her life to perfecting the art, now that she is practically in her dotage she seems to think that age gives her the unassailable right to be downright rude. A good many of us old ones suffer from that same delusion, of course,' he added, with a twinkle in his eye.

'Oh, not you, sir,' protested Harriet. 'I am certain that I have never heard you utter a truly vindictive remark and dear Lady Caroline sees only the good in everyone, so she is also exempt from your reckoning. I believe...' She stopped and her cheeks coloured.

Beldale, who had been contemplating his move on the chessboard between them, looked up at her hesitation.

'What is it that you believe, my dear?' he asked, his eyes suddenly alert as Harriet dropped her own in confusion at his scrutiny.

'I fear I seem to be growing too opinionated, my lord,' she stammered. 'And, unlike—certain of our acquaintances, I cannot plead the excuse of maturity.'

The earl looked at her in blank astonishment.

'Harriet, my love,' he said sorrowfully. 'You are in deadly danger of becoming ''one of them''.'

'One of whom, my lord?' asked Harried, puzzled.

'One of the great English sisterhood of niminy-piminy milksops,' said the earl, banging down his knight with such force that the rest of the pieces bounced off their squares.

'Oh, dear,' said Harriet, putting her hand to her mouth as her lips twitched involuntarily.

'Oh, dear, indeed,' said his lordship reproachfully. 'See how badly your ''best behaviour'' affects my play!'

Harriet burst out laughing and bent to retrieve the fallen chessmen. 'I believe you did that on purpose, sir,' she chuckled. 'I was near to victory, you must concede.'

Beldale regarded her fondly. 'Worth a dozen defeats to see you laugh again,' he said warmly. 'And now I demand to know who has been filling your head with this nonsense!'

Harriet was silent for a moment then, turning to look him squarely in the eye, she said, 'I'm afraid that Sandford and I have ''come to cuffs'' yet again, sir. He disapproves of my behaviour and—and—well, he has given me to understand that others might find it equally unacceptable. I was merely trying to m-modify...'

She caught his expression and broke into a grin. 'Well, if you will make me laugh, how can I possibly hope to improve?'

'Improve at your peril, my girl!' exclaimed his lordship, horrified at the prospect. 'If that young fool can't recognise a diamond when he has one in his hand, then he must resign himself to wearing paste! And I shall tell him so myself!'

'Please don't,' interrupted Harriet hurriedly. 'He would dislike above all things to know that I had been discussing him with you—and you must allow that he has had a great deal to contend with of late. I really do intend to try to conduct myself in the most dignified manner when I am with him but—I promise to save my worst behaviour for your lordship!'

'Excellent!' answered Beldale, with a delighted smile, 'Although I am bound to point out that the contemplation of your most dignified manner is enough to send one into the wildest hysterics!'

Ruefully, Harriet had to agree, although privately vowing that she would still endeavour to be on her very best behaviour that evening.

She dressed with care, choosing a pale turquoise crepe gown in the Grecian mode, with its gently draped bodice gathered under the bosom and its skirt flowing softly to her ankles. She elected to wear no jewellery, other than the obligatory ring, not wishing to be reminded of that other eventful occasion, and Rose, still bemoaning the absence of suitable adornment, brushed her mistress's bright locks into their new style and wove a silver ribbon through them. The result was one of simple but charming elegance.

Sandford, too, paid special attention to his toilette, discarding several neckcloths in his efforts to achieve the perfect knot. Kimble stood in silent reproach as, one after another, the snowy silk cravats were hurled aside until, breathing heavily, the viscount pronounced himself satisfied.

Kimble then helped his master into his exquisitely cut tailcoat, adjusting the lapel fronts carefully over the white silk waistcoat and smoothing away an imperceptible crease on the broad shoulders. Grudgingly pleased with the result, the valet stood back and gave a brief nod.

The viscount eyed him sourly for a moment, then emitted a deep chuckle. 'Oh, I've been a terrible trial to you this past week, haven't I, Kimble?' he said, with a sheepish grin. 'Accept my apologies, dear man—and have a tankard on me!'

He proffered a coin, which Kimble accepted with alacrity, although his countenance clearly displayed his affront at his master's suggestion.

'You know that I never frequent the local hostelry, my lord,' he said loftily. 'However, I shall be pleased to share a bottle of wine with Mr Rothman at your lordship's expense.'

He passed Sandford his fobs and signet ring and watched, eagle-eyed, as the viscount pinned a diamond stud into the folds of his cravat. Then he handed him his top hat and evening cloak and, opening the door for his master to leave, he executed his very correct bow.

Sandford, descending the stairs, perceived that Harriet had forestalled him and, to his intense irritation, he saw March step forward, take the cloak from her arm and carefully arrange it about her shoulders. Neither did he miss her smile of grateful thanks to the young footman, who retreated to his appointed place with what Sandford, gritting his teeth, could only describe as a fawning expression.

Great start, he thought wryly, shepherding the impassive Harriet out to the waiting carriage and handing her into her seat. He had been hoping for a more auspicious beginning to the evening, conscious that this could be his last chance to reinstate himself into her good books.

Seating himself opposite her, he leaned forward and smilingly complimented her on her appearance, which admittedly he had caught sight of only briefly before March's swift attentions.

She inclined her head in acknowledgement, but did not meet his eye, seeming to find the passing view of greater interest.

'I trust that you will find some reserves of your usual good humour before we arrive at Westpark,' he said uncomfortably. 'Judith will expect us to have—recovered from our—lover's tiff, or whatever she called it!'

'I can assure you that I am perfectly aware of my part, my lord,' she replied woodenly, clasping her gloved hands together in her lap. 'You will excuse me, however, if I save my performance until we have an audience. You need have no qualms as to the propriety of my behaviour—I shall be everything that is correct, I promise you.'

'Oh, good God, Harriet!' cried Sandford, flinging himself back into his own corner in exasperation. 'How long do you intend to keep this up?'

Unmoved, she regarded him in silence, her green eyes inscrutable. 'Only for a few more days, I hope, my lord,' she said, again without expression. 'My grandfather cannot be far from Beldale now and I hope that I can prevail upon him to remove me to some—other accommodation—until he is ready to return us to his own home.'

Sandford stared in hopeless frustration at her rigid countenance. 'Oh, that will create a fine impression of our hospitality, won't it?' he said sarcastically. 'I'm sure it will please my parents wonderfully!'

Harriet's face flamed resentfully and she glared at him from under her dark lashes.

'Oh, a veritable hit, my lord!' she said scornfully. 'Although it will probably come as a great surprise to you to know that neither Lord William nor Lady Caroline seem to share your low opinion of me...'

'Stow it, Harriet,' he cried hoarsely, his own cheeks flushing, 'you know damned well that I don't have a low opinion of you!'

'It has improved, then, since yesterday, my lord?' she asked witheringly. 'For I seem to remember that you thought me totally beyond the pale only twenty-four hours since!'

'I'm not proud of what I said yesterday,' he exclaimed heatedly. 'I was angry—you know I was angry!'

'It appears to be a particular failing of your lordship's,' she rejoined. 'However, perhaps you could manage to hold yourself in check for the next few hours, as I see we have arrived at our destination. If I could have your hand, my lord?'

Sandford was obliged to stifle the retort that was forming on his lips and, inwardly seething, he sprang out of the carriage to give her his hand.

Judith swept into the hall to welcome them. Harriet was delighted to observe that her friend seemed to have put off her blacks for good, for she was wearing a most becoming gown of lavender silk. The two girls devoted the next few minutes to comparing styles and laughingly exchanging extravagant compliments with one another.

Sandford, handing their cloaks to the waiting Finchley, quickly registered the return of Harriet's normal lively disposition and, in spite of the earlier setback, was once more determined to take full advantage of any opportunity that might arise.

'Come along into the drawing-room,' smiled Judith. 'Mother and Charles are waiting for us...'

'Charles is dining with us?' asked Sandford, in some surprise.

Judith nodded, a slight blush staining her cheeks. 'The more the merrier, wouldn't you say?' she said, as they entered the room. 'And, since you have lived in each other's pockets all week, I was afraid that you might begin to feel deprived if you were separated for too long!'

'Very amusing!' Sandford said with a grin, striding forward to present his compliments to Lady Butler. 'Evening, ma'am, I trust I find you in good health?'

Her ladyship gave him a pale smile.

'Glad to see that *you*, in any event, are in such good spirits,' she said, fanning herself ostentatiously. 'I myself find this warm weather quite overpowering—I believe your Miss Cordell suffers from a similar weakness—if we are to believe what we hear?'

She looked towards Harriet, who appeared to be involved in some sort of amusing wordplay with Ridgeway. An expression of contempt came into Lady Butler's eyes as she continued, 'I cannot think what possessed Judith to invite her bailiff to eat his dinner with us. Although, I am obliged to point out that it is all of a piece with her conduct since you brought your—young *lady* back with you to Beldale. A certain laxity of standards, you might say—I must suppose that *she* has been filling my daughter's head with some sort of foreign egalitarian nonsense!'

'Surely Judith has been far too well brought up by your own good self to be influenced by the word of a mere soldier's girl?' returned Sandford, who was, as usual, intensely irritated at Lady Butler's appalling rudeness but, at the same time, fiendishly interested to see how far on to her own cleft stick he could pinion her. He was gradually beginning to understand how Philip had handled the old harridan and why his father found her so amusing.

She glowered at him in silence for a moment or two, fidgeting with her fan. 'How very like your brother you are,' she said diffidently. 'That he should perish on his own doorstep in a carriage accident, while you escaped unscathed after ten years of war in some foreign land, strikes me as being grossly unfair—but life is so, as I am constantly reminded!'

Sandford, staggered at her outrageous insensitivity, was momentarily lost for words. 'I'm afraid that I cannot find it in me to apologise for my survival, ma'am,' he managed eventually. 'As to unscathed, I can assure you that I have a fine scar on my leg...' He gently patted his right thigh.

'Really, sir!' she protested. 'I have told you before that I will not have such unsavoury topics in my house!'

'My brother's house, I believe, madam,' he corrected her with stiff politeness, 'Or, in any event, Judith's, to hold in trust for his son!'

As this rejoinder seemed to have the effect of re-
ducing her ladyship to an affronted silence, he decided
that he had done more than his share of duty insofar
as she was concerned, especially as the uneasy pause
allowed him to become increasingly conscious of the
sounds of merriment that were emanating from the
group at the pianoforte.

'May I bring you a drink?' he forced himself to ask
Lady Butler, his natural good manners once more to
the fore. 'I see Pinter hovering with a tray and our
Cousin Charles is always so reluctant to push himself
forward—unlike myself. Lemonade, perhaps?'

She shook her head ungraciously, unfurling her fan
and fluttering it affectedly to and fro across her fleshy
cheeks—looking for all the world like some giant puce
porpoise floundering on a rock, he thought ungallantly
as he made his way across the room.

Harriet and Ridgeway were seated together at the
pianoforte, attempting to construct a duet, the former
never having had a lesson in her life and the latter
unable to recall many of his. That they were managing
to produce anything resembling a tune was due partly
to Harriet's excellent ear and, mainly, to Judith's hastily mouthed instructions to Ridgeway. Much laughter
ensued and Sandford pessimistically predicted that his
appearance would be certain to create a damper.

To his astonishment, however, Harriet leapt at once
to her feet as he approached and, taking him by the
hand, pulled him over to the instrument, begging
Ridgeway to relinquish his seat.

'—for I now have a *much* more proficient partner in *Robert*!' she cried gaily, apparently oblivious to the look in his eyes as he sat down beside her. 'Come now, dearest. Show how it is *perfectly* possible for two to devise a tune between them. I shall choose the chords and you must add all the terribly clever trills and runs that you are so good at! We have done this on *many* occasions so I *know* that it is not beyond your capabilities!'

Not quite out of his depth, for he was a competent pianist, Sandford waited until she struck her first chord, a C major and, thinking swiftly, he tentatively executed a few notes of a popular tune, hoping that the expected G would follow. It came on the beat without hesitation and so, between the two of them, the little ditty was rendered almost perfectly, to the delight of the two spectators, who clapped most heartily at its conclusion.

'Now that you see how it is done,' Harriet said to Judith, 'you and Charles should do far better than we did, for you both have the benefit of a musical education and you, I know, play beautifully.'

So Judith and Ridgeway took their places and their little piece was performed with more zest than skill, due to the laughter that accompanied its execution, but they jubilantly managed to finish at one and the same time, just as Finchley entered to announce that dinner was served.

Judith insisted that, as their number was odd, formalities would be dispensed with and that they must all go directly to the dining-room without further ado; she herself would accompany Lady Butler. Several of the leaves had been removed from the large mahogany table, which enabled the small group to disport themselves within comfortable speaking distance of one another, and still allowed for the prodigious number of side dishes to be positioned within reach.

Judith took the head of the table with the two men seated, one on each side of their hostess, at the top, Lady Butler to Ridgeway's left and Harriet to the viscount's right.

Harriet, true to her word, gave a dedicated impersonation of a loving bride-to-be in addition to keeping up her cheerful bonhomie. She was momentarily disconcerted, at various intervals throughout the splendid meal, to find Lady Butler's disapproving eyes upon her. However, all through the soup, fish, meat and game courses she continued with her amusing repartee, occasioning Judith to upset her wine glass because she was laughing so much, and her friend's mother to tut-tut even more vigorously at everyone's unseemly behaviour! Ridgeway, alternately grinning at Harriet's witticisms and smiling into Judith's shining eyes, was happy simply to be at his goddess's table.

Sandford, on the other hand, was in a perpetual state of nervous tension. One minute he was laughing along with the others and the next finding himself contemplating Lady Butler's rigid disapproval of the merriment at the dinner table. Most of all, however, he was acutely conscious of Harriet's vivacious and captivating nearness, her deliberate and pointed use of his given name and the constant flashing of her smile in his direction. For which dedicated attentions, he reflected gloomily, he would surely be paying dearly before the day ended so he decided he might as well make the most of them and set about entering into her pantomime with gusto.

At last the desserts were brought in. The lively exchanges had continued through a widely ranging number of light-hearted topics, everyone carefully avoiding the more contentious issues of corn prices, royal scandals and the like, any of which could be guaranteed to depress the spirits. The latest novels were touched upon briefly and, when local matters arose, Sandford, catching the flicker of concern in Harriet's eyes, was quick to steer the conversation away from her woodland escapade, in spite of Lady Butler's prurient curiosity in that event. Instead, he regaled them with the story of his own confrontation with Josh Potter when the old man heard that Bottom Meadow cottages were about to be pulled down.

'Such ripe language as he used is not for repetition in mixed company, of course,' he concluded teasingly. 'But I feel sure that, could he but walk the distance, he would do his utmost to disrupt the entire proceedings.'

Ridgeway and Judith joined in his laughter, but Harriet's face became suddenly serious and she stared at them reproachfully.

'Oh, but I can readily sympathise with his feelings!' she exclaimed.

'That much is clear, for the whole village is agog with your kindness to him.' Judith smiled fondly at her friend. 'It was such a—well—a *Harriet* sort of thing to do!'

Harriet blushed and lowered her eyes as the two men grinned at Judith's choice of words. Lady Butler, however, pricked up her ears.

'What kindness was this?' she asked, in saccharine tones. 'Do tell me more.'

'There is really nothing to tell, ma'am,' disclaimed Harriet hurriedly. 'I merely returned one of his damaged possessions to him. He—he was a little effusive in his gratitude, that is all. Please do not laugh. It is a dreadful thing to lose one's home. I, myself, know this only too well!'

In the ensuing silence Sandford, his eyes full of compassion, reached out to clasp her hand and she made no attempt pull away from him.

Her ladyship studied her thoughtfully for a moment then, turning to the viscount, she reverted to the topic of the cottages.

'You intend to replace them or merely to clear the site?' she asked. 'I was under the impression that the new ones in the upper meadow were already a replacement.'

Ridgeway answered for his clearly distracted cousin. 'That was the idea originally, ma'am,' he said. 'But as more of our lads return from the continent, we are finding that accommodation is scarce, especially for youngsters wanting to get wed and set up their own homes. And you know that Beldale likes to take care of his people.'

'I should have thought it would be difficult to justify such an expense at the moment—I hear that Beldale is threatening to cut back as it is!'

She sat back in her chair, satisfied that her words had hit their mark.

Sandford looked ill at ease and, raising accusing eyes to his sister-in-law's, he encountered her shocked and guilty expression.

'I didn't say "cut back", Mama,' she said, in some confusion. 'I merely mentioned that Robert and Charles were devising some sort of consolidation for the estates—at least—' she turned to Sandford '—that is what I inferred from our conversation?'

'That's all it is, Judith,' he returned, with feigned good humour. 'Just one of several ideas we're considering. I told you to forget about it. You must know that we would consult you about anything that might affect Westpark.'

'But, of course!' Lady Butler was at pains to point out. 'Although it is hardly for our bailiff to be making major decisions regarding our property!'

There was an uncomfortable pause as Judith coloured violently and Ridgeway, eyes fixed on the table in front of him, clenched his fists between his knees.

The meal was completed in subdued undertones, Sandford ruefully conscious of all the effort that Harriet had spent in contributing to the evening's earlier success. Looking sideways at her pensive expression, he had a desperate longing to take her in his arms and soothe away her hurts and fears, in spite of her angry declaration that he was 'not that man'.

Finally, when all the covers had been removed and the decanters placed at the gentlemen's elbows, Judith rose to escort the ladies from the room. Lady Butler, with her usual officious manner, deemed it necessary to linger behind to point out some deficiency or other to Finchley and instructed the two men not to linger over their drinks, before following her daughter from the room.

Left to themselves, Sandford and Ridgeway relaxed and the viscount, pouring his cousin a large glass of brandy, grinned sympathetically and said, 'You look as though you need that, old chum! Get it down you and let's talk!'

'I'd drink the whole bottle if I thought it would answer,' said Ridgeway, with a grimace. 'But it didn't serve my father, so its efficacy is clearly in doubt!'

Sandford contemplated him gravely for a moment or two before taking a sip of his own drink. 'What do you hear about this Potter business—with Harriet?' he asked casually. 'I know she picked up a memento when I showed her the cottages—but I'm damned if I can see why it should have set the whole village on its ears!'

Ridgeway looked up in surprise and, seeing that his cousin was clearly ignorant of the whole matter, furnished him with the details with which Lady Eugenie herself had supplied him, she having got them first-hand from Meggy Watts.

'And you say you didn't know any of this, man?' exclaimed Ridgeway, in amazement. 'What do you do? Walk around with your eyes and ears closed?'

'No need to be offensive, old chap,' said Sandford calmly. 'I don't have a houseful of chattering females to bring me the latest *on-dits* like you do and I've been stuck in the outfields most of the week, don't forget.'

'But you were at Mrs Watts' cottage the other day—you spoke to old Josh himself! Didn't he mention it?'

'Well, apart from damning me to perdition, he did suggest that I wasn't worthy of a certain lady's regard—something about not being ''fit to lick her dear little boots'' springs to mind—but since I'm well aware of that fact, I didn't pay a great deal of—why are you looking at me like that?'

'What's going on, Robert?' asked the older man sharply. 'You and Miss Cordell have been at daggers' drawn all week—any fool could see that. Last week it was much the same, if I'm not mistaken and—I have to say this, old chap—you don't act like a man newly in love!'

'Do I not, indeed?' drawled Sandford coldly and for the merest moment his eyes looked bleak as they studied his cousin's concerned face. Then, with a sudden urgency he leaned across the table and said decisively, 'Fill your glass, Charles. I have a tale to tell you—but it must go no further than this room.'

Chapter Eleven

Judith could not imagine what could be keeping Sandford and Ridgeway so long at the table, particularly since Charles had earlier given her the impression that he would be happy to spend every minute of the evening by her side and she had supposed that Robert must wish to do likewise with his new betrothed, yet the tea tray had come and gone and still the gentlemen had not appeared.

She was perfectly content to sit and chatter to her young friend, of course, but, of their own volition, it seemed, her eyes constantly wandered to the clock on the mantelshelf. Her mother, she observed, must also have registered their non-appearance, for Judith was aware of that lady's continual glances towards the door whenever the slightest sound penetrated from without.

Harriet, too, had marked the long absence but, since she knew that inquiries about her assailants were still in progress, she assumed that this must be the topic that engrossed them. She had no objection to Sandford's absenting himself for as long as he chose, she told herself, for she had found that, having expended

205

all of her energy and resources in keeping up the performance of constant good humour which she had promised him, she now felt quite drained and was perfectly happy to relax into exchanging idle pleasantries with Judith, for this required no false effort on her part.

'The gentlemen appear to prefer their own company, I see,' Lady Butler intoned peevishly.

'I'm sure they will not be long, Mama,' answered Judith, attempting to soothe her. 'I dare say they have become involved in estate matters and forget the time.'

'They must be very deeply involved—for even Miss Cordell's skills at the keyboard seem have to have lost their former attraction!'

Harriet laughed, one of her soft infectious chuckles. 'I know you jest, your ladyship,' she said. 'I do not pretend any skill at the keyboard. That was but a game we played whenever we found ourselves in possession of a piano—which was very seldom, as you can imagine.'

'Do tell us,' begged Judith, as much to pass the time as anything. 'This would have been while you were wintering in Lisbon, I collect?'

'Yes, and I cannot claim to have been the inventor of the game,' said Harriet, nodding in reminiscence. 'Some of the young officers could play, of course—those who had been given lessons in the schoolroom—so they would teach us certain chords, the very simplest of all and, therefore, quite easy to memorise, and our musical game developed from this. One of us would strike a chord and any available pianist would be challenged to extemporise. It was all done to keep the younger ones amused, although we *all* thought it rather fun—I was quite young myself at the time, of course. The more often one plays the game, the better one gets and, although it was never possible for me to be given proper lessons at the pianoforte, Mama did try to teach me some of the basic principles—and we sang a great deal, of course.'

She was silent for a moment, then turned to Lady Butler with a sweet smile, saying, 'Such a silly game bears no comparison with real music, of course. Perhaps we could persuade Judith to play for us. I love to listen to her—as I am sure you do.'

Lady Butler grunted, temporarily mollified at this request. 'Well, to be sure, she had the best of teachers, and a great deal of money was spent on her education—but it is true that she performs excellently, although she gets little enough practice these days. Yes, dear Judith, do play for us—something soothing, perhaps—I believe we have had more than enough jollity for one evening!'

And so, when Sandford and Ridgeway made their appearance shortly afterwards, they perceived Lady Butler slumped fast asleep with her chin on her chest whilst an envious Harriet, standing beside the piano admiring her friend's virtuosity, was the sole audience to Judith's expensive musical education.

At their entrance Judith immediately stopped playing and rose from her seat. She came towards Sandford anxiously, with a finger to her lips as she motioned towards her sleeping mother.

'What has kept you so long, Robert?' she almost whispered, and he found himself replying in kind.

'Sorry, Judith, we—got chatting and, well—you know how it is.'

Judith's eyes flew to Ridgeway, whose face held a very shamefaced expression.

'*Is* there something wrong? I do believe there is something that you are keeping from me...'

Sandford took hold of her hands and shook his head at her.

'Judith, I promise you there is nothing for you to worry about. I told you that if there was a problem with Westpark—'

'*Problem with Westpark!*' Lady Butler's ringing tones interrupted him. 'What problem with Westpark? Explain yourself, young man!'

Sandford controlled himself with difficulty. 'As far as I am aware, your ladyship,' he said carefully, 'there are no problems at Westpark—as I was just trying to impress upon Judith. Why everyone insists upon inventing problems where none exist, I cannot imagine! Charles and I were discussing something quite other, I promise you—and I—*we* apologise unreservedly for our outrageously bad manners in having deserted you for so long.'

Ridgeway nodded his agreement. 'It's true, Judith— Lady Butler—there was absolutely no mention of Westpark in our conversation and I, too, apologise for our lengthy absence.'

Lady Butler gazed at them both with narrowed eyes, as if by doing so she could read their minds, then, collecting together her various belongings, she got heavily to her feet.

'Hmm, well—I suppose you also wanted a little peace and quiet after that earlier boisterous display— frankly, I'm not surprised you stayed away for so long. However, it is now time for us to wish you good- night—it is, as you see, very late.'

She stared pointedly towards the clock and Judith, looking at Ridgeway, gave an embarrassed little shrug, as he smiled in sympathy.

'Lady Butler is quite right, Judith,' he said, as he bent over her hand. 'The time has flown so quickly and, indeed, I am very sorry that I didn't spend more of it in your company—it would have been infinitely more enjoyable, I assure you.'

'Couldn't have put it better myself, sir,' laughed Sandford, bowing to Lady Butler and kissing his sister- in-law's cheek. 'Many thanks, Judith. In spite of our prolonged absence, may I pronounce the evening a great success?'

Harriet, having also bidden her adieux, was escorted out to the waiting carriage by both men, but was sur- prised to find that it was Charles Ridgeway who stepped forward to hand her into her seat.

'If ever you need my assistance,' he said in a low voice, as he moved away from the door, 'remember that I am always at your disposal,' and, bowing, he walked off to collect his gig.

Harriet was still pondering over his words as Sand- ford climbed into the carriage and took his seat oppo- site her. It was too dark to see his face.

'Have you told Mr Ridgeway how it was that we met?' she asked him curiously.

'Has he said so?' Sandford sounded taken aback.

'Not exactly—but he seemed—different, somehow, and you were away so long I wondered...'

'I felt that it was time to take him into my confidence,' admitted Sandford. 'I am no nearer to tracking down your assailants than I was a week ago—I thought that he might have some new ideas...'

'And has he?' Harriet asked eagerly.

''Fraid not—he latched on to the Middletons, of course—just as I did—but now we're agreed that everything seems to point to someone from the House.'

They were both silent for several minutes then Sandford spoke again. 'Harriet?'

'Yes, my lord?'

'Oh, God! Not still?' She heard the thud as he struck the cushion with his fist.

'I beg your pardon?'

'Harriet—we have to talk—preferably somewhere I can see your face. Will you come into the library when we get back?'

'I am rather tired, sir,' she said mutinously. 'Can't it wait until morning?'

'No, it damned well cannot!' Sandford exclaimed. 'Do you want me to come over there and persuade you?'

'I would prefer that you remained in your own seat, my lord,' she said shakily. 'If I may remind you that I am under your protection...'

She heard his gasp and waited in trepidation for his reply, but there was only a heavy silence in the darkness. All of a sudden an unaccountable sensation of longing welled up inside her.

'Lord Sandford?' Her voice was hesitant.

'Miss Cordell?' he answered patiently. He was hurt and angry, but determined not to rise to any further strictures she might cast at him.

'I want you to know that I am very grateful for all the trouble you have taken on my behalf—no, please let me finish!' She had heard his attempted protest. 'It's just that I'm sure that it must have crossed your mind that had I never come to Beldale—had you never picked me up—you would not have had to spend all your time trying to extricate me from these other mishaps—I realised this some days ago. What I am trying to say is that I want you to stop wasting any more of your time on this endeavour. My own feeling is that it has all been a series of unfortunate and disconnected incidents—no real harm has been done to me—obviously none was really intended, otherwise it could easily have been achieved...*oh!*'

Sandford had leapt across the space between them and had his arms tightly about her.

'No, don't say it,' he said, his voice muffled in her hair. 'I have had nightmares enough. I do not consider it to be a waste of time to find and punish anyone who has tried to hurt you—they will be lucky to escape with their lives!'

'Sir! You must not say so!' Harriet's heart seemed to be leaping about inside her ribcage and she could hardly breathe. She tried to push him away, but her arms were trapped against him. 'Please release me—I beg you—Robert—please!'

At once he loosened his hold and moved a little way from her, still keeping one arm around her shoulders. She could scarcely make out his silhouette in the gloom, but knew that he had his face towards her for she could feel his warm breath on her cheek.

'You must listen to me,' she cried breathlessly. 'My grandfather will be here shortly—I shall keep Davy with me if I go anywhere, I promise. I know I should have done so when you asked me—but in a few days you will be free of me...'

'Free of you!' Sandford choked. 'I don't want to be free of you—I want *never* to be free of you. What I want is...'

But the viscount was unable to finish his passionate words as the carriage had drawn to a halt and Pritchard, the groom, was opening the door and letting down the steps for him to alight. Barely controlling his impatience, Sandford held out his hand to Harriet and led her into the house.

'Won't you come into the library—just for a few minutes?' he pleaded. 'There is something I must say to you.'

Harriet shook her head resolutely and moved towards the stairs. This is all madness, she thought, in a panic. In a few days my grandfather will come for me. I shall return to Scotland with him. That is what I set out to do. That is what I must do.

Sandford, his heart heavy, saw his hopes crumbling away as he watched her climb the staircase, for he realised that, from now on, she would be very much on her guard in ensuring that she did not find herself alone with him again. He turned away from the unremitting spectacle of her rigid figure, divested himself of his cloak and hat and, handing them to the patiently waiting March, dismissed the servant for the night.

Much later, sprawled in his father's high-backed chair in the library, he emptied another glass of brandy and reviewed his situation for the umpteenth time.

Trounced by a pair of green eyes, by God! After all his years in the field! Plenty of other fish in the sea, of course—and they'd be queuing up, once he let it be known he was hanging out for a wife—which he wasn't—didn't need one. Beldale's future was safe—Phil's boy was a fine enough heir—Ridgeway would help him run the estates.

Ah, yes, Ridgeway! His lips twisted as he remembered. *He* was being mighty friendly to Harriet this evening—supposed to be in love with Judith, too—very interested when he heard the engagement was a sham. Too interested, perhaps? Maybe I shouldn't have mentioned her inheritance, he thought, but he shan't have her—I'm damned if I'll let him have her—damned if I'll let anyone....

March found him slumped in the chair the following morning when he came into the room to open the curtains. The footman stared down at Sandford in distaste and picked up both the fallen glass and the empty decanter.

'He's had a skinful, I'll be bound,' giggled Lizzy, the young housemaid who had accompanied him, but he frowned at her and motioned her to be silent. She flounced away pertly with the tray he had handed her.

'My lord!' March gently shook the viscount's shoulder. 'Your lordship!'

Sandford's bleary eyes dragged open and he blinked rapidly to focus them upon March's expressionless face. Struggling upwards into a sitting position, he groaned as his head roared out its protest.

'What—time—is—it?' he croaked, carefully and slowly.

'Six o'clock, my lord,' March's answer came back smartly. 'Shall I bring you a pot of coffee, sir?'

Sandford started to nod, then quickly changed his mind as the battery of cannon exploded violently across his temples. He flapped a slack hand at the man and closed his eyes once more as March bowed and, with a very unsympathetic grin on his face, walked towards the door.

His lordship breathed deeply for several minutes, trying to remember why he should have chosen to sleep in the library, in such a damned uncomfortable chair when he had a perfectly good bed upstairs. His eyes were still closed when he heard the sounds of the door opening and footsteps approaching.

'Just put it on the table, March, thank you,' he murmured weakly.

'I shall do no such thing,' came a bright and well-known voice.

His eyes flew open in shock and he tried to rise, but Harriet's hands pressed him firmly back into his seat.

'Sit still,' she said, calmly pouring out a cup of coffee and, to his surprise, taking a sip of it herself.

'This is for you.' She indicated and handed him a tall glass full of an evil-coloured liquid.

Sandford sniffed at it and pulled a face. 'What is it?' he asked plaintively.

'It is vinegar and raw eggs—and it is quite horrid,' she said, with a laugh in her voice that woke him up immediately. 'Drink it!' she commanded and came down on her knees beside his chair.

'I can't—it would make me—that is—I should...'

'Yes, I know—you would be sick! Well, my lord, you will either bring it up or keep it down—whichever way, it will still cure your hangover.'

Manfully, he struggled to down the contents of the glass, hypnotised by the laughing gleam in her green eyes. She removed the tumbler from his shaking hand and put it carefully on the side table, but remained on her knees studying his face with a very serious expression upon her own.

'I came down early, to see if I could catch you before you left,' she said, after a minute or two. 'March told me you had spent the night in here—and that you were feeling somewhat...under the weather!'

'Did he, indeed—blast him!' gritted Sandford, who was fighting a desperate battle with the contents of his stomach and determined to win. 'I suppose that foul concoction was his idea?'

'No,' she said sweetly. 'It was mine!'

He blinked in astonishment at her answer and discovered at the same time that his head was indeed beginning to clear.

'Set on poisoning me, are you?' he asked roughly, his eyes engrossed with the nearness of her face.

'Of course.' She started to get to her feet, but when he beseechingly put out his hand she smiled and remained at his side. 'You'll survive, I'm sure.'

'Only with the right treatment, I think—and it may take a very long time.'

She laughed softly and the explosions in his temples were reduced to mere firecrackers. Tentatively he took her hand in his.

'Why were you hoping to catch me before I went out?'

'I thought you might allow me to ride with you—but I fear you are not up to such vigorous exercise just yet. Perhaps in an hour or two?'

'And until then?' Sandford asked hopefully, but Harriet thrust his hands aside and jumped to her feet.

'*You* will go and lie down on your bed.' She dimpled at him. '*I* shall go and eat a substantial breakfast and, perhaps, take a walk on the terrace—with the faithful Davy, of course—and await your return.'

'With bated breath?'

'There is always that possibility!'

The viscount rose gingerly, holding on to the back of the chair with great deliberation. He certainly felt a good deal better than when he had been woken by March, but perhaps a short rest and a change of raiment would be the best plan to follow at the moment. He looked at Harriet, trying to make sense of her mood.

'You have had a change of heart, perhaps?'

She shook her head at him and pointed to the door. 'Go now and have your rest—I shan't say another word on the subject until you return!'

Somewhat perturbed, but too confused to argue, he allowed himself to be shepherded to the foot of the staircase where he found Kimble waiting in frowning disapproval.

'Your arm, my lord,' said his valet stiffly and proceeded to help his young master slowly up the stairs.

Harriet watched until the pair had disappeared from sight, then turned and smiled at the ever-present March and said, 'Is Davy Rothman about, March? I should like to go for a walk after breakfast, if he is available?'

She still wasn't totally at ease with the idea that Beldale's servants were there for her to command and she regarded the idea of one wasting his time just walking along behind her as perfectly ridiculous, but since she had agreed to it she was prepared to fulfil her part of the bargain.

March's face creased with concern at her request. 'Young Rothman, Miss Cordell? I'm dreadfully sorry, but his father sent him down to the village just five minutes ago—we didn't expect you to be rising this early, miss—after being so late last night and all.'

Harriet laughed and put her hand on his arm. 'Don't look so worried, March—it isn't the end of the world.

I shall have my breakfast and, if Davy hasn't returned, surely you have another youngster who is prepared to give up his duties to be my shadow for an hour?'

'Of course, miss.' March's face cleared. 'I know just the lad. You would like your breakfast now, miss? I shall inform Mr Rothman.'

With that, he bowed and left the hall and Harriet strolled into the breakfast parlour where the early morning sunshine was just beginning to filter its pale light through the rear windows of the house.

She stood for a while, watching the gardeners tidying the terrace flower-beds, and marvelled at the amount of work that had to be done in a great house before the occupants rose. Dusting and polishing, sweeping, cooking and even gardening—and so many people involved, so many people dependant upon so few for their daily bread. A terrible responsibility, she realised, and was no longer so sure that she had come to the right decision, after all.

For, after a sleepless few hours, she had at last made up her mind. Sandford's continued protestations of love certainly seemed genuine and she was almost sure that he had been about to ask for her hand when they returned from Westpark last evening. Having searched her conscience thoroughly, she could see no good reason for refusing him. There were times when she actually *liked* him, although she found him very disconcerting too—and very high-handed, but that was to be expected in someone of his rank and position. He had been used to dealing with hundreds of men from different walks of life, many of them rather unruly and very badly behaved, as she well remembered. He would have had to be very strict and autocratic with some of them, she felt sure and, after so many years, it had probably become second nature to him. He wasn't always like that, as she herself could testify and he was often very amusing to be with. She was sufficiently level-headed to realise that refusing an earl's son would be considered absolute folly by the bastions of English Society and, although she knew none of these worthies, she felt that even her unknown grandfather would view such a refusal as somewhat puzzling from a girl with her unusual background. Besides which, she had to admit that the idea of immuring herself in a Scottish castle in a lonely glen was growing less appealing by the day, especially after having been in this glorious Leicestershire countryside for these past weeks.

She was not, she had to own, completely comfortable with the idea of marrying for the aforementioned reasons, especially after her high-flown speech about love and chivalry, and she was uneasily certain that Sandford would not be at all impressed to have any one of them offered to him as her justification for accepting his hand.

However, she was sure that they could learn to deal perfectly amicably together, which was more than a great many married couples could claim. She was well aware that her own parents' marriage had been most unusual in having been a love match and, in contemplating such a union between Sandford and herself, her cheeks grew hot and her heart seemed to skip several

beats. Her lips curving in anticipation, she allowed herself to visualise the wicked glint that would appear in
his eyes when she gave him her answer. Ridiculous!
She admonished herself for her foolish thoughts, vowing to concentrate on only the practical aspects of the
matter.

She finished the rolls and coffee that Rothman had
brought to her and went into the hall to see if young
Davy had returned from his errand to the village.

March shook his head. 'Sorry, Miss Cordell,' he
said. 'He's not back yet—but young Cooper would be
glad to accompany you—he's not that keen on polishing silver!' He grinned at her and she smiled in return.

'I can sympathise with that—a thankless task!'

March went to the back stairs to call Cooper up.
Harriet walked through the small parlour out to the rear
terrace, where a blushing young footman joined her a
few minutes later.

At this early hour the dew was still wet on the grass
and Harriet was glad she had pulled her riding boots
on before coming downstairs. Having dressed with a
view to being ready to ride at moment's notice should
Sandford have been available, she was still wearing her
riding habit. Not the most suitable skirt for a walk on
the grass, she realised, but since she would have to
change later to attend the church service she elected
not to waste any more of the beautiful morning worrying about a damp hem and set off across the park
with Cooper in train.

After some moments, the increasing absurdity of the
situation brought a smile to her face and she motioned

to Cooper to come alongside. 'I hear that you are not fond of silver-polishing.'

Cooper grinned shamefacedly and nodded.

'Will you enjoy being a footman, do you think?' Harriet persevered.

Cooper looked at her in surprise. Enjoying one's work had never been a question that any of the staff had given a great deal of thought to as far as he was aware. 'I think I should like Mr March's position, miss,' he ventured shyly. 'But it has taken him more than ten years to get to be first footman and I'm not sure I'd want to wait that long—or even if I'd be that good at it!'

'I suppose you didn't really have a lot of choice in the matter,' Harriet mused, more to herself than to the youth. 'What would you have done otherwise?'

'I suppose I could have gone in the stables—or the gardens, like my dad, but I'm not that keen on an out-door life,' said Cooper. 'What I'd really like, miss, is to be a carpenter—but I'd have to go for apprentice and it's not that easy these days.'

Harriet nodded sympathetically. The country had been in a state of unrest since the war ended. Prices had risen sharply and wages had fallen; returning sol-diers had been unable to find work and, in many areas, marauding gangs were set on inciting riots amongst the discontented and mob rule frequently prevailed. Bel-dale had, so far, escaped involvement with these crises, mainly because of the earl's policy of care for his ten-ants and servants—his 'people', as he called them. This was why Judith had expressed such concern over the possibility of laying men off and why young Cooper was grateful to have a job at all.

They strolled through the knot gardens, with Harriet pausing every so often to admire particularly attractive floral displays. When her young escort ventured to point out which of the gardeners was his father, she stopped to compliment the older Cooper on the magnificence of the late summer roses he was pruning.

'We've had a good year, miss,' he said, knuckling his forehead to her. 'Plenty of sun these last few weeks—although I shouldn't be surprised to see rain before the day's out.' He indicated the clouds gathering over the hill. 'If you're going riding, miss,' he warned, having observed her costume, 'you'll be wise not to venture far afield, if you'll pardon my saying so.'

'How very good of you to mention it.' She smiled at him and, much moved, he bent to clip a perfect specimen from one of the bushes and offered it to her.

'For your buttonhole, miss—almost matches your pretty hair,' he said, ignoring his son's impudent grin. 'It's called ''Beldale Sunset''—one of our own varieties.'

Harriet was deeply touched. 'How lovely!' she exclaimed, inhaling the delicious perfume before carefully tucking the flower into the braiding on her jacket. 'Thank you—for the compliment as well as the rose— I'm honoured that you should clip one for me.' She bestowed another of her captivating smiles upon him and was about to turn away when she happened to catch young Cooper's low and hurried parting words to his father.

'—news of young Tatler?'

She saw the older man's frowning shake of the head as he knelt to resume his work. An odd premonition overcame her and, as they walked on through the gardens, she questioned the young footman.

'Were you referring to Billy Tatler? Has something happened to him?'

Cooper shuffled uncomfortably. Visiting gentry didn't usually concern themselves too much in local problems and he was unsure of the wisdom of passing on rumours, but Harriet's eyes were fixed upon him in such a steadfast way that he found the words tumbling from his lips before he could stop them.

Harriet's eyes grew round with horror as his tale unfolded. It appeared that the lad Billy had gone missing two days previously but, because of his errant lifestyle, his mother had not begun to worry about his absence until late the previous night when she had expressed her concern to Ridgeway on his return from Westpark. He had, it seemed, chosen to regard the boy's disappearance as a much more serious matter than the rest of the household would have expected and had immediately set several men on to searching Billy's known haunts. Mr Ridgeway himself, Cooper told Harriet, had been out most of the night.

'But has no one informed their lordships?' she asked, walking quickly back towards the house.

'Mr Ridgeway wouldn't have them woken up, miss,' panted Cooper, hurrying to keep up with her. ''Tisn't usual for any of the family to be up this early—he'll have left a message with Mr Rothman, I'll be bound.'

Harriet hesitated, and then turned towards the stables where she found quite a flurry of activity. Apprehending a passing stableboy, she instructed him to saddle up her horse at once, while Cooper looked on in dismay.

'But I can't ride, miss,' he stammered. 'That's why Davy—Rothman was picked. Shall I go and see if he's back, miss?'

Harriet nodded. 'Yes, do, Cooper—and tell him to follow me to the Dower House. I shall take the back lane—and tell March to give the same message to Lord Sandford when he wakes,' she called over her shoulder as she mounted.

Wheeling Clipper in the direction of her proposed route, she headed for the short bridleway that led to the south of the Beldale estate, where the Dower House was situated. She had not gone far, however, when she was halted by one of the large group that was milling around the courtyard. A young groom, by the look of him, he signalled urgently to her to stop and she reined in beside him.

'If you're wanting Mr Ridgeway, miss,' he volunteered, 'he's just gone up to Top Meadow along North Lane. You'll soon catch up with him if you take a short cut through the copse—shall I tell Davy when I see him, miss?'

'Oh! Yes, please, would you?' Harriet swung Clipper in the opposite direction and, spurring her mount into a gallop, headed for the woods that led out to the north side of the estate.

Chapter Twelve

Urging Clipper swiftly through the woods, Harriet soon arrived at the dry-stone wall that bordered the estate. Clearing this without difficulty, she cantered up the lane that led, firstly, past the gated entrance to Westpark Manor, then past the old Butler property, Staines, and eventually towards the forked track that separated the crumbling cottages of Bottom Meadow from the newer dwellings in Top Meadow.

There was no sign of Ridgeway as yet, but she supposed that she could not be far behind him. She assumed he was making for the ruins—such buildings being a magnet for small boys. She hoped that Billy had not fallen and hurt himself, but this fate would be infinitely more preferable than her present thoughts concerning a more sinister explanation to the lad's disappearance. Like Ridgeway, she had straight away connected his absence with the mysterious stranger at the lake and was afraid that either Billy or his friend had somehow discovered the man's identity, which would have placed the two boys in serious danger, especially if this was the same man who was involved with her attack in the copse.

However, the track to Bottom Meadow was deserted and, although she could tell that there were stirrings of life in the new cottages further up the lane, she could see no indication of Ridgeway's presence—nor any sign of his big, raw-boned grey. Momentarily undecided, she stared down at the derelict buildings, remembering that Meggy had warned Josh Potter to stay away from the dangerous ruins and, conscious of the fact that she had once again broken her promise never to leave the house without a groom, she reluctantly started to pull Clipper's head up from the dew-sweet grass which the mare was presently enjoying.

Then she heard it. The faint sound of a cry of distress. Hesitating no longer, she dismounted and, throwing Clipper's reins around an overhanging branch, she kilted up her habit skirt and sped down towards the ruins. Again came the cry—from the back of Potter's cottage, she could swear. Gasping for breath, she rounded the end of the buildings and saw that the small cellar hatch at the rear of the cottage had been lifted from its mountings.

Kneeling at the portal, she called down into the gloom, 'Billy? Billy—are you down there? Are you hurt?'

If there was any reply she did not hear it, for something very hard caught her a stunning blow on the back of her head and she felt herself tumbling down and down into the depths of unconsciousness.

* * *

Small hands were shaking her. She was dreaming about Billy Tatler. How strange! Her head hurt badly and one of her shoulders felt rather sore. She opened her eyes, but darkness still prevailed. She tried to sit up, but waves of concussion overcame her and she sank back on to her hard and lumpy mattress, insensible once more.

'Miss! Oh, miss—do wake up—please don't be dead, miss—oh, miss!'

The sobs cut through her clouded brain. Small hands *were* shaking her! Very gingerly Harriet reached out towards them. They were real enough! As was the pain in her head! The darkness was only too real.

'Is it you, Billy?' she ventured weakly, as her fingers were grasped tightly.

'Oh, miss!' came the child's relieved cry. 'I fort you was dead—I were that scared, miss! Will we get out, miss? Mister Ridgeway will find us, won't he, miss?'

Harriet drew the boy towards her and put her arm across his thin shoulders. His whole body was shaking and, although she herself was experiencing the same terrors as he was, she knew that he was depending upon her for his salvation.

'Everyone will be searching for us, Billy,' she said, with as much calm as she could muster. 'They have been searching for you all night—I found you first, it seems.' A thought occurred to her. 'Was there someone here with you when I—fell—into the cellar?'

'You din't fall, miss—he whacked you one! I saw him behind you with a bit of wood! He pushed you in and fixed the trap-door back!'

Harriet tentatively put her hand up to the back of her head. There was a sticky, wet mess of hair around a considerable contusion. Grimacing at the pain, she supposed she had better fashion some sort of a bandage for herself. She wriggled uncomfortable as she felt the lumpen mass beneath her.

'What are we sitting on?' she asked her companion. 'It doesn't feel like coal or logs.'

'It's turnips, miss—put down last year, I should think. Maybe potatoes, too, somewhere.'

'I'm going to stand up for a minute, Billy—stay where you are. I just want to wrap something around my head—it seems to be bleeding a bit.'

She slipped off her petticoat and, tearing it into strips, set about padding and binding her wound in the well-remembered procedure that she had learned from her mother. She wondered just how long she had been unconscious and whether Sandford would have recovered sufficiently to come in search of her. She was reasonably confident that it wouldn't be long before somebody found them. Then she remembered, with a tremor of fear, that *somebody* already knew where they were and that *he* would be doing everything in his power to ensure that they were *not* found!

'The man at the lake, Billy,' she said, as she seated herself next to him once more. 'Who is he—and how came you to be in the cellar?'

'Well, miss—' Billy was feeling much more cheerful now that he was no longer alone in the cold and the dark '—me and Nick—him as was with me at the lake—fort we'd better find him before he found us, miss, but he took some finding, I can tell you! Turns out he's one of the gardeners—but he's a right queer cove and no mistake. Never goes down to the village—not even to the *Fox*. Probably drinks them queer potions and things he makes...'

'Queer potions?' interrupted Harriet, suddenly alert.

'Yeah—he's got bottles and bottles of 'em all on the shelves of his hut—sort of a tool-store place at the far end of the gardens at Westpark. Grows all these herbs and things—and works in the kitchen gardens, too. Anyway, we seen him talking to the old butler bloke and we followed him to his hut.'

'That was a very silly and dangerous thing to do. You should have informed Mr Ridgeway at once!'

'Yeah—I know that now, miss.' Billy wriggled uncomfortably. 'We just fort it were a bit of a laugh, see? Only—well, he saw me and came after me. I weren't even that scared then, you know, 'cos I'm pretty quick on my heels—as they'll all tell you...'

Harriet smiled sadly into the darkness as the young urchin attempted to puff up his consequence.

'Yes, and I seem to recall that you're a slippery little eel, too!' she said in a matter-of-fact tone. 'However—go on with your story.'

'Well, we didn't know who you was then,' said Billy, much affronted. 'An' it was 'cos we found out *who* you was that we went looking for him in the first place.'

Harriet managed to persuade him that she was not at all angry with him over his part in the lake incident and pressed him to tell her the remainder of his tale.

Both boys had escaped the strange gardener's clutches, it seemed, and had hidden themselves in the shrubbery of the old Butler property until nightfall when hunger pangs had tempted Billy to venture out. His friend Nick, it appeared, was a somewhat more cautious adventurer and had said he would remain hidden until he heard Billy's 'owl-hoot' from the lane before he elected to join him.

'Only he never heard it—'cos "matey" grabbed me when I jumped down off the wall. He must have been waiting there all the time!' said Billy indignantly.

Harriet patted his shoulder. 'Poor Billy,' she said sympathetically, 'and after all that time in the shrubbery.'

Billy snuggled up to her, his eyelids beginning to droop. After almost two days without proper sleep he was exhausted and, now that there was an adult present and a gentry-mort at that, he felt reasonably sure that all would be taken care of, for no harm would be allowed to befall the viscount's new lady, he was certain. Harriet interrupted this cosy reverie.

'Just one thing, Billy,' she said, gently shaking him awake. 'Did he hurt you? How did he get you into the cellar?'

'There was two of 'em, miss—his dafty friend was there wiv an 'orse,' he said drowsily. '*He* was the one what brought me up here, threw me down the hatch— but I fell on the pile of bracken so I weren't hurt...' His voice tailed off and he was fast asleep.

Harriet's arm was beginning to go numb with the effort of holding the boy and she was eventually obliged to lay him down upon the sacks of turnips or whatever they were. Her head ached abominably and she too would have been glad to close her eyes and go to sleep, but she knew that this would be a very foolish thing for her to do in the circumstances.

In the circumstances! Good heavens! How could she have forgotten? She had been shut in a cellar before! Voluntarily, of course, and Mama had been with her as well as Martha—when the French were sacking the village near Badajoz where they were quartered. The thing to do first is to acquaint oneself with one's situation, she recalled her mother's words.

Carefully she rose and felt to her right, moving slowly until she made contact with the wall, which was only a foot away on that side. The sacks of vegetables seemed to be piled up in a corner, so she elected to work her way clockwise around the walls until she returned to them. This she did, cautiously and very nervously feeling her way and counting her steps until she could gauge the size of their prison, which appeared to measure approximately eight feet by twelve. This would be directly below the scullery, she surmised, desperately trying to recollect the layout of the cottage. The hatch, she knew to her cost, was at the rear of the property and there was certainly no other way out of the cellar—the log-ladder, as she quickly ascertained, having been removed. The pile of bracken or brushwood just below the hatchway must have been stored there for kindling, she thought, her brow furrowing. Although that in itself was odd, since it smelled fresh and, surely, none would have been brought since Josh left?

The floor of the cellar was quite dry and for this mercy, Harriet was very thankful, for, she suddenly realised, it was becoming very cold and, remembering old Cooper's warning that a storm was brewing, she wondered if rain would seep into the cellar and make their incarceration even more miserable.

Surely she had been missed by now? She had no way of reckoning the hour, but knew that by the time of the morning service somebody would have noticed her absence. Sandford, if he had recovered from his night's libation, would certainly have expected her to keep her promise to meet him on the terrace. Young Davy would have been sent up to North Lane after her, for the young man had assured her that he would pass on her message...

She stopped her conjecturing at this point as a chill disquietude overcame her. The young man who had directed her to the cottages—who was he? Could he be one of the men who had attacked her in the woods— and possibly the same one who had brought Billy to this place? He had been eager to suggest that she went through the woods to North Lane—perhaps there was a quicker route which he had used to arrive here without her knowledge. He could have travelled over the fields, she realised, so that she would have remained unaware of his presence until he was upon her and, as she had learned from Billy, he had an accomplice who might already have been here!

Sandford would not be best pleased with her actions, she admitted to herself ruefully, and he was, of course, right as usual. Her irresponsible and impetuous behaviour had really dished her this time and his lordship, she was sure, would be forever bringing it up for the rest of their lives—given that he found her and still wanted to spend the rest of his life with her! All at once, the thought of any alternative filled her with the most terrible heartache.

A rustling came from the turnip sacks and Billy's voice cut across her dismal thoughts. 'Miss! *Miss*—are you there?' He sounded terrified and she went to him immediately.

'It's all right, Billy,' she said, with a confidence she was far from feeling. 'I was just trying to work out the size of the cellar.'

The boy started to weep. 'I fort I was dreaming, miss,' he sobbed. 'Why ain't nobody come for us? I fort they'd come for you—even if I weren't important!'

'You are important, Billy,' said Harriet, gathering him to her, with tears in her eyes. 'Your mother must be in an awful state of worry.'

'Well, I'm hungry, miss,' came the snivelling reply. 'I ain't had nuffing to eat since Friday morning!'

Glad of the change of topic, Harriet set her mind to Billy's present problem and quickly came up with a solution.

'We are sitting on a bed of vegetables, Billy,' she reminded him. 'We shan't starve.'

'Turnips, miss—and not even cooked!' Billy was not impressed.

'Let me tell you, young man,' said Harriet, unmoved by his cavalier attitude to such largesse, 'that when I was in Spain, such bounty would have kept a whole brigade in fodder for a week—including the horses, probably, so I beg you not to turn your nose up at it!'

She felt in her skirt pocket for the 'necessaire' which she had, in her youth, learned to carry at all times. This particular little roll, containing scissors, needles, pins and thread, she had constructed as a replacement to her own long-serving lost one as soon as she had been able to collect the required items from the housekeeper at Beldale House, regarding it as a vital accessory, for it had proved its worth many times in the past and was like to do so at present. She carefully unrolled the strip of cotton and, feeling for the scissors and a nail file, she extracted them and returned the 'necessaire' once more to the safety of her pocket.

'Now,' she said, with a feigned cheerfulness, 'we have the tools—so we can eat our dinner!'

Billy attacked the turnip sacks with misgivings but once opened, it was clear that their contents were still in good condition and quite edible. Harriet had eaten worse things in her time and entertained Billy with several stories of much more inferior provender she had been obliged to consume when she was not much older than he was now. Highly impressed, he tucked into sufficient of the vegetables to stay his hunger and begged for more anecdotes of her Peninsular experiences.

In this way Harriet managed to allay the boy's fears, although, as time passed, she found herself growing more and more concerned at the absence of any rescue. Where are you now, my reluctant hero? her heart cried out forlornly, but her battered head responded immediately with the sure and certain belief that Sandford would not rest until he found her. Clinging to this knowledge, she found some comfort of her own.

Chapter Thirteen

The first clap of thunder penetrated Sandford's brain and his eyes flew open with a start. Just for the merest moment he had believed it to be the sound of cannon-fire. Then, smiling and relaxing with a lazy yawn, he sat up and stretched and wondered where the devil Kimble had got to, for surely his valet should normally be busying himself about the bedchamber at this hour. He had to shake his head once or twice to clear away the remaining cobwebs and, as he did so, the night's events came rushing back to him. Leaping out of bed, he hastened to the window, which overlooked the rear terraces. It was pouring with rain. He sighed. No sign of Harriet, of course, she must be waiting in the salon. He glanced down at his pocket-watch on the dresser.

Good God! It was almost three o'clock! Why had no one woken him for morning service? Chagrined, he now had vague recollections of Kimble trying to rouse him from his stupor. She'll be furious, he thought, angrily pulling at his bell-cord for the third time, and we'll be at daggers' drawn again, just when it all

236

seemed to be coming about. He cursed his own stupidity.

The door opened and Kimble entered. Sandford was about to give him a piece of his mind when, to his astonishment, he saw his sister-in-law following the valet into his bedchamber.

'Judith?' he said, somewhat taken aback at this unexpected invasion.

'Harriet's missing,' said Judith, without preamble.

'M-missing? How do you mean?' Sandford gripped at the bedrail to steady himself.

'Wake up, Robert, for God's sake!' said Judith angrily. 'We've been searching since eight o'clock—the whole village is out looking for her!'

Sandford sank down on to his bed weakly and stared at her in uncomprehending horror.

'I don't understand,' he said at last. 'She was going to wait on the terrace—she *promised* she wouldn't go anywhere without Rothman—where the hell *is* Rothman? So help me, I'll *kill* him!'

'That will be a great help, I'm sure,' said Judith unkindly. 'Just get yourself dressed, man, and come to Lord William's room as quickly as you can!'

Sandford looked down and realised with a shock that he was clad only in his dress pantaloons. Glowering at Kimble, he grabbed the proffered dressing-gown and covered himself in one swift movement.

'Save your blushes, Robert,' said Judith, turning to leave. 'We have more important things to think about.'

After quickly splashing cold water over his face and scrambling into the garments Kimble passed him,

Sandford was ready in minutes and hurried to his father's chamber where the astonishing sight of a great crowd of people met his eyes.

'Father? Mother?' He walked forward anxiously. 'What is it—what has happened?'

The earl eyed him sourly. 'You picked a fine time to take to the bottle, my boy,' he said. 'The whole village has gone mad—and no one is in charge, it would seem.'

Sandford looked around the room, hardly recognising half of those present. 'Where's Charles?' he said heatedly. 'Surely he—'

'Charles has disappeared, too,' said Judith, her voice shaking, and immediately the rest of the group started to add their various and unconnected pieces of information until Sandford could stand it no longer.

'*Enough!*' he roared. 'Not another word until you are asked!'

The hubbub ceased at once and Sandford's eyes swept quickly amongst the expectant faces, desperately searching for Tiptree, and it was with overwhelming relief that he saw his stolid groom step forward.

'Tip? What's going on, man?'

In his clear but unhurried fashion, Tiptree related the events that had preceded Harriet's disappearance, culminating in Cooper's return to the kitchen and Davy Rothman's setting out, as instructed, for the Dower House.

'He couldn't have been more than five minutes behind her, guv—but there was no sign of her. He searched the bridleways on both sides of the lane and went to the top of Bell Hill—nothing, sir. He's taken it real bad, too,' finished the groom.

'Go on,' said Sandford grimly, caring less than a jot for the inadequate Rothman's finer feelings, but realising that nothing would be gained by losing his temper.

'Mr Ridgeway came back from Westpark and when he heard what had happened he set everybody from the yard and out of the gardens to search the copses—even some of the footmen went into the hayfields to look. When word got down to the village, they *all* turned out and the Reverend had to cancel the service because there was no congregation!'

He studied his master's face anxiously. 'We've been everywhere, my lord,' he said gently. 'The whole place has been combed over twice or more. One of our stable-lads thought he had seen Miss Cordell heading in the opposite direction—up towards the Top Meadow—but we've had searches going on up there, too. They're refusing to stop, guv—even though it's pouring with rain, as you see, sir.'

Sandford shot a cursory look out of the window, then turned once more to face Tiptree. 'You said Mr Ridgeway came back.' He frowned. 'Then where did he go?'

'He took two men down to search the lake area, sir—Beckett and Hinds, from Westpark—but he left them to it and said he was going up to Staines—nobody had looked there, apparently.'

'And he didn't return?' Sandford was finding it difficult to breathe.

'No, sir,' said Tiptree, shaking his head. 'And I went there myself, guv, and searched the place from top to bottom and inside out—the tenants were very co-operative.'

'And no sign of the horses—Mr Ridgeway's big mare?'

'He wasn't riding Bess, guv—she'd been out all night. He'd picked up one of our two-year-olds, but nobody can remember which one.'

'And no sign of Clipper?' demanded Sandford hoarsely.

Tiptree was silent for a moment. 'Miss Cordell's mare has just been found in West Wood, sir—during the second search there. She's been given something, guv—can't tell what, exactly, Smithers is seeing to her—and her saddle was missing.'

Sandford, white-faced, had collapsed on to the empty chair beside his mother, who leaned forward to put a tentative hand on his knee. Her eyes were full of tears for she could find no words with which to comfort him.

'The men are waiting for new orders, my dear,' she said softly. 'You must take charge now.'

There was a tense silence as the expectant assembly now focused its attention on the distracted viscount. The minutes dragged on until a violent clap of thunder suddenly reverberated above the roofs. Everyone in the room started with shock and, at the same time, Sandford leapt to his feet.

'Everyone—downstairs, into the hall,' he commanded, in a voice of steel. 'Tip—on my desk in the office, the lists and the maps—fetch them. And I want to see the lad who saw Miss Cordell ride off.'

He turned to his parents and his face softened momentarily. 'We'll find her—try not to worry. I'll keep you posted and—*forgive me*, Father!' This last was uttered on a low, choking breath just as he turned and left the room.

Chegwin closed the door behind the last of the visitors.

'He'll do it, my lord,' he said. 'He'll find her—you mark my words.'

Lady Caroline clasped her hands together tightly. 'Please God, may you be right, Chegwin—but where can she be? Oh, where can the poor child be?'

Downstairs, the same question was occupying the minds of the now increasing throng, which had gathered, not only in the hallway, but also on the steps and at the front of the building.

Sandford was issuing orders in a sharp staccato manner. 'All Beldale men to my left and Westpark to my right. Mr Ridgeway's men on the steps here in front of me. I intend to have a roll call. When you hear your name, step forward and identify yourself and form into lines of six—Tiptree will call the Beldale staff, I shall deal with Westpark and...' Who could he trust? he wondered, and felt a hand on his arm.

'You can depend on me, your lordship,' came March's steady voice. 'May I take the Dower House roll-call? I am acquainted with most of the staff there.'

Sandford, without hesitation, handed the shortest list of names to the young footman.

'Quick as you can, March,' he said gruffly and turned to deal with his own group.

Much moved by everyone's eagerness to assist in the search, the viscount was impressed at the speed with which the lines of men were formed. Some of them had been with the military, of course, which helped a great deal, but even the very young and quite old men found their places with alacrity, and in less than ten minutes the division was complete.

'Who's missing?' Sandford wanted to know.

Tiptree's list of Beldale absentees consisted mainly of Davy Rothman and the young grooms and stable-boys who had gone out with him, Rothman having re-fused to give up his search. Smithers was in the stables, having suggested that his time would be better spent attending to any problems with the horses and Chegwin was, of course, upstairs with the earl.

Ridgeway had only a few men working at the Dower House and they were quickly accounted for. Sandford studied his own list carefully as Judith, who had been watching the procedure in silence, came forward to offer her assistance.

'Who's missing from your staff, Judith?'

She cast her eyes down the list and over the assembled ranks of the Westpark men.

'Finchley and Pinter—they're still at home, of course.'

'Why "of course"?' demanded Sandford suspiciously.

Judith flushed. 'Mother said she needed them,' she said defensively. 'But they're both quite old men, Robert, they wouldn't be much use to you.'

'What about these others—Freeman, Hinds, Purley and Beckett?'

'Freeman—he's Head of Stable—I imagine he's doing exactly as Smithers is. There are a lot of very tired horses, Robert—he'll be trying to keep them on their feet. Purley and Beckett—I believe they work in the gardens—and Hinds—I'm not sure...' She looked towards her head gardener for guidance.

'Jack Hinds—works in the stable, ma'am,' came the answer. 'Came from Staines—along with Matt Beckett—bit of a slow top, but no real harm in him, I'd say.'

Sandford digested this information for a moment then, turning to Tiptree, he asked, 'Didn't you say that Hinds and Beckett were with Mr Ridgeway before he went off to Staines?'

Tiptree nodded, a deep frown furrowing his brow. 'They *said* he had gone to Staines, guv—I'm just wondering...'

'So am I, Tip. So am I. They need to be found...'

Just then a commotion at the back of the village crowd caught their attention and, as the group parted, the wet, bedraggled figures of the two men in question came forward. Beckett hurried up the steps and removed his soaking cap, while the other, younger man stood nervously below.

'Just got back, your lordship,' he panted. 'Been up North Lane again—searched all the ditches right up as far as Top Meadow—then crossed over and came down the south side. Still no word, sir?' His expression was full of concern.

Sandford shook his head wearily, and then faced the assembly once more. 'I want each and every one of you to know how grateful his lordship and myself are for your dedication and hard work. The search will begin again, but first you must all have something to eat and change your coats, if you can—leave your wet things with the laundry staff, they will deal with them. Food and drink will be provided here in the kitchens until further notice—extra help from your wives will be very welcome. Your horses will be fed and watered in the stables. Search parties will go off at regular intervals to comb specific areas and return—this way you will all have time to dry out and take some sustenance. And, please, don't forget that we are looking for three people—Billy Tatler has still not been found.'

There were some caustic mutterings at his last remark, for many of those present believed that Billy Tatler was the root cause of the whole mystery. Although how he could have spirited the young lady away no one was prepared to guess, but most were in agreement that a good thrashing might have served him well.

Sandford had collected the boards with the large-scale maps of the area from the estate office and had set them up in the hall, where they could be studied by all. With Tiptree's assistance he had divided the estates into small workable sections and he had only one stipulation to make as to the composition of the search parties. He insisted that each party must comprise of an equal number of staff from both houses, with the men from the Dower House fitting in wherever they could, along with any volunteers from the village. Only in this way could he feel confident that any possible subterfuge would be immediately exposed. With this, Tiptree was in total agreement, recognising the military precision with which his guv'nor was masterminding the vast operation.

As darkness began to descend over the woods, Sandford felt his spirits lowering in keeping with the dusk. He had been obliged to remain at Beldale, in order to co-ordinate and structure the searches and to keep his parents informed, although he desperately wanted to be the one who found Harriet.

Lady Caroline had insisted upon throwing open all the ground-floor rooms as rest areas for the volunteers and, as night approached, Mrs Gibson had willingly released so many candles from her precious store to light up the huge reception rooms that the house had become the beacon which lit the last returning searchers home.

It seemed that almost the entire village population was gathered in Beldale House and yet there was very little noise. Weary men, in old felt jackets, leaned their backs against pale damask sofas as they sipped at their tankards of ale. Some were too tired even to drink and fell asleep on the Aubusson rugs. Others conversed in hushed, whispering groups in various parts of the hallway, while a never-ending stream of maids and volunteer matrons replenished and removed plates and mugs.

It had been agreed that the search would be renewed at first light and that those who were able to do so would continue with their efforts. Very few of the volunteers had chosen to quit and those who had been obliged to go to their homes to attend to their own domestic matters had promised to return without delay.

Sandford stood watching a group of sleeping youngsters and his heart turned over as he recalled similar watches before dawn offensives in a far-off land. Who could have imagined that this lovely, sleepy Leicestershire village could ever resemble a foreign battlefield! He turned away from the poignant sight with a lump in his throat and was about to go up the stairs to report to his parents when he felt a tug at his sleeve.

'Your lordship.' Davy Rothman was at his elbow, his dark eyes red-rimmed from both weariness and the tears he had shed.

At the sight of the young footman Sandford had great difficulty in controlling the surge of rage that threatened to overcome him. The boy had been missing all day although every group had been on the look-out for him.

'Where the devil have you been, Rothman?' The viscount's voice was curt.

'Everywhere, sir—anywhere.' Davy's voice broke. 'I'm sorry, sir—sorry I wasn't here—I should have been with her—I know...'

Sandford's eyes searched the boy's face and Davy returned his master's gaze without flinching. Sandford sighed and put his hand on the boy's shoulder.

'Have you been out all day, lad?'

Davy nodded and his eyes filled with tears. 'Yes, sir—but I'll go out again—whenever you're ready.'

'Go and find something to eat, Davy and try and get some sleep,' said the viscount wearily, 'You'll be no use to Miss Cordell in your present state. I'll have you called as soon as it's light, I promise you—you'll be the first.'

The youngster bowed and turned to go to the kitchens, but was stopped in his tracks by Cooper, the gardener, who was staring intently at Davy's uniform cap.

'Where'd you get that flower, young man?' he said fiercely, pointing to the withered blossom tucked into the boy's maroon hatband.

Davy coloured as several interested faces turned in his direction. 'I picked it up on the lane—what's it to you?'

'That's a "Beldale Sunset" that is,' Cooper said mulishly. 'I want to know how you came by it.'

With a heavy sigh, Sandford started back down the stairs. Surely we can do without an altercation about staff filching flowers, he thought in frustration.

'What's the trouble, Cooper?' he asked, with a patience he was far from feeling.

The elderly man pointed at Davy's cap. 'It's the flower I gave her, sir—the "Beldale Sunset"—on account of it matching her hair. I gave it her just before she went missing—I saw her tuck it into her buttonhole. Where'd he get it from—that's what I'd like to know!'

Sandford approached the scarlet-faced footman and all conversation ceased as everyone within earshot turned towards the little group at the foot of the stairs.

'Well, Davy?' the viscount spoke very softly.

'I told him, sir,' gabbled Davy almost hysterically, terrified at finding himself in this spotlight. 'It was up at the fork—I picked it up because—it was...' His voice tailed off.

'The colour of Miss Cordell's hair?' Sandford could hardly bring himself to say the words, but the boy nodded eagerly.

'I thought it was a sign, you see, and I started searching the derelicts, but somebody else was already there and hadn't found anything, so we came away together, but I kept the flower—for luck.' He stared defiantly at the gardener.

Sandford chewed at his lip. Another dead end, he thought, helplessly, but just then Tiptree stepped forward.

'Begging your pardon, sir,' he said, in his slow careful manner. 'I wonder if young Davy here would be able to point out the other party he was mentioning— the man he met at the cottages?'

Davy stared helplessly around the hallway at the dozen or so men now sitting with their backs to the wall or leaning their weary frames against the great pillars which held up the ceiling.

'It wasn't anyone from our house, sir,' he said, with a shaking voice, as Tiptree drew him into the largest drawing-room and led him amongst the rest of the volunteers. He gazed from left to right with meticulous attention as he made his way through the sleeping groups. Eventually he shook his head. 'Can't see him, sir,' he said, with obvious reluctance.

Tiptree took Sandford to one side as Davy was motioned off to get his much-needed refreshment.

'We kept a list of the men who left, sir—shall I get it?'

Sandford nodded bleakly and sat down on the stairs with his head in his hands. It's hopeless, just hopeless, he thought, in misery. Where are you, my love? Are you hurt and all alone in the dark? Are you thinking what a poor sort of hero I turned out to be? He closed his eyes, willing his brain to convey a message through the darkness—I'll find you, my darling! I promise you I'm coming to find you!

'There's something keeps nagging at me, guv,' came Tiptree's voice at his elbow.

The viscount opened his eyes and frowned questioningly at his groom.

'Well, sir, it's these two blokes from Westpark— Hinds and Beckett. They seem to be everywhere—and nowhere—if you get my drift?'

'Keep talking,' said Sandford grimly, as he rose to his feet.

'It's like this, sir—we know that Mr Ridgeway went down to the lake with them and they sent us on a wild goose-chase to Staines. Thing is, guv…'

'—we haven't searched the pavilion!' Sandford finished, clapping him on the back. 'Get some lanterns, Tip. We'll do it now!'

Striding through the rear salon, over more sleeping villagers, the two men hastened out on to the terrace into the pouring rain, which was still lashing down in a relentless torrent. Sandford raised his lantern and looked down the steps at the pools that were forming on the grass below him.

'Quicker to walk, wouldn't you say?'

Tiptree agreed that horses would be useless in these conditions and, hats down and shoulders hunched against the drenching downpour, they had just started to make their way across the park towards the lake when the viscount's attention was caught by a pale movement on the lawn in front of him. In the meagre glow of his lantern he beheld a sight that stopped him dead in his tracks.

A gasping Charles Ridgeway lay at his feet, his clothing soaking wet and caked with a thick, black mud!

'Sandford?' came his choking voice. 'Help me up, old man—I'm done in.'

Together Tiptree and his master half-dragged and half-carried the exhausted Ridgeway back up into the house, laying him carefully down on to one of Lady Caroline's best damask sofas—a passing thought which did cross Tiptree's mind but knowing better than to mention it, he motioned instead to a nearby footman to bring some brandy.

Sandford himself held the glass to his cousin's trembling lips and gently allowed some of the restorative to dribble into his mouth. Ridgeway was struggling to sit up, his panic-stricken eyes flashing from side to side as he attempted to take in his surroundings. The viscount pressed him firmly back against the cushions.

'Wait just a moment, Charles,' he cautioned. 'Take your time—another sip.'

'No—time, Robert,' rasped out his cousin. 'Beckett and Hinds—they're our men—took me by surprise— knocked out—the pavilion—swam back...' He swooned away once more as Sandford stood up.

Several of the searchers were now beginning to rouse themselves, having heard the commotion, and word quickly circulated that Charles Ridgeway had returned. A crowd began to gather around the couch.

Sandford beckoned to Tiptree. 'Where does this Beckett live? He's a gardener—does he reside at Westpark?'

Tiptree shook his head. 'Dunno, guv. Hinds lives over the stables there. Some of the gardeners live out— Top Meadow, maybe...?'

'No, he don't, sir,' interposed an eager voice and Cooper senior stepped forward. 'Matt Beckett—he's Finchley's nevvy—shares a room with his uncle over at Westpark—got a hut out behind the shrubbery at Staines.'

'A hut?' said Sandford in exasperation. 'What the devil has that got to do with anything?'

'Grows things, your lordship,' replied Cooper, unmoved. 'Herbs—for horse liniment and such. Saw him put an old dog to sleep once—knows a thing or two about sleeping potions, I'd say...' Other heads nodded and wagged in agreement behind him.

'Has the hut been searched—for Billy—or Miss Cordell?' Sick with apprehension, Sandford turned to Tiptree, who assured him at once that it had.

'Couldn't hide anyone there, sir,' he said. 'Full of bottles and pots. Seem to remember that Beckett showed me himself—very keen that I marked it off, now that I recall.'

'Get the horses saddled, Tip,' said the viscount curtly. 'I'm going up to Westpark myself...'

'It's pretty dark, guv. Might be better to take a carriage round the lane—we'd have the lamps.'

Sandford considered this for a moment, then shook his head. 'Take too long,' he said briskly. 'And they'd hear the carriage coming.'

On the couch beside them, Ridgeway stirred and his eyes flew open in shock. 'You don't think Judith is involved in all this, for God's sake?' His voice cracked with horror as he struggled to sit up. 'I'm coming with you!'

Sandford regarded his cousin frowningly. 'If you think you can sit a horse,' he said without expression and turned to leave. 'Better change out of those things, too—you've got five minutes. We'll be in the stables!'

Apart from a single lamp which hung above the rear entrance, Westpark Manor was in darkness when the three men arrived. Tiptree, still carrying the poled lantern that had guided the riders along the bridleway, swung himself down from his horse and hurried to assist Ridgeway, who was near collapsing with exhaustion.

'I told you not to attempt the journey,' said Sandford unsympathetically, as he himself dismounted. 'You can hardly stand!'

'I'll be fine,' gasped his cousin, leaning against his mount. 'I had to come—you must see that!'

Tiptree glowered at his master. 'Give him another drop of that brandy, guv,' he suggested. 'That'll sort him out for a while.'

Sandford complied, handing his flask to Ridgeway who, after taking a hefty swig of the restoring spirit, took a deep breath and straightened himself up.

'I still think it would be better if you were to wait out here, Charles,' said the viscount, preparing to open the door.

'Not a chance, thank you, coz,' replied Ridgeway indignantly. 'Judith might need—somebody.'

The three men entered the silent house and made their way to the hall, which had the customary single candle burning in its holder on a side table.

'Do you intend waking the whole house?' asked Ridgeway, in a hushed voice. 'The children…?'

Sandford shook his head. 'I expected to find Finchley here,' he admitted. 'If he is involved, along with his nephew, it's unlikely that they will have gone to their beds!'

'That's true.' His cousin nodded. 'Shall we go back and try the kitchen?' He turned to retrace his steps along the passageway that led to the servants' quarters but, just as the other men were about to follow him, a voice came from above their heads.

'Who's there? I warn you, I have a pistol! Come out where you can be seen!'

It was Judith. Standing at the top of the stairs in her night attire, she was firmly brandishing one of her late husband's duelling pistols in one hand and a branch of candles in the other.

Sandford immediately stepped forward into the shallow pool of light.

'It's me, Judith,' he called out in a soft voice. 'Put down your weapon.'

'Robert!' she gasped. 'What are you doing here? You have found Harriet?' She hurried down the stairs, gaping in astonishment as she beheld her other uninvited guests.

'You, too, Charles? Where have you been all day? And what are you all doing, creeping about the house in this manner?' She spun angrily round to face Sandford. 'Robert? Are you searching Westpark for Harriet? You cannot think that she is hidden here, surely?'

'It appears that some of your men are involved, Judith,' said Sandford uncomfortably. 'We are looking for Beckett. I understand that he sleeps here with his uncle—Finchley.'

Ridgeway reached out to take the pistol from Judith's shaking hand at the same time as Tiptree relieved her of the candlestick. She sank down on to a nearby settle and looked at Sandford in distress.

'Are you certain—Beckett? But he's only a gardener—why would he...?'

'They left Charles for dead in the lake pavilion, Judith,' replied Sandford awkwardly. 'They are clearly dangerous men—and if they've got Harriet…!' His voice trembled and Judith's shocked eyes travelled to seek Ridgeway's.

'You are injured?' she inquired anxiously, but he shook his head.

'Bruised—tired—I'll survive,' he said, dismissing his pain. 'Finchley's room, Judith?'

She rose at once to her feet and pointed to the steep stone stairway that was situated beside the door to the kitchens.

'The men's rooms are on the top floor—second or third door—I'm not sure…'

'Tip—check the rooms,' instructed Sandford. 'Try not to wake anyone.'

Tiptree ran lightly up the stairs and disappeared from view as Sandford and Ridgeway turned back in the direction of the kitchens but, once again, they were stayed by a voice from above. This time it was the harsh, stentorian command from Lady Butler that stopped them in their tracks.

'Stand still, whoever you are!'

'Mother!' gasped Judith, running back into the hall just as Lady Butler, swathed in a massive purple dressing gown, began to descend the stairs.

Sandford, raising his eyebrows in despair and swearing fulsomely under his breath, reluctantly stepped forward to reveal himself. Judith's mother blanched at the unexpected sight of the viscount coming out of the shadows.

'Judith! What is the meaning of this?' she hissed. 'In your nightwear—go to your room at once, miss!' and, turning to Sandford, 'You, sir, how dare you come creeping…' but Sandford had had enough.

'Be silent, madam!' he uttered curtly. 'You are wasting precious time. Come down, if you must, but kindly keep your comments to yourself! Light some more candles, Judith!'

Lady Butler, silenced by the viscount's tone, clutched at the banister as she trod heavily down the stairs, then, shakily seating herself on the settle, she watched mutely as Judith hurried to fulfil Sandford's request. The hall was soon adequately illuminated and, upon perceiving that Sandford was not the only night visitor, her ladyship started with undisguised dismay.

'Ridgeway…?' she began, but Sandford gave her a quelling glance and she was once again silent, staring apprehensively at the estate manager as he assisted her daughter in the lighting of more candles.

'Nobody up on the top floor, guv.'

Tiptree had returned from his mission and Sandford, nodding, motioned Judith to one side.

'Look after your mother. I didn't mean to frighten her but we don't want the whole house woken.' Then, to Ridgeway, 'You stay on this side of the door in case one of them comes through—Tiptree, behind me.'

The two men sidled along the passageway and pushed open the heavy oak door that led into the kitchen. They were at once confronted with the unappealing sight of Finchley and Pinter lashed to their chairs with clothes-line, both totally unconscious, but snoring loudly. A sniff at the contents of the tankards on the table in front of the servants provided Tiptree with all the information he needed as to the reason for the old men's condition.

'Strong ale, sir—been doped, too, I shouldn't wonder, if "matey" has had anything to do with it.'

Sandford tried slapping the men's faces in an attempt to wake them, but to no avail, and Tiptree had to restrain his now furious master from delivering a more violent punishment to the old servants.

'Leave it, guv,' he insisted, pulling the viscount away. 'We don't know that they're to blame.'

Breathing heavily, Sandford sank down on to a chair and closed his eyes, his shoulders sagging in defeat.

'It's hopeless, hopeless,' he groaned. 'He's ahead of us at every turn—he'd probably left before we even arrived. What now, Tip?'

'Back to Beldale, sir—can't do anything until it's light. At least we know who's behind it all.'

'Do we, Tip—but do we?' His lordship's voice was weary as he led the way back into the hall, where another distasteful sight met his eyes.

Judith was on her knees, attempting to pacify her distraught mother who was now moaning loudly and rocking herself from side to side, demanding to know what was to become of them all. Ridgeway stepped forward to meet the viscount, thankfully leaving the old woman to Judith's administrations.

'What is it, old man?' he said, quickly taking note of his cousin's dejected air. 'You did not find them?'

'Finchley...' began Sandford, his tone heavy, then he staggered back in surprise as a suddenly upright Lady Butler elbowed Ridgeway aside and all but threw herself at him.

'He lies! Whatever he has told you—it is all lies!' she panted, clutching at his lapels.

Ridgeway gripped her roughly by the arm as Sandford wrenched himself away from her clawing hands and Judith stared at her mother in shock.

'Wh-what are you saying, Mother?' she gasped. 'Do you know something about all this?'

'Nothing—nothing!' wailed Lady Butler, vainly trying to pull herself away from Ridgeway's grip. 'I tell you the man lies—he's an incompetent old fool—you cannot believe a word...'

Her voice trailed away weakly as Sandford, eyes glittering, reached out and took hold of the neck of her night-rail.

'You despicable old woman!' he ground out. 'It was you! My God, it was you all the time! What a fool I've been—where is she? If you've hurt her I'll kill you— I swear I'll kill you myself!'

'Robert! For God's sake!' came Judith's voice in protest, as both she and Ridgeway leapt to extricate Lady Butler from the viscount's furious grasp while Tiptree struggled to hold his master back.

'It's your own fault!' spluttered the woman, from the comparative safety of the settle where Ridgeway and Judith had finally managed to deposit her. 'You should have married Judith—I didn't mean any harm...'

Judith stepped away from her mother in dismay, her hands covering her trembling lips.

'What are you saying?' she whispered. 'Are you to blame for Harriet's disappearance?'

'No, I am not,' rejoined the old woman obstinately. 'I didn't tell him to take her away. I only wanted to put Sandford in dislike of her—make her look cheap and common—which she is!' She stared defiantly at the grim-faced viscount who was still fighting to remove himself from Tiptree's iron hold.

'Have done, guv, do,' said the groom, in exasperation. 'You've the whole night to spare. If you want to find out where Miss Cordell is, you've got to hear her out.'

At these words Sandford ceased his struggles and Tiptree at once released him.

Lady Butler shook her head. 'I don't know where he has taken her. I never intended anyone to get hurt—Beldale was a mistake. Beckett should never have…!'

'You were responsible for Lord William's accident!' Judith, horrified, collapsed into Ridgeway's outstretched arms. 'Mother! What have you done?'

'*I* didn't do anything—I merely pointed out to Finchley how much better off we would all be once you became countess—Beckett took it upon himself to feed Beldale's horse with one of his potions and Beldale went down. No one expected him to recover—well, he is very old.' Lady Butler shrugged, as four pairs of eyes stared at her in shocked incredulity. 'When Sandford came home with *her* I could see that I would have little difficulty in showing her up for what she is—having her fall into the lake was just a lucky chance. Beckett happened to see her on the path, but the fool let the whore's brat get away—*and* he told me that his lordship here only *laughed* when he saw her appalling state—so you must see that it was necessary for me to think of something else.'

'I can't believe I'm listening to this,' groaned Sandford, with his head in his hands, as Lady Butler nodded at her audience in cheerful unconcern. '*You* arranged Miss Cordell's mishap in the woods?'

'Well, it *is* true that I wrote the note—rather a clever idea, I thought.' She shrank back as Sandford moved angrily towards her. 'And I did help Elspeth to give her the pink biscuits. That was *very* tricky—because Elspeth...' At these words Judith gave a frightened gasp. 'I would never have allowed *her* to eat one, my dear—surely you do not think that?'

Her daughter gave a strangled moan and buried her face in Ridgeway's chest as her mother coolly continued her incredible tale.

'Hinds picked up the gloves *she* had dropped in the stables—another lucky chance—and it proved very useful in my clever little tryst scene. Beckett failed to get the emerald ring, of course—that was a puzzle to me for I had seen her wearing it—but I knew that the whole thing had succeeded when I heard that you had taken each other in such dislike!'

Judith, who had known nothing of these events, was staring at Sandford in consternation. '*That* was why you had quarrelled,' she said weakly. 'But you made up—I saw you—and when you came to dinner...!'

'That was when everything started to get out of hand,' cut in her mother, calmly straightening her nightcap. 'Finchley told me that Beckett had caught the trollop's brat and was waiting to know what *I* wanted him to do. Well, I told him that it was their problem and nothing to do with me—which, of course, it isn't, for *I've* done nothing wrong at all and...' she glared resentfully at Sandford '—you can shake me all you like, but I still don't know where he is or where he has taken her!'

'Do you really believe that you will go unpunished for your part in these events?' asked Sandford incredulously. 'People have been hanged for less! You must be insane!'

'Robert!' Judith's face was white. 'She is my mother!'

'For which you have always had my sympathies,' said her brother-in-law tartly, ignoring his cousin's angry look. 'What time is it, Tiptree?'

'Close on one, sir—at least three more hours before dawn.'

'We'll get back to Beldale then,' said the viscount wearily. 'I'm leaving you in charge, Charles—make sure *she's* still here when I get back. See to those two in the kitchen—and for God's sake don't let any word of this get out!'

'Now, look here, Robert,' exclaimed Ridgeway, in protest. 'Judith is very upset about all this—her mother, dammit!'

'What would you have me do, Charles?' said Sandford icily. 'Offer her a viscountcy? Apparently none of this would have happened if I had done so!'

'That is very true,' said Lady Butler, unperturbed at her daughter's obvious distress. 'You see how you have brought the whole thing upon yourself!'

'I think not, your ladyship,' rejoined Sandford softly. 'Although it pains me to have to say this, it appears to be entirely thanks to you that I have other plans for the title.'

Lady Butler frowned. 'Why ''thanks to me''?' she asked. 'I have explained that I had nothing to do with any of this business!'

The slightest flicker of a smile crossed Sandford's lips as he prepared to leave. 'You tell her, Charles,' he said, 'although I doubt that the lady will appreciate the irony.'

'Aye.' The older man nodded, holding Judith's hand firmly in his own. 'I'll willingly do that for you, man— and mebbe add a few words on my own behalf!'

Sandford, hunched in his damp riding-coat, did not utter a single word on the homeward journey and, since Tiptree's whole attention was dedicated to keeping the poled lantern low in front of his horse's head to guide the two beasts along the bridleway, the groom kept his thoughts to himself.

Chapter Fourteen

In the cellar time passed interminably, for Harriet and Billy were unable to tell whether it was day or night, being aware only of the endless waiting in impenetrable darkness. They could hear the persistent and ominous rumble of thunder, even within their earthen cave, although the torrential rain that accompanied it they could only imagine, until intermittent dripping of water from various parts of the roof indicated its overhead presence.

'You would think that a cellar would be watertight,' observed Harriet crossly, as she moved their now bracken-filled sacks for the umpteenth time. 'One does, after all, expect to keep logs and certain perishables throughout the winter.'

'Yeah, but you have to remember that the roof has gone on this cottage,' Billy pointed out. 'And some of the other wooden bits must have dried out in the fire—them that didn't burn, I mean.'

Harriet considered this. 'Meggy Watts told me that the flagstones had fallen through to the cellars in some of the other cottages. I hope the ones above our heads don't take it upon themselves to come down on top of us!'

She regretted having given voice to these thoughts as Billy at once let out a loud wail and clung to her like a leech. She was obliged to sit him down and pet him for some time until his terror abated. She dashed away the tears that persisted in forming in her own eyes and leaned her still desperately aching head against the now dank and streaming walls. The thought of falling flagstones kept recurring, however, and eventually gave birth to an idea.

She settled the fitfully sleeping child down on to the damp sacking and felt her way back to the corner where the rest of the vegetable sacks were heaped. Carefully climbing on top of them, she raised her hands and realised, to her joy, that she could feel the underside of a large flagstone. The cellar was hardly more than six feet high! How stupid of her not to realise that this would be the case!

Moving her fingers across the under-surface of the stone until she felt the floor timber that supported it, she widened her search until she could feel another. Twelve inches apart, she judged, and the joists probably nine or ten inches wide. The flagstones must be about twenty-one inches square and heavy enough to rest on the oak timbers without moving—two or three-inch-thick quarry stone, probably—would she be able to move one upwards?

She sat down upon the turnip sacks to weigh up the possibilities. She was no weakling, in the ordinary way, but thought that it was likely that she had lost quite a bit of blood as she had twice felt it necessary to renew her makeshift head-bandage—in addition to having subsisted on raw turnips for who knew how long.

The problem was one of leverage, she supposed, and she had no tools available. She had scoured the floor of the cellar on hands and knees, with Billy's assistance, to scavenge for anything that might have come in useful to them but, unfortunately for her cause, Potter had proved to be an inordinately tidy housekeeper and none of the usual debris of broken shovels or brooms had been found in his underground storeroom.

Harriet made up her mind. Hoping that the sounds of activity would not penetrate the sleeping urchin's brain, for she was reluctant to raise his hopes unnecessarily, she began to rearrange the sacks of turnips into a more stable platform for herself. This was heavy and cumbersome work, for the sacks were unwieldy and unco-operative, in addition to being very wet, and she was forced to stop frequently to rest and recover from the attacks of swimming fatigue that overcame her. But her perseverance was finally rewarded when, some immeasurable time later, she found that her solid pile of sacks would raise her three feet closer to the roof.

She could only crouch at the top, of course, but this had been her intention for she knew that this was the only way in which she would be able to apply any upward movement to the slab, given that her arms could sustain the weight. Where would be the best place to push? she wondered, not wishful of having a quarry-stone come crashing down on her fingers to add to all her other miseries. If she could lift one at its junction with a neighbouring slab, would it be possible to slide it over the top in the same movement? She was well aware that, even with all the will in the world, she had no real hope of holding up such a heavy weight for more than a moment or two, but if she could just get one into position on top of its fellow it would surely be possible to slide it along the timbers and out of the way. Then, even if she could not make her own escape through the aperture, there might be sufficient room for Billy to do so.

She gnawed at the unappetising turnip in her hand, wondering if she would ever be able to bring herself to face the taste again then, smiling at her foolishness, remembered having had the self-same thoughts about stewed rabbit many years ago—what she would not give at this moment for a dish of that delicacy!

She drew a deep breath, at the same time feeling in her pocket for her riding gloves and, pulling them on so that she could get the best possible grip, she positioned herself carefully and, with all her might, she strained her muscles against the unyielding object.

Nothing! A sob of wretchedness escaped from her lips and her eyes filled with tears. Please, God—oh, please, dear God, she prayed, give me the strength— please help me! She applied herself once again and, gritting her teeth with anguish, she heaved at the slab above her head until her arms began to give way and her head swam.

Then she felt, or rather, heard the movement and

either her prayers or her desperation must have given her some sort of divine power for, with a grating lurch, the flagstone did indeed lift and move away from her, only a fraction but enough to balance its front edge precariously on top of its neighbour.

She slid down on to the sacks in a half-swoon, her ears pounding, choking for air and was unable to move for several minutes. She heard Billy stirring and his anxious voice calling her, but could not answer him for she had no strength left in her body.

'Miss? Miss—where are you? Did you hear a noise? Where are you, miss?'

He had found her platform of sacks and was clambering up to reach her. Weakly she put out her hand to reassure him and he huddled himself as close as he could get to her limp body.

'What you doing up here, miss?' he asked in shocked amazement.

'I—think—that—we—may—be—able—to—get out!' she gasped, her voice rough with exhaustion. 'But I—must rest—for just a little while—before I can go on.'

'Is it your head, miss?'

Billy couldn't imagine what had happened to Miss while he had been sleeping. This surely was not his stalwart saviour, who had been so strong and resilient up until now. If she folded, he was ready to believe that they were doomed to remain in their underground prison forever and that they would fade away and die— if 'matey' didn't come and finish them off first!

But Harriet was at last beginning to recover from her Herculean efforts and was gradually able to sit up and explain, in simple terms, what she had achieved.

'And I do believe,' she said, trying to make her voice sound bright and cheerful, 'that if we can push the slab from this end, we might slide the whole thing back and make good our escape!'

'Ooh, miss—let's do it. I can help—see! I can easily reach if I stand up next to you! Both of us should be able to push hard enough!'

Harriet fervently hoped so, but begged him to allow her to get her breath back before they attempted the task. She gave him a turnip to nibble while she closed her eyes for a few minutes in a concentrated endeavour to mobilise her few remaining resources. Her arm muscles felt as though they were made of water, the back of her head was causing her considerable discomfort and she knew that she would be able to summon up sufficient effort for only one good push and, after that, how long would it be before her strength returned, in these conditions?

Resolutely, she positioned herself again and gave Billy explicit instructions as to where to put his fingers, even going so far as to insist that he wear her gloves to cushion any impending damage. Curiously, she also removed the Beldale emerald ring and wrapped it safely in her 'necessaire' before proceeding—a future Hurst bride might not care for a scratched or chipped ring, she told herself sadly, should their endeavour fail and any other rescue prove to be in vain.

'One good push, Billy,' she said. 'Then we must rest. When I say ''now'' you must push straight forward with me—are you ready? Take a deep breath—*NOW*!'

With their combined weight they heaved at the slab together. It did indeed move but, sadly, only an inch or so, and both Harriet and the boy collapsed weakly on to the sacks beneath them, neither of them capable of rational speech for some time.

Gradually, however, Harriet became aware that the deep blackness of the cellar had lightened. Only to a dark grey gloom, it was true, but light was actually penetrating through the small slit. Was it grey dusk or grey dawn? she wondered despondently, then sat up in rigid shock as she heard the unmistakable sound of a man's voice almost directly above them. She reached out towards Billy and placed a warning finger against his mouth as her ears strained to catch the words.

'I told her, old girl—if I want to come up home I will—I don't need her to tell me what I can do. Look what's happened to our little nest, love—all your dear things—gone. Soon be gone meself, shouldn't wonder—but I'll be with you, my Milly...'

It was Joshua Potter! In defiance of his daughter's instructions he had come back to his old home again and was muttering away to himself as he ferreted amongst the remnants of his possessions.

Harriet pulled herself back up to the flagstones above her head and placed her mouth to the gap. 'Josh! Josh!' she called urgently. 'In the scullery! Come into the scullery!'

There was a deathly silence, then all of a sudden the sound of stumbling footsteps came towards their corner.

'Milly?' came a breathless voice. 'Have you come for me? Where are you, lass—can you show yourself? I'm ready to come with you!'

Harriet experienced a momentary pang at having to disenchant the old man of his simple belief in his late wife's visitation but, since he was likely to be their only hope, she resolutely dashed this feeling from her thoughts.

'It's me, Mr Potter—Harriet Cordell!' she cried through the slit. 'I am imprisoned in the cellar—with Billy Tatler. Can you see the raised flagstone in the corner of the scullery?'

Please God he has a light of some sort, she thought, and found herself sobbing with relief as she saw the stump of candle in his hand as he bent towards the gap. The flickering light was sufficient for him to see the reflection in her green eyes, now brimming with tears as she recognised his wrinkled old visage.

'It is you, indeed, miss!' he gasped in amazement. 'Everyone's been looking for you—how'd you get down there, miss?'

But Harriet had no heart to indulge in an explanatory conversation from her present uncomfortable position and begged the old man to open up the cellar hatch and, with some difficulty, eventually persuaded him to shuffle off to comply with her request. Presently, however, he came back to inform her that, unfortunately, a large mass of timber was wedged against the trap-door and that, try as he might, he had been unable to remove it.

Harriet beat her fists against the roof timbers in impotent frustration. 'Can you not find something with which to lever up the slab?' she called out in anguish but, as with a growing sense of hopelessness she listened to the old man stumbling about amongst the debris above them, she soon realised that this task would be equally beyond him.

'Josh!' she called out again, unable to bear the tension any longer. 'You must go for help—but *only* to Lord Sandford—do you hear? On no account tell anyone else of our whereabouts and—please—I know it will be difficult for you—but, *please*—hurry!'

'I'm on my way, miss,' came the wheezing reply. 'I'll fetch himself—don't you worry, miss.'

But Harriet was extremely worried and wondered how quickly a tired old rheumatic with chest problems could possibly cover the four miles to Beldale House—even supposing that Sandford was to be found there!

'Will he get back, d'ye think, miss?' asked Billy in a plaintive voice. 'He can't walk proper—it'll take him forever!'

'Well, Billy,' said Harriet grimly. 'We seem to have forever—we certainly aren't going anywhere—so we'd better think of new ways to pass the time.'

She dwelt on this problem for a moment, then brightened. 'Do you know ''Black Jack Ladderback''?'

'Can't say as I do, miss. What is it?'

'It's a round song we used to sing as we rode or marched along. I'll teach it to you. It goes like this...'

"Black Jack Ladderback
Took the acorn that he found
Dug a little hole and put
The seed into the ground
And the sun it shone, and the rain it rained
And in time it came to pass
There grew beside the wishing-well
An oak tree on the grass."

And in this way she kept him happily entertained for a full hour as he learned how Black Jack saw first a branch, then a twig followed by a leaf until, inevitably, he found another acorn and the whole song was repeated ad infinitum. This revelation caused Billy great amusement and he insisted on frequent encores. Harriet, for whom the song was less of a novelty, steadfastly put away her tedium and encouraged him to sing out with gusto, all the while wondering for how much longer she would be obliged to keep up his spirits.

By way of their little gap in the flagstones the cellar had slowly lightened sufficiently for each of them to just about make out the other's person in the gloom and this in itself was cheering. They were boisterously chanting out the words of the song for possibly the fifth time when they heard the sound of the trap-door being swung away. Harriet held her breath as she pulled Billy back into the furthest corner.

A sneering voice fell on their horrified ears.

'Sing-song, sing-song! What a pretty sound! Here's a little present for you!' and a load of brushwood and bracken was thrown through the opening, followed by a considerable quantity of dry straw.

With a sinking heart Harriet realised immediately what their captor's intention was. He meant to fire the cellar and leave them to their fate! Frantically scrambling down from the makeshift platform, she dealt firmly with her initial terror at the thought of being burnt to death and, with Billy's help, set about dragging as much of the scattered brushwood and straw as far away from immediate incineration as was possible.

Fear and the deep-rooted instinct for survival had instantly renewed her strength and with a determined obstinacy she then started pushing all the damp and sodden sacks directly below the cellar hatch, reasoning that should their assailant be about to hurl a firebrand into their underground prison, there was an evens chance that it would land on the not-so-readily-combustible pile of vegetables. Although only a few extra minutes might be gained from such a diversion, it could be enough to make all the difference to the outcome.

She held her breath as the trap-door re-opened and, with mounting horror, she saw that the shadowy outline above them had, indeed, set fire to a tarry faggot, for its flickering light enabled her to register the man's grinning countenance just before he tossed the kindling into the cellar and, with a snigger, slammed down the door once more.

She was certain that she had seen him somewhere before—but where? He was not the man who had directed her to ride up here—but she had no time to dwell upon this puzzle as another, far greater problem was facing her.

Sparks from the firebrand had ignited some of the scattered straw that still lay on the cellar floor and she had to engage her whole concentration in stamping out the various pockets of flame as they took hold. Billy, too, was thrashing his wet sacking at the defiant flickers that were creeping towards the dry brushwood at the far side of their prison.

Above them they could hear the sound of debris being piled once more against the trap-door and, at the sight of flames licking around the cracks in the framework, Harriet's heart sank, for she knew that as soon as the flimsy wooden structure burned away the whole mass of burning timber would fall through and, if that happened, nothing could save them.

Thick, acrid smoke was pouring from the faggot that had fallen beside the turnip sacks. The combination of wet earth and damp vegetables had caused the flames to expire, but the glowing, tarry embers that remained were eating their way along the edges of the sacks, causing choking palls to rise up and, mingled with the smoke and stench from all the other sources, the cellar was soon filled with an atmosphere in which no one could hope to survive for long.

Harriet grabbed at another of the empty, wet sacks and wrapped the choking Billy into its folds, pushing him into the corner furthest away from the burning hatchway and ordered him to keep himself rolled up.

She dragged off her smouldering boots and, lifting up her riding-skirt, she threw it over her head, sinking down on the cellar floor beside the howling urchin and prayed as she'd never prayed before.

Chapter Fifteen

Sandford stood at the window of the drawing room, watching intently for the first faint streaks of dawn to break across the dark sky. Never in his whole experience could he recall having lived through a longer night. With his brain in a whirl from Lady Butler's revelations, he had been unable to rest without recalling the disasters that had occurred during his earlier torpidity and, like a demented wraith, he had paced the crowded and bedimmed rooms, inwardly cursing his stupidity, weakness and every other fault or failing he could attach to his own ineptitude. Tiptree, dozing in a corner, had continually roused himself to point out in his usual blunt manner that Sandford would be as much use as a tinker's reject by the morning and that he would do better to harness his thoughts for an hour or two, but the viscount found it impossible to attend to this excellent advice.

His eyes were ragged from staring out into the darkness for any perceptible lightening of the black landscape before him until, all of a sudden, his senses quickened as he realised that he could, indeed, separate

276

sky from land. As the pale dawn began at last to spread its pearly pink glow across the low horizon, he turned in relief to give instructions for the first searchers to be wakened.

Very soon a crowd had gathered both inside and outside the yellow drawing-room and Davy Rothman stepped forward in some urgency.

'It's light enough, sir,' he said to Sandford. 'Can we go out now?'

The viscount nodded and Tiptree began issuing new directions and commands to the waiting groups, but his orders were suddenly interrupted by the sounds of a violent altercation issuing from the hallway.

Sandford frowned impatiently. 'Now, what the devil…?'

The crowd in the doorway parted to reveal the sight of Joshua Potter struggling with his son-in-law Seb Watts, who was attempting to prevent the old man from entering the room.

'I *will* speak to him—I *will*!' croaked Potter, who was in a state of near hysterics. 'Get your hands off me, young Seb. I *gotta* speak to himself—*she* said only *himself*!'

Sandford ripped through the crowd that divided him from the contentious pair and frantically grabbed at Potter's arm.

'Who?' he jerked out roughly. 'Speak up, man—for God's sake!'

'She's in the cellar, sir,' gasped the old man, collapsing to his knees. 'Along of Billy Tatler. I come as fast as I could—she said *only you*, sir!'

'He wouldn't tell me what it was, your lordship,' said Watts, screwing up his face. 'Meggy sent me up the lane with the cart, to see if he'd gone up to the cottage again, and I found him half-dead on the verge. He made me bring him—but I wasn't sure...' His voice tailed off as he saw Sandford making for the door, at the same time exhorting every man with a mount to get saddled and ride at once to Bottom Meadow.

Please, God, let me be in time, he prayed, as he gave Pagan his head along the bridleway that was the short cut to both Westpark and to the lane that led to Bottom Meadow. Tiptree and some of the men followed the viscount whilst the rest of the riders had been instructed to take the longer route along the lane.

It was almost full dawn by the time Sandford wheeled his stallion across the meadow that separated the two estates. He did not turn towards Westpark, however, but took his mount at a gallop over the stone wall into North Lane and on towards the fork at the top where, to his utter shock and horror, he could clearly see the thin column of smoke that was spiralling viciously from the vicinity of Potter's cottage.

From the sound of the shouts behind him, it was obvious that the others had also registered the sight. He spurred his horse on furiously, raising his arm in order to thrash down his crop against Pagan's sweating rump when, somewhere inside his head, he could hear Harriet's voice: 'Horses shouldn't be whipped— shouldn't be whipped!'

'Come on, boy,' he urged, as his arm dropped. 'Give me everything you've got!'

Ears flattened and tail streaming, Pagan positively flew the final half-mile and at last the derelicts came in sight and every one of the horsemen could see that the end cottage was aflame! Timber and debris had been piled up against the cellar trap-door and it was a raging bonfire! In one swift movement Sandford had leapt from his mount and, with Tiptree at his side, he had rounded the cottage and was tearing at the flaming brands with his gloved hands.

'Harriet! Harriet!' he called out, ignoring the searing pain in his fingers. 'Can you hear me?'

'Lord Sandford, sir,' came an urgent voice from inside the ruined building. 'We can get in from here—lift the flagstones, lads.'

Coughing and spluttering as the acrid smoke rose from the cellar, willing hands hoisted the flagstones from the scullery corner as Sandford dropped the smouldering branch he was holding and dashed into the cottage. On to his knees he fell, clutching at the sides of the floor timbers, peering desperately into the gloom of the smoke-filled interior.

'Harriet!' His voice was hoarse. 'Are you there?'

A faint moan from below was the only reply. Without hesitation, Sandford swung himself down into the suffocating smog and, as he landed, he narrowly missed falling on a soft, curled-up bundle. It was Billy Tatler, wrapped in damp sacking! He was conscious and groaning, his breath coming in ragged gasps. In one swift movement Sandford had lifted the bundle and thrust the boy through the opening to the outstretched hands above him before crouching and feeling his way around the immediate vicinity. His eyes were streaming and he could scarcely breathe and the heat from the hatchway was growing intense. Through the smoke he could just make out the eager flames licking through the cracks in the old timber and realised that the trap-door would soon disintegrate and drop its burning embers into the cellar. Suddenly his fingers made contact with a wet, stockinged foot and, with his heart almost at bursting point, he threw himself down to examine the motionless form beneath him. She was still breathing! Quickly he raised her in his arms and called for assistance and many eager hands reached down to help lift Harriet's limp body out of his grasp. Gasping for air, he took hold of the joist to pull himself out of the choking atmosphere when, with a roaring explosion, the burning trap-door fell into the cellar and immediately set the straw alight. The force of the blast threw the viscount to the ground where, for several interminable moments, he lay completely stunned. It was only when the sound of Tiptree's voice screaming at him from above finally penetrated his fading senses that he managed to right himself sufficiently to enable the horrified groom to haul him from the inferno. Then, for the first time in his life, he swooned dead away.

Chapter Sixteen

Lord William was very troubled. The extraordinary events that had overtaken his household during the past few weeks were becoming quite beyond his comprehension and, following the recent and most terrifying episode, there appeared to be no one with whom he could discuss the situation for, apart from his son's groom, there was no man in whom he was prepared to put his trust. Even his loyal nephew Charles had refused to answer his summons, sending to say that he had more pressing matters to attend to at the moment and would come as soon as he could.

Tiptree was aware of his lordship's difficulty and, although flattered that he had been chosen to be the earl's confidante, his only concern at the moment was for his guvnor's recovery and he was barely interested in what he thought of as a 'local skirmish' for, in spite of having been a witness to Lady Butler's breakdown, he still had the feeling that Miss Harriet was really to blame for all of this turmoil and the sooner her grandfather arrived to remove her the better it would be for everyone.

The earl had been obliged to hold court in his bed-chamber, owing to his inability to manage the stairs without the assistance of two sturdy footmen but, since he had vehemently protested against that particular system of conveyance and scathingly pointed out the awkwardness and inconvenience it would cause all round, all conferences were henceforth held in his room.

Mrs Gibson despaired of keeping the carpets in any sort of order as a succession of muddied footwear beat a path to his door but, with two other invalids in the house, she supposed she must cope and, as her concern for his young lordship was greater than her concern for the carpets, she instructed the housemaids to do the best they could under the difficult circumstances and to be sure to be extra quiet outside the poor viscount's door.

Tiptree had helped to carry his master up to his room himself and had curtly told Kimble to 'clear off, if he knew what was good for him'. Since Kimble had always known what was good for himself and, moreover, had never been able to stand up to Tiptree, he reluctantly complied and betook himself off to the boot-room, where he spent much of his time in tearful but dedicated drudgery, polishing and re-polishing his lordship's Hessians and top-boots until the leather was like to wear away. Apart from Sandford's parents and the physician, whom he was powerless to prevent, Tiptree mulishly refused to allow anyone to enter the viscount's chambers.

'He never needed anyone but me for nigh on ten years,' he said stubbornly, when Sir Basil had suggested that it might be better to send to Market Harborough for a pair of nurses.

Lady Caroline was too wise to allow the two men to argue across her son's sickbed and had gently persuaded the physician that Sandford could not hope to get better care from anyone other than Tiptree. Everything that the groom required was, therefore, provided without question and, apart from insisting that they be given regular reports on the viscount's condition, the earl and countess forced themselves to remain as much as possible in the background.

A whole day and a night had elapsed since Sandford and Harriet had been carried back from Potter's cottage and his lordship was still in very poor shape. He had suffered a mild concussion in his fall and one of his hands had been badly burned, but it was the problems brought about by the smoke inhalation that were causing Sir Basil the gravest concern.

Harriet had managed to avoid breathing in great quantities of smoke, owing to her final inspiration of throwing her damp habit skirt over her head before crouching down beside Billy, and the wet sacking in which she had wrapped the boy had protected him from the excesses of both heat and smoke.

Sir Basil had bound up her head and, in spite of her protests, had insisted upon her remaining in bed until, with nourishing broths and custards, her strength should return. She desperately needed to go to Sandford, to talk to him, if possible, or even just to see him, but Rose had informed her of Tiptree's adamant refusal to allow the viscount any visitors. Harriet, her heart filled with despair, was constrained to wait for her share of the all-too-infrequent reports on his lordship's welfare.

Now, glumly supping some of the restorative chicken broth that Cook appeared to be making by the cauldron-load, she contemplated her sadly ravaged hands, which had suffered greatly from her exertions in the cellar. Cracked and broken fingernails, blisters, grazes and callouses—a very unlovely sight, she sighed, putting down her bowl and tucking the offending objects beneath the bedsheets, wondering whether Sir Basil would allow her to get up and take a bath.

Rose had sponged away most of the filthy grime before putting her mistress to bed, but Harriet was still conscious of the unpleasant stench of smoke and burning timber and felt an overwhelming need to wash her hair. She was busily speculating on the possibilities of this delightful prospect when Rose burst into the room.

'Oh, miss!' Her eyes were shining. 'They're here! Your grandfather has arrived! Her ladyship is taking them into the drawing-room this very minute!'

'Them?' Harriet was confused, but not for many moments as the door was suddenly thrust open and her own dear mama almost ran across the floor to her bedside.

'Dearest girl!' her mother cried, holding her tightly. 'I was so worried! Let me look at you! Oh, heavens! What have they done to you?'

Little by little, in between the tears and the exclamations of shock and horror, Harriet unfolded her tale and when it had been brought up to date she begged

Lady Middleton, for, sadly, this was now her mother's title, to account for her own presence at Beldale.

'For I was expecting only my grandfather,' she said, still gripping her mother's hands. 'I can hardly believe that you are really here!'

Her mother smiled in recollection of the momentous day when her father had descended upon Middleton Hall to extract his long-lost daughter from Sir Chester's clutches and she related her own story with undisguised relish.

'It was quite amazing—he burst in—literally! Swathed in his cloak and tartan kilt—Middleton was terrified! *I* recognised him immediately, of course, and he simply *ordered* me to get my cloak and bonnet and get into the carriage!'

Harriet stared at her mother, wide-eyed. 'He sounds very high-handed,' she said, thinking of such another.

'There was no other way to deal with the situation,' said Lady Middleton, laughing at the expression on her daughter's face. 'Father told Sir Chester what he thought of him, and—oh, Harriet, it's so wonderful— he says he can probably have the marriage annulled— because he's a Lord of Court or something—isn't it marvellous? We're to go back to Craigburn with Father as soon as you are well enough to travel!'

Harriet took a deep breath. 'I'm afraid I cannot do that, Mama,' she said, her voice firm.

Her mother stared at her in consternation. 'But of course you can, dearest,' she said. 'Her ladyship will not expect you to remain here now that we are come for you!'

'I cannot leave until I know that Rob—Lord Sandford is recovered,' said Harriet obstinately. 'He saved my life, Mama—you must see that I cannot go until I can thank him!'

Sarah Middleton stared closely at her daughter in frowning curiosity, then a sudden smile lit up her face. 'Yes, of course, dearest,' she said, almost absentmindedly. 'I do see that—and we must all thank his lordship!' She looked about Harriet's bedchamber and beckoned to the waiting Rose.

'I think Miss Cordell might have a bath, Rose—could you see to it, please?'

The smiling girl curtsied and went below to make the necessary domestic arrangements while Harriet's mother examined her daughter's wounds, exclaiming sadly at the loss of her pretty ringlets.

'Papa so loved your hair,' she said, her eyes suddenly glistening, and Harriet reached forward to clasp her hand.

'I know,' she said gently, 'but this is so much easier to deal with—in fact, you might like to try it yourself,' she added teasingly. 'Lord William says that I remind him of a marigold! Oh, Mama! You will love him—he has such a sense of humour and he is so wise!'

'The whole family has been very good to you, Harriet,' said her mother, beaming again. 'Lady Caroline did not stop singing your praises until I begged to come and see whether this paragon was indeed my own girl—for it seems that the entire local population has called to deliver flowers or to wish you well! How we will ever be able to thank them, I cannot imagine!'

With Rose and her mother both vying in their efforts to assist her, Harriet soon found herself bathed and dressed in her favourite primrose muslin. Sarah agreed that the now shining mop of curls did indeed suit her daughter and decided, after some deliberation, that the head-bandage was an unnecessary ornament, and elected instead to dress the wound with a light dusting of basilicum powder. Standing back to survey the finished effect, she heaved such a heavy sigh that Harriet was immediately filled with apprehension.

'What is it, Mama?' she said anxiously. 'You think that Grandfather will not approve of me?'

'Oh, I am sure he will, dearest.' Her mother tremulously smiled. 'I was merely wondering how long we would—but no matter—we must go down. Father will have been waiting with such impatience!'

As Harriet descended the stairs, gripping Sarah's hand tightly in her own, she was filled with very mixed emotions but she need not have worried, for as soon as she approached the door of the salon a huge giant of a man came bustling out and clasped her to his chest.

'Child, och—child,' was all he seemed able to utter, as he rocked her against him. Then he held her away and stared down at her with such affection in his eyes that she almost wept.

'Grandfather?' she whispered timidly.

'Och, you're a sight for an old fool's eyes—that's for sure,' he said, as he led her to a sofa and sat himself down beside her, gently holding her damaged hands in his own huge ones. 'You've the looks of your dear grandmother—same wicked eyes, I see!' And he let out a great bellow of laughter at her shocked look. 'Och, now—that's a good thing, believe me, lassy—your grandmother broke a few hearts with hers, I can tell you! But she chose me—and I'm gey thankful that she stayed long enough to produce the two of you!'

Harriet looked up at her mother in blushing consternation, but both Sarah and Lady Caroline were regarding Ramsey with such fond amusement that she at once relaxed and began to warm to the old gentleman.

'It was very good of you to come so quickly,' she began, but he brushed aside her attempts at gratitude and berated himself for having been such a stubborn old fool to waste so many precious years and promised that he intended to do his best to make up for his past obstinacy.

'For I can be a bit of a block-head, as your mama will confirm,' he confessed, twinkling his blue eyes at Sarah. 'I sometimes canna bear to admit that I'm wrong, you see—and I'm a great one for digging my toes in!'

'Oh, but I'm exactly the same!' exclaimed Harriet, in astonishment. 'I do try to curb my impetuosity, of course, but it usually gets the better of me,' she finished, somewhat shamefacedly recollecting the most recent disaster.

Lord Ramsey patted her hand. 'There, there,' he said comfortingly. 'Ye can hardly be blamed for what you've inherited from your grandsire—as long as you're not such a fool as to allow it to blight your life. And remember, lassy—obstinacy can be regarded as a great strength as well as a weakness. Ye just have to learn to judge when to use it—and I'm mebbe not the best teacher!'

They all laughed and Harriet leaned forward and kissed him on his cheek.

'I'm so very glad to have met you at last,' she said, with a catch in her throat, for she could hardly help thinking that if only her other hopes were realised it was possible that she would not be returning to Craigburn with him as he obviously expected.

With this thought now uppermost in her mind, she turned to the countess and inquired as to the latest reports from Lord Sandford's sickbed and learned that the viscount was improving, but that Tiptree had continued to deny admittance to visitors for, as he had said, 'Seeing as he can hardly breathe, my lady, there's not much use expecting him to hold a conversation.'

Harriet's mother, noting the shadow that had crossed her daughter's face at this news, tentatively put forward her own suggestion.

'I wonder if Sergeant Tiptree would allow me to assist him with his patient,' she said. 'He knows that I have had a good deal of experience with this condition—he may be willing to trust me.'

The countess was perfectly agreeable that Sarah should petition Tiptree and, leaving a fretting Harriet to relate her misadventures to her grandfather, the two ladies left the room.

'Dinna fash, lassy,' said Ramsey, soon noting her distracted air. 'Your laddie is in good hands—and he's no weakling, so I'm told.'

Harriet, blushing, shot him a look of startled gratitude. 'I feel that his injuries are my fault,' she confided
in him. 'If I had not been so hot-headed—if I had
waited for Davy...'

The old man shook his head and placed his finger
on her lips to silence her. 'Life is full of "ifs and
buts",' he said, 'and it does no good to dwell on
them—what's past is over—look to the future. Having
wasted years meself, I'll not be happy to see you do
the same. Now tell me the whole tale—for you must
acknowledge that these have been gey queer happen-
ings!'

He listened intently to her story from its wayside
beginning to its fiery conclusion and, apart from frowning and nodding and occasionally shaking his head, he
chose not to interrupt her flow of words. When she had
quite finished he closed his eyes for a moment or two
before he spoke.

'Ye've had a lucky escape, lassy,' he grunted. 'But
I don't doubt that ye have your father's courage in
ye—aye, I'm prepared to own he was a fine man—fer
all he stole my daughter!'

However, his bright blue eyes were teasing her as
he said this and, delighted at his words about her dear
papa, Harriet beamed back at him as he stood up and
held out his hand to help her to her feet.

'I think we might go and pay Beldale himself a
visit,' he said. 'I fancy I've a few questions that I'd
like to put to him. He'll be eager to take a good look
at you too, I shouldn't wonder.'

The earl was, of course, delighted to see that Harriet had suffered no great ill effects from her misadventure, and insisted that she sit on his footstool, close beside him, where he could stroke her head and hold her poor ravaged hands at one and the same time.

'For I am constantly reminding myself,' he told Ramsey, 'how near we all came to losing her and I swear I shall have nightmares for many weeks to come!'

Ramsey sat down on the chair in the embrasure next to them, his huge bulk almost blocking the light.

'Aye—ye'd have had some explaining to do,' he grinned. 'But put away your dismals, man—we have her here safe with us—and I hear that your boy is improving by the hour—so all's well that ends well, as they say!'

'If, indeed, it has ended,' said Lady Caroline, who was also present, having recently deposited Sarah with a surprised and grateful Tiptree. 'We are still no wiser as to the reasons behind this man's abduction and—attempted *murder*—for that is what it was, dear child!' She had seen Harriet's shocked expression. 'He is still at large—I, for one, shall never feel safe until he is captured!'

'I cannot believe that he would dare to show his face anywhere in the vicinity,' cried Harriet, trembling at the thought. 'Everyone in the village would surely lynch him after what he did to Billy!'

'I doubt it would be Billy they had in mind while they were stringing him up, lass!' Ramsey's eyes met

Lord William's in some amusement. 'I hear that some of them have a bit of a fondness for yourself!'

'Goodness me, yes,' said her ladyship. 'They have been coming to the doors—both back and front—in droves. The vicar, Squire Bevans, young Cedric Lambert—and most of *his* friends—not to mention old Potter's family and Lady Eugenie's ''ladies''—it will take you a month to go round and thank them all for their good wishes!'

Harriet beamed. 'I shall be pleased to do it,' she said. 'They will have been concerned for the little boy, you know—he was so afraid. It was a dreadful thing to do—to put such a small child in a dark nasty place like that—he must be a very evil man and Lady Caroline is right! How can we go on as normal when we do not know why he did these things? If he is a madman on the loose, then surely Judith and her children could be in very grave danger?'

Ramsey was scratching at his beard and nodding his head at his granddaughter's words.

'That's true,' he said. 'I've been pondering on this very thing and a thought occurs to me. This Lady Butler I keep hearing about—your daughter-in-law's mother—she wouldn't have been one Ernestine Carr, I suppose? Married Freddy Butler—you remember him, Beldale—very serious sort of fellow—got a knighthood for some Egyptian relics he dug up?'

'Yes, of course.' Lady Caroline clapped her hands. 'Fancy you knowing Sir Frederick—and Lady Butler too. We knew her name was Ernestine, of course, but we would never have dreamt of using it—she wasn't our most favourite person—I always felt so sorry for Judith.' She turned to Harriet. 'Her father persuaded us to let her study with the twins' tutor—her governesses were totally incapable of controlling her. Her mother spoilt her so dreadfully—it's amazing that she turned out so well, although her father was such a dear sweet man—how he can have married…!'

'Aye—I was coming to that,' interrupted Ramsey. 'I wondered if ye possibly didn't know the whole story— it was quite well hushed up, as I recall.'

'Well, don't keep us all in suspense, man,' said Beldale, leaning forward in eager anticipation. 'I knew she'd committed some unpardonable sin—or crime— out with it!'

Laughing, Lord Ramsey shook his head. 'Nay, Will,' he said. 'She was quite a wee peach, if my memory serves me right—just out of the schoolroom at the time and in her first Season. Anyway, her family managed to get her engaged to Jack Fellowes—Viscount Moffat, that was…'

'Moffat?' asked Lady Caroline wonderingly. 'But surely he…?'

'Aye—I see ye remember—he eloped with an opera-dancer and went off to the Americas—jilted the Carr lass at the altar.'

'I never heard that part of the story,' exclaimed her ladyship. 'How dreadful for her—but I collect that she was well into her twenties when she married Sir Frederick…'

'Well, no doubt she was holding out for a better offer—her mother was mighty keen for her to be a countess, as I recall!'

'Poor Lady Butler,' said Harriet, who had been listening to her grandfather's tale with her eyes full of sadness. 'No wonder she always acts in such a grand manner—it must have been an awful shock for her to have her sweetheart…!'

'Sweetheart!' Beldale hooted. 'I cannot imagine the Butler in love with anyone but herself!'

'Do not be so unkind, William,' chided Lady Caroline. 'We do know that the Butlers lost two babies before Judith was born—that was why *she* was so spoilt, of course,' she added, in explanation to Lord Ramsey. 'Apparently Lady Butler insisted upon travelling abroad with Sir Frederick when he was involved in those archaeological diggings—even when she was with child. As a result, she lost both of Judith's brothers at birth, which must have been quite unbearable for her!'

'Oh, poor lady!' Harriet was greatly moved by this tale. 'No wonder she is always saying that Life is unfair—to her it must seem dreadfully so! To lose two babies, her husband, then her son-in-law…!' She stopped in dismay, remembering that Philip had also been the Hursts' son. 'I'm terribly sorry, ma'am,' she said to Lady Caroline. 'How thoughtless of me!'

The countess gave her a gentle smile. 'But it is true, my dear,' she said. 'Philip was her son-in-law. I believe she grew quite fond of him—although Robert would have been her first choice, I suspect!'

Harriet nodded. 'Yes, Judith has said so—and I believe that Lady Butler still has aspirations in that respect—although Judith has confessed to me a certain fondness for Charles Ridgeway— Oh, dear! I should not be telling you this!' Her hand flew to her mouth in confusion.

Three pairs of eyes looked at her.

'Judith and Charles!' exclaimed Lady Caroline. 'But of course! That would be perfect!'

Harriet laughed at the countess's obvious delight, but then her face became more serious as she continued, 'I'm afraid that Charles does not think so, my lady. He is very concerned at his lack of fortune. He says he cannot offer for Judith. Perhaps *you* can persuade him otherwise?'

Beldale regarded her in some amusement. 'Still determined to right the world's wrongs, little one?' he said, patting her hand gently. 'I can see we shall have to keep a tight rein on you until Sandford recovers. As to Ridgeway's lack of fortune—it has always been my intention to leave him well provided for. He is my sister's son, after all, and has earned his share of the estate—although it is odd in him not to have answered my summons. He must know that I need to talk with him!'

'I hear he has his hands full,' Ramsey consoled him. 'He'll still be looking for the Beckett chappie—as well as trying to oversee all the estates—and I'm told that he took a bang on the head himself! Would ye care for me to ride over and see if he needs anything—I've four big lads of my own with me who have always proved very handy in an emergency!'

It was agreed that Ramsey should go to Westpark. Harriet did her best to persuade her hosts to allow her to accompany her grandfather, but Lady Caroline was adamant in her refusal.

'Until the man Beckett is safely under lock and key,' she said, 'we cannot think of letting you out of our sight and, in any event...' she cleverly played her trump card '—supposing Robert were to ask for you?'

'Oh, yes, of course!' Harriet nodded in instant agreement. 'He will surely be himself soon—Mama is the *best* nurse!'

'Tiptree might argue with that,' laughed the countess, 'but I'm sure that between the two of them they will soon have him on his feet again.'

Chapter Seventeen

Sandford was sure he must be dreaming. He could see Mrs Major at the foot of his bed. She was calmly rolling bandages and was in deep conversation with Sergeant Tiptree, who seemed to have given up wearing his uniform!

The viscount tried to struggle upright, but found that one of his arms was encased in strapping, added to which was the desperately uncomfortable sensation of burning inside his chest every time he tried to take a breath.

'Tip?' he groaned. 'What's happened—the men...?'

As the two heads turned towards him, his brain cleared in a sudden flash and he threshed his limbs in a frustrated effort to lift himself.

'Harriet! Oh, dear God!' he gasped, fighting to get some air into his lungs.

'Keep still, your lordship,' came Sarah's voice, and his eyes widened in alarm as he realised that it was indeed Mrs Major standing beside him. If Harriet's mother was here at Beldale, it could mean only one thing! Harriet had not survived the fire!

He sank back on to his pillows in weary defeat and screwed up his eyes, unable to prevent the unmanly tears from welling up. Locked inside his crushing misery he ignored the cool, damp cloths that were being applied to his face, but was eventually forced to respond when he felt Tiptree's strong arms reaching behind him to raise his shoulders from the pillows. He was startled to observe the wide smile on Sarah's lips.

'Another pillow, my lord,' she said. 'The more upright you are, the easier you will find it. In a little while we will get you into a chair by the open window where the air is fresh and clean. Will you take a sip of water?'

Sandford shook his head, his eyes on her face as she held the glass to his lips.

'Harriet?' he croaked, dreading her answer.

'Harriet is very well, my lord,' said Sarah, with a gentle smile at Sandford's hoarse gasp. 'We are all extremely grateful to you—you undoubtedly saved her life.'

As the waves of relief flooded through him, Sandford allowed himself to take a sip of the cooling draught. Thank God, oh, thank God! She was safe! He had not failed her. All would be well! Dismissing his pain, he tried to rise.

'Where is she?' he demanded. 'I must see her.'

'She is resting, my lord,' replied Sarah, soothingly. 'She, too, needs to recover from the dreadful experience.'

For a moment Sandford was silent. Then, 'The boy? Was he hurt much?'

'Right as rain, sir,' came Tiptree's assurance. 'Strutting round the village fit to burst, I hear!'

Exhausted, Sandford lay back, eyes closed, as he digested this piece of information until another thought flashed into his mind.

'Tip! The man—Beckett—you have him?' he shot out anxiously.

Tiptree shook his head. 'Gone to ground, sir,' he said glumly. 'Hinds—the stable-lad—he's been collared but he's refusing to talk—not too bright, you see, sir. Mr Ridgeway's holding him at Westpark, but what with his lordship out of action and yourself, sir...'

'Good God, man—let me up!' protested Sandford, as both Tiptree and Sarah held his shoulders back against the pillows. 'How long have I been here?'

'All day yesterday, sir—and coughing fit to die, if I might mention it,' replied Tiptree calmly. 'It's now Tuesday noon and Miss Cordell's mother and grandfather arrived not two hours since. You can't get up, sir, not until you can breathe proper—and you will no doubt be pleased to know that I stopped the quack from bleeding you—so if you could just keep still for a bit longer, you'll be as right as rain.'

The viscount ceased his struggles and glared truculently at his man.

'Well, get me over to the window—I can't stay here forever—and what's the damage to my hand?' He waved his left arm at them.

He learned that, although his riding gloves had taken most of the punishment from his ruthless handling of the burning timbers, the left one had finally disintegrated, leaving him with suppurating blisters on the palm of his hand.

'You need have no fear, my lord,' said Sarah comfortingly. 'You will not lose the use of your hand, for we have applied goose-fat and its healing powers are well known in such cases.'

'But I need to see Harriet now!' rasped their patient petulantly. 'Why can't I see her?'

Tiptree shook his head. 'Question is, sir—if I might be so bold—whether you would want Miss Cordell to see you, sir—seeing as how you're not exactly in your best looks…!'

Sandford cast him a baleful look. 'What the devil do you mean by that, damn you?'

'Oh, a bit of a singe here and there, guv,' returned Tiptree cheerfully. 'Nothing that Kimble won't be able to deal with—soon as it grows back, of course!'

Groaning, Sandford threw himself back against the pillows. 'I have to speak to my father,' he said weakly. 'There are things to be done—the man is still out there!'

'And Harriet is quite safe here, my lord,' said Sarah soothingly. 'Just take a sip of this, it will help your throat.'

'No drugs,' he slurred, as his eyes closed. 'No drugs, Tip…' and he was asleep, once more.

'He has an aversion to opiates and such, ma'am,' said the groom, straightening the sheet which covered his master's form. 'And he won't be cupped, neither— regular pig-head, sometimes.'

'Well, he's a strong, healthy young man—he shouldn't need any of those things,' replied Sarah, putting down the glass of lemonade that the viscount had refused. 'Perhaps when he wakes up again we could get him into a chair by the window—I wonder if the earl has one of those wicker chairs they use on the Bath promenade—the ones with wheels?'

'Not that I know of, ma'am—but I'm sure they'd soon get one if we asked—Lord William could have done with one of them himself these last few weeks.'

They settled themselves comfortably beside a table at the window, Sarah engaged in some sewing she had brought with her and Tiptree immersed in the latest broadsheet from London. She applied herself to her stitchery for some minutes, then looked up and said to him, 'Harriet seems to think that you hold her responsible for Lord Sandford's injuries.'

Tiptree flushed, and looked uncomfortable. 'I'm sure I've never said so, ma'am,' he replied, frowning.

'But you do think so?' Sarah persisted.

'Well, I will say that his lordship has been behaving very strangely these last couple of weeks—forever losing his temper and drinking—quite out of character, ma'am—and the hours he's spent looking for these chaps...!'

The groom stopped, remembering Sandford's warning that Lady Butler's disclosures were not to be repeated.

Sarah regarded him silently for a few minutes. 'These two—Beckett and Hinds, isn't it?' At his sudden start, she smiled. 'Lady Caroline has only repeated what I suspect everyone in the village knows by now, sergeant, and you cannot prevent servants gossiping. The story is that his lordship and yourself found two of Mrs Hurst's elderly menservants attacked and left for dead, as a result of which Lady Butler suffered some sort of seizure and was taken to the Dower House and placed under Lady Eugenie's care. Mr Ridgeway, it appears, has apprehended the—minor—culprit, who he has under lock and key—am I correct, so far?' She studied his reaction keenly.

'No keeping secrets from house staff, it seems,' replied Tiptree, shrugging his shoulders and picking up his newspaper again. Behind its sheets he was privately congratulating Ridgeway on his quick thinking—the story was quite credible!

'The stable-boy—Hinds—is, apparently, a little—how shall I put it...?'

'Feeble-minded,' finished Tiptree shortly. 'Wouldn't say "boo" to a goose, so they say. Can't get anything out of him, apart from "Matt'll sort it out"!'

'Matt?'

'Matt Beckett, ma'am—seems he's the real villain of the piece—the one who fired the cellar!'

Sarah shuddered. 'How close she came to death!'

Tiptree cleared his throat. 'They all three did, ma'am,' he reminded her, then, after a pause, 'We once had this old colour-sergeant who used to believe that everyone is born with an allotted time-span—quite a comforting thought for a soldier, I used to think—nobody goes before his time is up, whatever happens!'

'Barring accidents, surely?'

'No such thing as an accident, he used to say—all part of a great big masterplan—everything connected to something else—all pre-determined!'

'So we all have a part to play in everyone else's destiny—and they in ours?'

'Ah, well,' grinned Tiptree sheepishly. 'I admit it gets a bit deep.'

'No, I'm fascinated—did you agree with him?'

The groom shuffled uncomfortably under her thoughtful gaze. 'Well—I dare say it sounds a bit high-flown for a soldier, ma'am, but I suppose I've been inclined to go along with it. I'm still here, at any rate—though what my destiny might be is anyone's guess!'

'Would your sergeant have said that someone who saves a person's life is helping them to fulfil their destiny, I wonder?' Sarah mused, as she poured herself a glass of lemonade.

'Doubtless, he would, ma'am,' said Tiptree, girding his own thoughts as he looked towards the now peacefully sleeping viscount.

Sarah studied his pensive face. 'Do you recall, I wonder,' she said gently, 'our retreat to Corunna?'

Tiptree frowned at her. 'I'm hardly likely to forget it, ma'am,' he said, in some surprise. 'Pretty much the worst days of my life, I'd say.'

'Yes, it was a terrifying time,' agreed Sarah. 'You may recall helping to get the baggage wagons across the River Duoro in full flood?'

'Aye—I do that. We lost most of it, if my memory serves me right—and a host of good men in addition. Freezing cold water right up to the saddles...' He shuddered in sudden recollection of that awful night. 'Eight years ago that was—December '08—right?'

Sarah nodded. 'One of the wagons was carrying children,' she reminded him. 'You were riding alongside.'

He stared at her, taken aback. 'Funny you should think of that, ma'am,' he said. 'I hadn't realised you were with that train!'

'Do you remember what happened, sergeant?' she asked softly.

He lowered his eyes. 'I don't like to think of it, ma'am,' he said. 'Them poor little ones...!'

'You and Lieutenant Sanders saved almost all of them—and, if you really believe in your colour-sergeant's Destiny theory, you have no reason to reproach yourself—you were not responsible for the dreadful torrent that swept the two youngsters away.'

He pondered gravely over this, and then his face brightened. 'Do you remember that little lass—the one who jumped in after the baby's basket? She was a plucky bit and no mistake!'

Sarah's lips curved. 'You pulled them both out—half-drowned, they were, the pair of them! Were you fulfilling your own destiny, sergeant, or helping them fulfil theirs, I wonder?'

'Bit of both, wouldn't you say?' Tiptree grinned at her. 'I wonder what became of them?'

'Oh, the baby was Lord Chadwell's son—I believe he's at Eton, now.'

'Fancy that—and that girl must be a young woman by now—nineteen or twenty, perhaps? Probably married, with babies of her own!'

'Twenty years old last May, sergeant,' she said, her eyes twinkling, 'and no—not yet married.'

For a moment he stared at her in shocked disbelief. 'Miss Harriet?' he stammered. '*That* was Miss Harriet?'

Sarah nodded. 'Her father used to say that he hoped she had a cat's nine lives to go with the eyes—and, since you have now been closely involved in saving at least *three* of those lives, sergeant—what do you think Harriet's destiny might be?'

Tiptree swallowed and his glance travelled once more to the figure on the bed. 'I'd say that it's becoming clearer by the moment, ma'am,' he replied gruffly.

Chapter Eighteen

Patience was not Harriet's forte. She had resigned herself to remaining quietly in the library while her grandfather paid his visit to Westpark and her mother attended Sandford. Disconsolately picking up one book after another, she found it impossible to give her full attention even to her most favourite authors and the onerous ticking of the wall-clock merely served to emphasise how slowly the minutes dragged by.

She had paid a lengthy visit to the kitchens to offer her grateful thanks to the smiling staff and both young Rothman and Cooper had insisted upon accompanying her to the stables where her tributes were gently brushed aside by the grinning Smithers and his men, who were all delighted to see her 'up and about' again.

'Don't you worry about him, miss,' said the head groom, in answer to Harriet's questions about Beckett. 'He'll not dare show his face round here again. My guess is he's left the country—probably signed up on one of His Majesty's ships and gone to one of them there voodoo lands—suit him just about right, we're all thinking!'

'Leaving young Hinds to shoulder all the blame,' Harriet pointed out, as she stroked the now recovered Clipper's nose. 'I do pity him—he must be so confused, poor boy!'

Smithers regarded her in astonishment. 'But there's no doubt he was involved, miss,' he said, in some consternation. 'He was with Beckett when Mr Ridgeway was attacked—we all know that!'

'Yes, I know, Mr Smithers,' replied Harriet awkwardly. 'It's just that—well, you know everyone agrees that he isn't very bright—perhaps he didn't appreciate what Beckett was doing?'

'Aye, well, you may be right,' said the man, shaking his head. 'I doubt we'll ever know what was behind it all, what with Beckett sloping off and Hinds playing mummer. We're all sorry that you got caught up in their shenanigans, miss, and that's a fact. Please God their lordships will soon be back on their feet taking charge again and we can all get back to normal.'

'Amen to that, Mr Smithers,' replied Harriet fervently, as she turned to leave.

Now, sitting in the heavy silence of the library, flicking idly through the pages of *Chesterfield's Letters*, she wondered how long it would be before her mother could persuade Tiptree to allow her to visit the viscount. Sarah had left her patient briefly to join Lady Caroline and herself for a hurried repast and had assured them both that Sandford had not been badly damaged and that as soon as she and Tiptree had seated him by the open window of his room his breathing had rapidly improved. He had taken some nourishment and was, apparently, impatient to 'get back in the saddle', as Tiptree had put it, and, whilst Harriet was overjoyed to hear this news, she was somewhat disconcerted that his lordship had not asked for her.

She was beginning to fear that the outcome of her latest escapade must have given the viscount such a violent dislike of her that he could not bring himself to face her and this lowering thought was unendurable. During her incarceration in the cellar she had suddenly realised, with a terrible clarity, that Robert Hurst was, indeed, the only man she could ever love. Now she was miserably certain that any passion he may once have felt for her must have been utterly quashed by his recent horrifying experience caused, he would surely have realised, by her wilful disregard of his instructions. It was no wonder he was refusing to see her!

She had been reluctant to voice any of these fears to her mother because it would have involved revealing certain unflattering particulars about her own conduct, which she had been careful to omit from her earlier narration. She shuddered as she once again recalled the foolish and defiant words she had thrown at Sandford and, with equal distaste, shrank from the memory of her cold-blooded resolution to accept his expected offer of marriage. How could she have considered herself suitable for such a position? she wondered, now amazed at her own arrogant presumption.

A tap on the door disturbed her melancholy reverie and she looked up to see March ushering Judith Hurst into the room. Harriet sprang to her feet in delight.

'Oh, how glad I am to see you!' she exclaimed, holding out her hands with pleasure. 'How is Lady Butler? And Charles? He has recovered?'

'Sit down, silly girl,' responded Judith, with a little smile at her friend's exuberance. 'You are supposed to be resting—I promised not to get you excited!'

'Oh, pooh to that, Judith—I am bored to distraction and in such a fit of the dismals! But, what are you doing here? No one can see Sandford—Tiptree's orders!'

'I came to see you!' said Judith. 'Your grandfather said that you were up and dressed, so I came as soon as I could. What a charmer he is, to be sure—he is still deep in conference with Charles at the Dower House.'

'But Lady Butler? What happened?'

Judith's face at once became serious. 'Mama has had a stroke,' she said quietly. 'Two of our menservants were overpowered—I don't know how much you already know?'

The young widow was still badly shaken by the events that had occurred and had readily agreed with both Sandford and Ridgeway that the shocking revelations were not for public broadcast. Her mother's involvement in the conspiracy had horrified her, especially when she understood the futile reasoning that lay behind the scheme, namely that Harriet's being sent packing would be bound to bring about a match between her brother-in-law and herself.

Following Sandford's return to Beldale on that fateful night, Judith had railed long and hard at her mother and, after informing the hysterical Lady Butler that she had every intention of accepting Charles's hand, should he still care to offer for her, she had stormed off to the kitchens to assist Ridgeway with the two elderly servants, neither of whom could recall a great deal of what had befallen them. After rousing other members of staff, she and Charles had managed to get the stupefied pair to their bedchambers where Charles had ordered a watch to be kept on them at all times. Both he and Judith doubted that either of the old men were capable of giving any trouble, but feared that their accomplice might try to contact them for some reason.

On returning to the hall where she had left her mother, Judith had found the said lady surrounded by a bevy of maids and footmen, in the throes of some sort of apoplectic fit. Charles, at once taking charge, had sent for Sir Basil and also for his mother who, being the first to arrive, had recommended that Lady Butler should be removed to the Dower House immediately, where she herself would be pleased to look after the poor woman.

'For 'tis clear that she has had a paralytic seizure,' asserted Lady Eugenie, taking one look at Lady Butler's twisted countenance. 'You will never get her up to her room—she must be brought to the Dower House—a flat conveyance is all it requires. Don't worry, Judith, I shall take care of your mama—these dreadful events must have been too much for her!'

At Charles's warning glance, Judith kept her counsel and Lady Butler had been carefully conveyed to the Dower House, where she presently lay, paralysed down one side and able only to offer a savage gurgle in response to Lady Eugenie's kindly inquiries as to her feelings and requirements.

Judith had, naturally, suffered agonies of guilt over her mother's condition, believing her own outburst to be the cause of the seizure and she was only partly mollified by Charles's gentle suggestion that Lady Butler had already worked herself up into a fever pitch well before her daughter's intervention. As the news of Harriet's imprisonment and rescue gradually found its way to Westpark, Judith's feelings of guilt and sympathy for her mother dwindled to those of shame and remorse.

'How can I face them all?' she wept, upon hearing of the unfortunate trio's brush with death. 'My own mother! It is too awful to contemplate!'

Ridgeway's arms were around her in an instant. 'No one is to be told. Sandford was quite specific,' he reminded her. 'This is a family affair, Judith. Let's keep it that way.'

But now, face to face with Harriet, and having been furnished with the truth behind the girl's presence at Beldale, Judith was undecided as to how much of the story Sandford would wish her to know and, indeed, how much she already knew. She was aware that Lord Ramsey, a highly discerning landlord, had not been fooled for a moment by Ridgeway's ingenious tale about Lady Butler's seizure having been brought on by her shock at hearing of her servants' complicity in Harriet's disappearance.

'Try again, my lad,' he had said, frowning at Ridgeway. 'There's more in this than you're letting out.

Don't take me for a fool—that old woman is somewhere at the bottom of this—I can feel it in my blood!'
And, eventually, he had drawn the whole history from
the reluctant Charles.

Judith realised that it was going to be equally impossible to spin Harriet a Banbury tale. She steeled
herself to the prospect of the once-respected Butler
name being dragged through the mud for some time to
come and to the knowledge that dear Philip's children
would have to bear most of the ignominy. Nevertheless, she bravely set about providing her young companion with a brief explanation as to her continual mis-
fortunes during the past few weeks.

Harriet heard her out in silence, her green eyes, dark
and unfathomable, fixed intently on Judith's face
throughout the exposé. Judith's voice trembled as she
reached the conclusion of her confession and her own
soft brown eyes were filled with tears.

'Apologies are not enough, Harriet,' she choked. 'I
do not know what to say to you!' She delved into her
reticule for her handkerchief and turned her head away
from Harriet's impassive face.

'And you say that Sandford instructed you to hush
the matter up?' Harriet's voice was cool.

Judith nodded, dismayed but hardly surprised at the
girl's offhand manner.

'He told us—Charles and myself—not to speak of
it. Tiptree was present, of course and, apart from your
grandfather, you are the only other person who knows.
Even Aunt Eugenie believes that my mother's seizure
was brought on by—other things.'

'Their lordships would not care for a family scandal,' said Harriet, standing up and carefully straightening her skirts. 'Please do not worry yourself on my account, Judith. You must know that I will not breathe a word about Lady Butler's involvement if that is what Sandford wishes.'

Judith also rose to her feet and, laying her hand on Harriet's arm, she said pleadingly, 'Are we not to be friends any longer? I know how angry you must be and I do so beg your forgiveness! Harriet, please speak to me!'

'I'm very sorry, Judith,' returned Harriet evenly. 'I realise what it must have cost you to come here and tell me this and—I do admire you beyond measure for your courage in doing so—but, as you are probably aware, I shall be travelling to Scotland with my mother and grandfather shortly, so it is unlikely that our paths will ever cross again. Now, if you will excuse me...'

Turning her back on her visitor, she walked quickly through the open doorway on to the rear terrace, leaving the stunned and white-faced Judith to see herself out.

Shaking with anguish, Harriet hastened along the terrace, running almost blindly down the steps that led into the gardens, where she came to a sudden halt, uncertain as to her next move. With weary resignation she leaned against the stone balustrade and stared bleakly across the rolling lawns towards the lake, from where the sparkling reflections of the late afternoon sunshine glinted through the trees.

Of course he would wish to keep such information to himself! His family name and reputation, she knew, were everything to him. Was that why he had striven so desperately to save Billy and herself from the burning cellar? For of course, murder would have been impossible to withhold from the guardians of the law! But to allow everyone to believe that the villain was still at large when all the time he knew that she was safely imprisoned in her bed! And to think that she should have been so foolish as to believe that he had raced to her rescue for quite other reasons! Tears started into her eyes and she brushed them away angrily. No! She would not weep over him! The sooner she put him out of her thoughts the better, she decided, straightening her shoulders resolutely. She determined that she would return to Craigburn with her mother and grandfather as soon as they were ready to undertake the journey; in the meantime, perhaps she could persuade them to stay somewhere other than Beldale.

Drearily retracing her steps, she found herself unable to resist the temptation of casting a swift glance up towards Sandford's window, but she recoiled in shocked dismay as she saw that the viscount had observed her, for he was rising to his feet and appeared to be shaking his fists at her! Her face flaming with mortification, she quickened her pace along the terrace towards the library doors, frantic to remove herself from his wrathful gaze.

With a pounding heart she careered through the doorway, only to find herself immediately pinioned in the very strong clutches of a young man who was determinedly propelling her into the room. He must have gained entry from the shrubbery below the parapet whilst she had been standing out there! Her furious struggles proved futile and his hand over her mouth prevented her from crying out. He kicked the terrace doors closed behind him before thrusting her down on to a nearby sofa.

'Please don't make a sound, miss,' he warned her softly, as he sprang towards the hall door and turned the key in the lock. 'I have nothing to lose, it seems.'

'What do you want with me?' cried Harriet, shakily realising that her assailant must be the elusive Beckett. 'I have done nothing to harm you!'

As if undecided for a moment, he walked slowly towards her and stared down at her frightened face.

'I haven't come to hurt you,' he said heavily. 'I just wanted you to know.'

'I don't understand!' Harriet tried to rise, but he held her back against the cushions with one hand while his other delved into his coat pocket and brought forth a ragged sheet of paper.

'I have to make you understand…'

'I rather think not!' came Sandford's haughty drawl from the terrace. 'Move away from the lady, if you please! I have a pistol levelled at your head!'

Beckett spun round in fright, the paper fluttering from his hand and, as he sidled nervously away from her, Harriet was able to perceive the astonishing sight of the viscount lounging, apparently nonchalantly, against the door-frame, his good hand holding a pistol which was pointing steadily at the intruder.

'But how on earth...!' she exclaimed, as she leapt to her feet and rushed towards him.

'Down the ivy,' Sandford responded dismissively, not taking his eyes from the cowering Beckett.

'Down the ivy!' Eyes wide with shock, Harriet rapidly took in the viscount's appearance. His unbuttoned shirt was hanging loosely outside his breeches and he was in his stockinged feet! Patches of his soft brown hair had been trimmed close to his head, his face was ashen and through the unshaven stubble she could see beads of perspiration forming on his upper lip.

'Done it dozens of times,' he croaked, pressing his shoulders against the door-frame to support himself. 'Now, be a good girl and tie the fellow's hands—use a curtain cord—and don't put yourself between us!'

Harriet complied, with all the speed she could muster, having realised that Sandford was about to collapse at any moment. In a very few minutes she had whipped one of the curtain tie-backs from its hook and bound Beckett's hands behind him, motioning him to a chair, to the back of which she then secured the cord. He offered no resistance and seemed to be accepting his fate with calm indifference.

'Looks like he could do with a drink,' he said, nodding towards Sandford, as Harriet stood away from her endeavours. 'Better give him some brandy before he passes out!'

Harriet shot a startled glance at the viscount and saw that he was, indeed, having great difficulty maintaining his stance. She pulled a chair towards him and, after carefully helping him to lower himself into it, she hurried to the table to pour a generous measure of brandy from one of the decanters, returning swiftly to his side, where she knelt and gently held the glass to his trembling lips.

'I tried to warn you,' he gasped, after sipping some of the contents. 'Why did you ignore my signal?'

Harriet flushed. 'I thought you were shaking your fist at me!' she said, in a small voice, avoiding his eyes.

'Shaking my—what are you talking about, for God's sake?' His strength was returning and he dropped the firearm to the floor in order to grasp her hand in his good one.

'Take care! It could go off!' she admonished him, retrieving the pistol at once and, carefully pointing it away from him, attempted to defuse it. She raised her eyes to his in shocked astonishment. 'But it isn't loaded!' she exclaimed. 'You climbed down the ivy in *your* condition with an empty pistol! Are you mad?'

'Probably,' he nodded, with a weak grin. 'I couldn't manage to load it with only one hand—and I could hardly come unarmed, now could I? Why did you think I was shaking my fist at you—and why have you been refusing to come and see me?'

She stared at him pensively for a moment before sudden enlightenment dawned. 'Ask Tiptree,' she said sternly, getting to her feet. 'I thought that *you* didn't want to see *me*! He said you were too ill—thanks to this blackguard here!' She spun round to face their prisoner, having almost forgotten him in her concern for the viscount.

'Why are you still persecuting me?' she demanded of him. 'How could you let yourself be persuaded to do such awful things? What had you to gain from these devilish tricks?'

Beckett raised his head wearily. 'Nothing to gain, miss,' he said evenly. 'Plenty to lose, maybe—and not that it makes a hap'orth of difference—it wasn't me who fired the cellar.'

'Quite right,' interrupted Sandford, finishing his brandy. 'It makes not the slightest difference—you're in it up to your neck—which will end up in a noose, if I have anything to do with it!'

Beckett regarded his captor impassively. 'I realised *that* as soon as Jack told me he'd knocked Miss Cordell into the cellar,' he said wryly. 'I hadn't reckoned on him being that foolish!'

'Save your story for the magistrates,' said Sandford curtly, getting to his feet and heading towards the locked door, but Harriet forestalled him and, clutching at his sleeve, she shook her head and said, in some urgency, 'No, wait—*I* want to hear his story—it does concern me, after all—please, *Robert*!'

Sandford paused, his lips twitching. 'Minx!' he said, as he sat himself down in a more comfortable armchair. 'Very well—ask away, if you must. But be prepared to have the entire household trying to break the door down any minute—as soon as Tiptree gets back from his dinner and finds me gone!'

Harriet pulled up a stool in front of Beckett and sat down to face him. 'I know why Lady Butler wanted me out of the way,' she said, ignoring Sandford's start of surprise. 'But you made no attempt on my life on either of the first occasions—you simply set out to make me look foolish and ill bred—why did you alter your—designs?'

Beckett stared back at her, biting his lip as she carefully studied his expression. Suddenly her eyes softened and she briskly commanded him to tell her the whole.

'From the beginning and with no lies, if you please!'

His mouth twisted momentarily. Then, 'The old missus—Lady Butler—threatened to put us all off if we didn't come up with something, miss,' he said, in a matter-of-fact tone. 'I could probably have got work somewhere, but who would have taken Uncle Eddie or old Pinter on—not to mention a simpleton like Hinds? In the first place, she said that if Lord William was to have a ''little accident'' his lordship here—' he nodded towards Sandford '—would be sure to come back from London and keep up his visits to Westpark and that would be that. So I gave Jack—Hinds, that is—something to slip to the earl's horse when he left him in the stables, only his lordship fell awkwardly and he was out on the path in the rain for such a long time before they found him—I never intended him to be hurt so bad, sir,' he blurted out, flinching at the murderous look on Sandford's face.

Harriet turned her head and frowned a reprimand at the viscount before resuming her questioning. 'So Lord Sandford returned home—but with an unexpected complication in tow,' she said encouragingly. 'What then? Lady Butler told you to push me into the lake?'

Beckett shook his head. 'No, miss—that was my idea—spur of the moment, really. *She* told us—Uncle Eddie, Hinds and me—that it would be easy to find ways of making you look ridiculous—and it wasn't. Jack tried loosening your saddle girth after your first visit to Westpark but—like he said—it turned out that you're too good a horsewoman not to check your own straps before you mount, so that didn't work.'

'Cut out the compliments,' said Sandford frostily. 'Get on with it.'

Beckett shrugged and continued. 'Well, I thought if I gave the Tatler lad a shilling he'd be sure to keep quiet, but he ran off without it so I knew I'd have to find him before he put the finger on me—but he's a wily little monkey and he just kept out of the way. Her ladyship was getting really het up because by then everybody was full of admiration for the young lady and—it was actually old Pinter's idea—we all rigged up the pantomime in the copse. I gave Pinter the herb to put into the icing on some of the biscuits and her ladyship organised the breakfast. By the time you got to the bridleway the dope had taken effect—the rest was easy.'

He stopped, eyeing Harriet speculatively. 'Could you loosen this cord a bit, miss? My hands and arms are going numb.'

'Serves you right if they drop off,' grated Sandford savagely, recalling the wood episode with distaste, but Harriet was already on her knees busily untying her knots.

She studied Beckett uncertainly as he sat chafing his hands. 'You won't attempt to escape?'

'Where would I go, miss?' he replied in a tired undertone, wincing as the blood returned to his fingers. 'I know when I'm beaten!'

Harriet waited for a few moments before asking him, 'What did you intend to do to Billy when you found him?'

The young man shifted uncomfortably on his chair. 'There's lots of ways of frightening an eight-year-old boy, miss—*I* should know—I've been there.' His lips trembled momentarily, then he looked her full in the face. 'It was when I found out who you were, miss,' he said, with a tremor in his voice. 'I sort of lost control for a bit and Jack—well, he's not too bright, see—he thought he was doing me a favour—'

'How do you mean?' interrupted Harriet. 'You found out who I am?'

'Your father, miss,' came the astonishing reply. 'He had my dad shot and—I wanted you to suffer like my mum had!'

'Had your dad shot!' cried Harriet indignantly. 'What nonsense! When was this, pray?'

'It was in Ireland—my dad was a trooper in your father's company—they were garrisoned in Dublin— 1798, it was—I was six years old.'

'I *was* there,' said Harriet wonderingly. 'I don't remember—I was only a baby—about two, I should think.' She collected herself. 'My father was only a captain then—how could he have had your father shot?' she demanded fiercely.

'My mum got the letter from him.' He indicated the crumpled sheet of paper on the floor beside the sofa. 'I wanted you to read it. It says that my dad was shot for—desertion in the face of duty, it says, and there'd be no more pay for her. I'll never forget how she cried and then we were put out of our lodgings—we were destitute until Uncle Eddie got her some skivvying in the kitchens where he worked. Eighteen years I've carried that letter—and I swore I'd get even one day—now it turns out I'm just a coward—like my dad.'

His chin drooped on to his chest and Harriet, after retrieving the faded missive, looked at Sandford in confusion.

'Vinegar Hill, I should imagine—before my time,' he explained, with a frown. 'A local rabble attacked the garrison—only a bit of a skirmish, if I recollect my history. It isn't likely that your father could have had the man shot, though—needs to be a general or a colonel at the very least to issue that sort of order.'

Harriet nodded vigorously. 'That's what I thought— and Papa would only have written a personal letter to a next of kin if he had liked and admired the man!'

She unfolded the paper and stared down at the faded remnants of her beloved papa's well-remembered handwriting before turning once more to Beckett. 'My father probably didn't even believe in your father's guilt,' she cried accusingly. 'He must have written to your mother out of sympathy—and you have held a wicked grudge against him for all these years! I doubt that your father was a coward,' she said, and then added unkindly, 'He certainly wouldn't be very proud of his son!'

The man stiffened and his face turned scarlet, then he shrugged again. 'Likely you're right, miss,' he said, without expression. 'What are you going to do with me?'

'You still haven't told us why Hinds fired the cellar,' Sandford reminded him curtly. 'Or how Mr Ridgeway came by his injuries. You might as well finish the story.'

'Jack got into one of his panics when the whole village turned out,' said Beckett. 'After I'd told Miss Cordell that Mr Ridgeway had gone up the North Lane I sent Jack up the shortcut—he took one of the horses that were being saddled up. I cut across the hayfield on foot, but by the time I got there he had already pushed Miss Cordell into the cellar and boarded up the trap-door again. I didn't know then that he'd actually hit you, miss, I swear!'

His voice shook again at this point then, swallowing, he continued, 'Jack went over to the stables at Westpark to change the saddles while I went to find out what her ladyship wanted us to do—she washed her hands of the whole thing, of course,' he added bitterly. 'By that time all our men were over at Beldale, so we both rode back.'

'You rode Clipper back here!' Harriet was astounded. 'Weren't you afraid someone would recognise her?'

'The whole place was swarming with horses by then,' Beckett pointed out, 'and it had started to rain quite heavily, too. When Mr Ridgeway said he was going to search the boathouse I made sure everyone knew we went with him so that it would seem as if we'd been there all morning.'

'But why on earth did you attack Mr Ridgeway?' demanded Sandford. 'If he was your alibi...'

'Jack and him had rowed over to check out the island and the guv'nor remembered that no one had been up to search the cottages. Trouble was, Jack lost his head and hit him with one of the oars—then he locked him in the pavilion. I was waiting by the boathouse and when he came back and told me what he'd done I knew there was nothing for it but to clear out. We told one of the gamekeepers that Mr Ridgeway had gone up to Staines and then we cut across to Bottom Meadow and took turns in putting off any other search parties that turned up.'

Only the ticking of the wall clock disturbed the silence that followed this confession until Sandford cleared his throat and asked, 'This Hinds—I heard that he was a harmless sort of fellow?'

Beckett nodded. 'He is, sir—mostly. He gets a bit beside himself sometimes, when the youngsters torment him—hide his things and call him names and suchlike but, until now, I've never known him get violent—that's my fault, too,' he added swiftly, 'because I told him I was going to get even with Miss Cordell—only I didn't mean to kill her!'

'What did you...?' Harriet and Sandford spoke as one and Beckett shifted uneasily.

'I was waiting until the coast was clear—I was going to drug the two of them—you and Billy, miss—and take you to the city on a cart and leave you there!'

Harriet gazed at the man in a stunned rage. 'But why?' she wanted to know. 'What would have been the point of that? We would have woken up and explained and we'd have simply been brought back to Beldale!'

Sandford cleared his throat. 'Probably not, my dear,' he said, glowering at Beckett. 'I imagine you were thinking of leaving them in—how shall I put it—a certain area where Miss Cordell's protestations would be of less interest than her charms?'

Beckett nodded, keeping his eyes from Harriet's rosy blush. 'I wanted her to know the sort of life we'd been forced to lead—what it's like to starve and freeze in a filthy slum—and suffer as my mother suffered just to put bread in my mouth!' He put a hand to his lips to control the trembling and, in spite of her anger, Harriet felt a sudden surge of pity for the young man.

'I have had a little experience of the conditions you describe,' she told him gently. 'Not in the same way or for the same reasons, but enough to understand what you must have suffered. How old were you when you first came to Staines?'

'Eleven, miss. Uncle Eddie got the footman's job and mum was taken on as a kitchenmaid at first, then she became cook and I was given work in the gardens. I used to gather herbs for her to use and when Sir Frederick found out I was interested in such things he gave me some books and pamphlets from his collection. He taught me to read and write...' His voice tailed off and he sat slumped on his stool, his hands clenched between his knees.

Sandford stood up. 'None of this makes any difference, you know,' he told Harriet. 'The fellow's a criminal and he must be punished—along with all of his accomplices!'

'But I thought that you wanted to hush it all up!' exclaimed Harriet, in some surprise. 'Judith and Charles have been inventing all sorts of stories to keep Lady Butler's name out of it!'

'Damn!' Sandford sat down hurriedly. 'I'd forgotten about that! But that was before the fire—it's all too serious now, Harriet. Attempted murder and all that—you surely cannot mean them to get off scot-free?'

'Lady Butler has already paid dearly for her part, it seems,' Harriet reminded him. 'Hinds, if I understand correctly, cannot be held responsible for his actions—Lady Eugenie will know of a place where he can be safely housed and looked after, I'm certain—which leaves the two old servants.' She turned to confront Beckett, who had been listening impassively to her words.

'How did they—Pinter and your uncle Finchley—come to be bound and drugged on Sunday evening? Was that your doing?'

'I didn't want Uncle Eddie to be involved,' admitted the young man nervously. 'It was partly Pinter's idea. As soon as we realised that it was pretty well all over for us, he got me to drug the ale and tie them both up—as if they'd been attacked, he said, but I didn't hit them so I'm not to blame for the bruises they suffered.'

Sandford reddened and he leaned forward in surprise. 'How did you hear of their bruises?' he demanded truculently. 'Do you have another accomplice?'

Beckett shook his head. 'I was hiding in the oak settle,' he said, to the viscount's astonishment. 'When I heard you coming, there was nowhere else to go—I had to stay there until you left—and, when Mrs Hurst left her ladyship in the hall by herself, I knocked on the lid for her to let me out, but she started screaming fit to wake the dead and keeled off the settle in some sort of fit. All the servants came rushing in so I stayed there until everybody had gone. I heard Mr Ridgeway describing my uncle's injuries to the other servants.' He eyed Sandford pensively. 'I didn't hit them, sir, as you well know. I'm not a violent man!'

'*Not a violent man!*' Sandford gave a hoarse laugh. 'I take leave to argue with that!'

'Oh, but I don't think he is, Robert,' Harriet chided him. 'Oh, yes, I know he has given his potions and concoctions out rather indiscriminately, but he was rather *trapped* into it—surely you see that? I really don't see what good it will do to give him to the magistrate!'

'Very well, Harriet,' replied his lordship, with a sigh. 'What would you have me do with him—pat him on the back and give him the head gardener's position?'

'No, of course not—Mr Cooper would not care for— oh, I see! You were funning!' Having registered the smile that followed Sandford's remark, Harriet wrinkled her nose at him, then directed her attention to Beckett once more.

'You weren't intending to drag me forcibly from this room, I take it? You could have made your escape—why did you come back? Were you so determined, still?'

The young man shook his head emphatically. 'No, miss, I swear to God it wasn't that. I came to tell you—to show you the letter—I wanted you to know that I was sorry. I was going to ask you to help Jack—for there was no way that I could get to him!'

Harriet slowly rose to her feet and stood looking down at him for some moments before turning to Sandford. 'He's telling the truth, you know. I've had an idea.'

Without waiting for his reply, she laid her hand gently on Beckett's shoulder.

'Have you ever thought of training to be an apothecary or a pharmaceutist?' she asked him. At his look of amazement she smiled. 'It is possible, you know, and it is, perhaps, time your skills were put to the use Sir Frederick intended. We could make enquiries—perhaps there is somewhere in Bristol near your mother?'

'For God's sake, Harriet!' protested Sandford, clutching his head in despair as Beckett's eyes brightened and looked towards him hopefully. Heaving a great sigh, the viscount finally nodded, then motioned Harriet to unlock the hall door, outside of which they could hear the sounds of growing commotion.

'Better let them in,' he said in weary resignation.

Chapter Nineteen

Tiptree thrust open the library doors, angrily jostling Harriet to one side in spite of Sandford's attempted warning. He marched to the armchair in which his master was slumped and glared down at him in a fury. The viscount gave him a shamefaced grin.

'I know, Tip,' he said. 'But it was an emergency—and you weren't available—so I had to do it for you!'

The groom gave a puzzled frown. 'What, guv?' he said. 'Do what for me?'

'Well, I hear you seem to have made a bit of a habit of saving Miss Cordell's skin,' said Sandford, getting slowly to his feet and leaning on Tiptree's arm. 'Sorry to rob you of your fourth notch, but I had a fancy to even scores with you!'

'Young fool,' berated his man with a slight flush, then gaping as he recognised the third individual in the room. 'What's he doing here? What's been going on?'

'Tell you upstairs, old chap.' Sandford swayed momentarily and Harriet started forward in concern as Tiptree steadied his master. 'Just one thing—Beckett here is to be taken down to the kitchen for a hot meal but no one—and I mean no one—is to speak a word to him. Get young Rothman to watch him.'

He had observed the footman standing with the group of servants in the doorway, from where Lady Caroline and Harriet's mother had also been watching the proceedings in concerned silence. 'Now, if you will excuse me—I must go and lie down for a moment. Come along, Harriet!'

'I don't think so, guv!' protested Tiptree, helping the viscount to the stairs, but Sandford ignored him and held out his good hand towards Harriet.

'You're not moving out of my sight for an instant, my girl,' he said, quite firmly, smiling at her startled look. 'Bring a book—or your tatting—or whatever will keep you in the same place for more than ten minutes. Lady Cordell is welcome to join us if she can prevent you from disappearing!'

Sarah stepped forward at once, beaming with pleasure at the viscount's use of her former title.

'I think I can manage that, your lordship,' she said, motioning Harriet to follow the two men up the stairs, while the bemused countess gave orders for the remaining assorted members of her household to return to their duties and a jubilant young Rothman silently prodded what he subsequently referred to as his 'prisoner' through the baize door into the servants' quarters.

Sandford gingerly lowered his aching body on to his bed and finally closed his eyes, having assured himself that Harriet was, indeed, safely seated at the table by the window. Sarah, having exclaimed in horror at the state of his lordship's bandages, immediately set about replacing the ivy-stained rags with clean linen, while Tiptree stood sullenly to one side, waiting for his master's explanation.

The viscount, remembering his promise, opened one eye and registered the man's affronted demeanour. His mouth twitched as he said, 'Come on, Tip. Don't squabble over me—there's plenty to go round!'

'It's not funny, guv.' replied his servant mulishly. 'You could've killed yourself! Climbing about in your condition—what were you thinking of!'

'You know damned well what I was thinking of, Tiptree,' rejoined Sandford in weary good humour. 'And you might as well get used to the idea for it's quite permanent, I assure you! Now, go and make friends with the lady and I am sure that she can be persuaded to give you a good account of her latest adventure!'

With which advice he turned his head on the pillow and fell asleep.

His man, still bristling, stared down at him in brooding silence for some minutes until, raising his eyes and finding Sarah contemplating him with some concern, he gave a rueful grin and turned to leave.

'Looks like you can manage without me, ma'am,' he said with an obvious effort, indicating the neat bandage on his lordship's hand. 'Dare say he'll do pretty well now—I'll just take myself off to the *Fox* for a tankard or two—there'll be plenty of gossip to catch up on, I'll be bound!'

Harriet jumped up in alarm and hurried to block his exit. 'Oh, no, Tiptree—please don't go. His lordship would be so cross with us—you know he cannot manage without you! How can you say such a thing—tell him, Mama—*no one* can take his place!'

Sarah laughed at her daughter's consternation, but at the same time helped her to steer the unwilling Tiptree towards the window-seat.

'Harriet is quite right, sergeant,' she admonished him gently as he reluctantly sat down. 'Indeed, it would be a very foolish woman who imagined that she could—and I assure you that my daughter is no fool!'

'I never thought she was, ma'am,' said Tiptree morosely. 'It's mebbe me that's the fool! Reckon I'm getting too old for all this domestic brouhaha—it's set me thinking that mebbe it's time for me to be moving along—if the guv'nor's mindful to settle down here—well, he'll be needing a younger man than me!'

Ignoring his listeners' protesting denials, he went on, 'Then there's Kimble—now his lordship's got himself a ''top-o'-tree'' valet he won't have much use for an old batman—different sort of work, entirely. I'm no houseman, ma'am, been a soldier all my life...'

'Stop that at once!' interrupted Harriet crossly, drawing her chair towards him and, to his intense embarrassment, taking both of his hands in her own. Gazing earnestly into his startled eyes she said, 'You must not think such things! His lordship has terribly important work for you to do—something that he would never entrust to anyone else! If you forsake him, how will he manage? You must know how much he values your opinion! He certainly doesn't regard you in the same light as he does his—dresser!'

Tiptree scratched his head and frowned, regarding her in brooding silence for a moment before giving a resigned shrug. 'I'm sure I've never been one to shirk my duty, miss,' he said with a heavy sigh. 'I'll stay to do whatever his lordship requires—it's to do with that blackguard downstairs, I suppose?'

'It's for his lordship to give you your orders, of course—but if you will allow me to furnish you with the details of this afternoon's events? It has to be kept secret, Tiptree—but you already know that?'

Tiptree nodded, his curiosity immediately aroused, for he was as keen as anyone to know what had occurred in the library and, by the time Harriet had finished her discourse he was, at last, beginning to understand what Smithers and the rest saw in this seemingly indomitable young lady. She appeared to believe that there was good to be found in everyone! Even villains like Hinds and Beckett—who, apparently, was now not such a villain, after all—and that vicious old harpy! How anyone could extend sympathy to that one was beyond his belief! And to have persuaded the guv'nor to set the lot of them up all comfy and tidy-like—now that really was something to be marvelled at. Although, upon further reflection, he had to concede that it was probably the best way to keep such an unsavoury story out of the newspapers.

'It could work, miss,' he said, in grudging admiration. 'There aren't many who know the full truth—except that surely folk hereabouts will be expecting Beckett to get his come-uppance?'

'I thought of that!' Harriet assured him. 'We can tell them all he's been transported—which will be perfectly true, if he's transported to Bristol! Pinter and Finchley will be more than happy to be pensioned off to Mrs Beckett's boarding-house after this, I'll be bound, and poor Hinds...'

Sarah laughed at the man's shocked expression 'A little charity, sergeant?' she said, chastising him gently, as her daughter sought Tiptree's eyes pleadingly. 'The lad cannot be held entirely to blame—in his simple way he must have believed that he was following orders—which is all he is really capable of. When he heard Beckett say that he intended to ''get rid of'' Harriet and the boy, he must have thought that he meant precisely that!'

'And think how he must have suffered all his life!' Harriet put in. 'Forever teased and bullied by everyone—then finally to have found one friend who did not misuse him! No wonder he feels such loyalty towards Beckett! But punish him? I do not think so!'

'Well, I can't say as I agree with you,' said Tiptree, shaking his head doubtfully, 'but if that's what his lordship wants, then so be it. I dare say there are plenty of suitable places where the lad can be sent to see out his days, but it still seems downright odd to me that none of them are to be punished for what they did to you, miss!'

'No good would come of it, Tip,' Harriet tried to explain to him. 'It wouldn't achieve anything but more misery and unhappiness and surely we've all seen quite enough of that! I am convinced that none of them will do any more harm—they no longer have reason to do so—and I cannot forget that revenge and envy were the underlying forces behind their actions. For me to perpetuate those feelings would win me something of a Pyrrhic victory, I feel—I should lose more than I could possibly gain!'

'If you say so, miss,' he said, after mulling these words over. 'And truth to tell, I can't see a better way to deal with it—the guv'nor wouldn't take kindly to being involved in any sort of scandal—so, if you're willing to ''forgive and forget'', as they say, we'd best get it all cleared up as fast as we may!'

He then looked at her with a curious expression on his face, 'And if you'll pardon me saying so, miss, I must say that you certainly seem to have collected a fair bit of wisdom in your short life!'

At this, Sarah nodded in agreement. 'I've often thought so, myself, sergeant,' she said, smiling fondly at her daughter. 'Although it's clear that she doesn't always use it to her own advantage!'

Harriet blushed prettily, causing a broad smile to suddenly appear on Tiptree's face.

'I dare say you won't be sorry to get back to normal, miss?'

'I'm not sure I know what ''normal'' is in these parts, Tip,' she returned with a soft laugh, then put her hand over her mouth as the sound of a deep chuckle came from the vicinity of the viscount's bed.

'Oh, dear! Have we woken you, my lord?' Her voice was full of concern as she rose from her seat and hurried to his side.

'No, my little crusader, I've been awake for some time—still putting the world to rights, I hear,' he teased her, his heart leaping in hope as he registered the expression in her eyes.

'And you are feeling quite well?'

He thought he detected a tremor in her voice. 'Fitter than the proverbial fiddle—truly,' he assured her softly, reaching out his undamaged hand to take hold of hers.

'Ahem! If I might make so bold, sir,' came his groom's distinct tones.

'Tiptree!' Sandford's voice held a dangerous note.

'Sorry, sir.' His man was unrepentant. 'It's just that I see Lord Ramsey has returned—he's below on the terrace with Mr Ridgeway—and Lord William has been waiting for some time to speak with you.'

The viscount gave Harriet a rueful smile and swung his feet to the ground. 'Better get on with it, then,' he said, swaying very slightly as he stood up. 'I'm afraid I shall have to ask you ladies to excuse me while I attend to my toilette and—' turning to Sarah, he bowed '—my deepest thanks, ma'am, for—everything.'

His eyes held hers for a moment until a tiny smile appeared at the corner of her mouth and she gave an almost imperceptible nod.

'Come along, Harriet,' she said. 'We must also go and change. Her ladyship will have postponed the dinner hour to suit our convenience. We must not keep her waiting any longer than necessary.'

As her mother led her from the room Harriet cast a despairing glance towards Sandford, but he was already involved in selecting articles from his wardrobe.

Back in her own bedchamber, undergoing the cheery Rose's ministrations, Harriet wondered miserably when she would get an opportunity to speak to Sandford alone, for how, otherwise, could she discover his true feelings towards her?

True, he had climbed out of the window to come to her rescue, but he obviously felt that he had no choice—he had told Tiptree that it was an emergency. And he had needed very little persuasion regarding her suggestions as to Beckett's redemption—could that have been because he was tired of the whole matter and simply wanted rid of her!

Harriet trembled at the thought, and then her eyes brightened. He had called her his 'little crusader' in a very fond tone, but then she recalled that he was, in all probability, only half-awake at the time and her heart sank once more.

'If you don't keep still, miss,' chastised Rose, as she tied Harriet's hair ribbon for the third time, 'I shall have Mrs Gibson putting me back in the parlour—I'm making such a pig's pie of this!'

'I'm sorry, Rose,' said Harriet, endeavouring to comply with the girl's request. 'I'm still in the fidgets—it's been such an extraordinary day. Tell me what's happened to Beckett? Has he been taken away?' She wondered if Sandford's orders had been carried out.

'Davy has him under lock and key, miss—and won't allow nobody near him. Made me shiver just to see him walk past, it did, miss—wicked devil. Just think, if Granfer hadn't gone up to the cottage...!' Her eyes grew round.

Harriet nodded vigorously. 'It was terribly brave of him to come all the way back in the dark, Rose, and lucky for all of us that your mother sent your father out looking for him—I shall never be able to thank them enough!'

Rose's cheeks flushed with a combination of pride and pleasure.

'That's all right, miss,' she said airily. 'Granfer always says that good deeds usually find their way back home and isn't the Reverend forever telling us that "as we sow so shall we reap". You must have sown a lot of good deeds in your life—we all think so, anyhow!'

'Everyone has been so kind,' said Harriet, her eyes moistening at the girl's words, but then her own cheeks flamed in guilty recollection of her earlier treatment of Judith and she was, once again, deep in dismal self-reproach when Rose's voice intruded upon her thoughts.

'Shall you wear the emerald set, miss? It looks so well with this gown—and seeing as it's a special occasion—what with your mother and grandfather here and— Oh, miss! I nearly forgot to tell you! His lordship—Lord William, that is—he's going downstairs to dinner!'

'Oh, that's wonderful! I must go down at once!'

In her excitement Harriet barely noticed that Rose had already fastened the emeralds around her neck and wrist. She stood up hurriedly, hardly pausing to glance at her reflection, then, suddenly conscious that she had omitted to thank the girl for her efforts, she turned back to the mirror and said, with a sincere smile, 'Thank you Rose. Perfect, as usual.'

Rose's beaming face told Harriet that her instincts had not been wrong. 'You look that lovely, miss. It's such a pleasure to dress you!'

Sarah, arriving at the door just as Harriet was about to leave, was initially somewhat taken aback at her daughter's new finery. Then, secretly rather thrilled to see her one-time scamp looking so delightful, she studied the elegant figure before her with very mixed emotions.

'Papa would have been so proud of you, my dearest,' she said, holding the blushing girl at arm's length, her eyes moist. 'You have grown into such a lovely young lady—he would hardly recognise his romping girl!'

'I'm afraid she's still there, Mama,' laughed Harriet ruefully, 'underneath these fancy furbelows I'm the same impulsive hothead that I've always been—and I do not seem able to do anything about it! One minute I think I have succeeded in curbing my impetuosity and the next thing I know, I'm thick in trouble again!'

Sarah's brow furrowed. 'I do not think you can hold yourself entirely responsible for these extraordinary events,' she pointed out. 'Lady Butler would surely have held her grudge against any potential bride whom Sandford brought home with him?'

'Yes, but that lady would never have behaved as I did—I always have to get involved—with Billy, old Potter—even interfering in Judith's affairs!'

Harriet swallowed hard and turned anguished eyes to her mother.

'Do you think that Lord Sandford holds me in disapproval, Mama?'

Sarah hesitated and Harriet mistook her silence as a reluctance to proffer a blunt answer. Forcing a light laugh, she feigned a devil-may-care attitude as she ushered her mother towards the staircase as the sound of the dinner-gong reverberated throughout the hall below.

'No matter,' she said with seeming nonchalance, as they descended the stairs. 'It is of no real consequence. It is Grandfather's approval I must seek to gain.'

'I doubt you need have any qualms on that score, dear child,' laughed Sarah, as March threw open the dining-room doors.

Chapter Twenty

In spite of Cook having surpassed herself in the variety of dishes she had sent up to the table, Harriet found that she had very little appetite for any of the carefully prepared dishes.

Beldale, resplendent in full evening dress and back, once again, in his rightful place at the head of his table, exhorted her to 'take a little more of this' or 'a morsel of that' as each subsequent course appeared and, to please him, she accepted small servings of food, which she discreetly moved around on her plates in an effort to seem as totally absorbed in her food as her companions were.

Most of the leaves had been removed from the huge mahogany table in order to reducc it to a more convenable size and Lord William had insisted upon Harriet sitting at his right hand with her mother at his left. Lady Caroline, at the foot of the table, had chosen to sit Lord Ramsey on her left, next to his granddaughter. This arrangement had placed Sandford diagonally opposite Harriet but, since a large silver epergne graced the middle of the table, its branched bowls of fruit and flowers had the effect of obscuring him almost totally from her vision.

Because of the lateness of the hour and the difficulties involved in getting his lordship to his place, the initial greetings and social conformities had been dispensed with and they had come straight to the table and so, apart from the smilingly courteous bow she had received at her entrance, Harriet had been reduced to seeing little more of the viscount than the occasional wrist or elbow although, as she could clearly hear, he was obviously enjoying spirited conversations with his immediate neighbours. 'I have hardly seen you all day,' Lord William was laughingly scolding her, 'and Sandford tells me that you have settled this whole matter almost single-handedly!'

'Oh, no, sir!' Harriet was abashed. 'I merely put forward some suggestions to his lordship—I hope you do not think—it is not for me to decide...!'

'Oh, but I think it is,' said the earl, twinkling at her. 'You have been the chief victim of these dreadful wrongdoings and yet your heart is still full of forgiveness—you put some of us to shame, my golden girl. I have to own that I would have sought to wreak the usual revenge had you not petitioned on those devils' behalves—for I myself suffered considerable discomfort, as you know—and there were moments when I seriously considered that my brain had deteriorated!'

He guffawed at his listeners' horrified expressions. 'But enough of that! We will all hopefully learn something from the experience. And, thanks to you, my child, much good has been gained! Following your excellent suggestion, we have arranged for Tiptree to escort the penitents to Bristol at first light, with Pringle and Garvey—Ramsey's men—as outriders. I have a man of business at the port and I shall provide him with the necessary instructions as to their future welfare. I think we need give that particular matter no further thought.'

'Young Hinds won't be left to shoulder the blame, will he, sir?' said Harriet, her green eyes wide with anxiety. 'Even Beckett was most concerned that he should not suffer—that was his main reason for returning.'

'Don't worry, little marigold,' his lordship assured her. 'Eugenie has it in hand—the lad will be properly looked after, I promise you—but,' and here his expression grew very stern, 'before you even think of it, I flatly refuse to fulfil any pleas you may be contemplating on the Butler's behalf!'

'She has already been dealt her punishment, I fear,' said Harriet, with a deep sigh. 'Judith is so distressed— and I was so beastly to her when she came to see me!'

Ramsey, who had been listening to this exchange, smilingly patted his granddaughter's hand. 'Don't fret, sweetling, yon Ridgeway has already assured the lassie that you'd soon be back to your own sunny self! He's feeling pretty pleased with himself—these events won him a rare prize—he'd likely still be casting sheep's-eyes!'

Harriet looked towards the countess in delight. 'You mean that Charles has finally...?'

Lady Caroline nodded happily. 'Yes, my dear. They settled it this afternoon. He and Judith are to be married next month. Beldale's man of business is already working out the settlements. Lady Butler is to remain with Eugenie—Sir Basil is hopeful of a partial recovery.'

The room was suddenly silent and Harriet's eyes filled. Sandford, sensing the changed atmosphere, damned the entire guild of silversmiths to perdition and made to rise from his seat, but his mother laid a restraining hand on his arm and threw him a warning frown as Sarah began to speak.

'I believe Sergeant Tiptree would say that it was all meant to be,' she said, smiling across at her daughter, 'and a good many philosophers have agreed with his Destiny theory. If it is really so, it somehow helps to reduce the—horror—of these recent events, wouldn't you agree?'

'Well, I'm eternally obliged to any Destiny that saw fit to restore you to me,' laughed Ramsey, adding, as he twinkled at Harriet, 'A double bonus, which I'm sure I've done nothing to deserve!'

'I think Lord Sandford must claim some of the credit for that,' she said with a blush, glad that the viscount could not see her face. 'He was the one who rescued me from the ditch!'

Beldale, flicking a surreptitious glance at his son's furrowed brow, leaned forward and stretched out his hand to cover Harriet's. 'And we can only be thankful that he had the sense to bring you to us, my dear— such a pretty bonus—but I cannot help feeling that Fate has been dealing you some pretty poor cards lately. I pray that she intends to look more kindly upon you in the future—although I do not care to think of you quitting my house with such unpleasant memories!'

Sandford, rising at once to his feet, observed Harriet's downcast eyes and trembling lips.

'You have teased Miss Cordell quite enough, Father,' he said firmly, vacating his place. 'I believe I can manage without further assistance! I shall withhold on the port, if you will excuse me.'

He strode quickly round to Harriet's side of the table. 'And now, with everyone's permission, I must take it upon myself to remove the lady. She appears to be in need of a little air—would you care to step on to the terrace for a few moments, my dear?'

This last was to Harriet, who rose from her seat in silent relief and allowed the viscount to lead her to the dining-room doors. Four pairs of eyes watched in unconcealed amusement as Sandford gently shepherded her out on to the terrace, now bathed in moonlight.

'You were a little hard on her, William,' said Lady Caroline, signalling to Rothman to close the curtains. 'And Robert was beginning to look distinctly edgy!'

'I wondered if I was going too far,' agreed the earl, taking out his handkerchief and wiping his damp brow. 'But he's been taking so long to come to the point that it was making me nervous. Just thought he needed a bit of a push—maybe they both do! Don't remember being such a slowtop myself!'

The countess raised her brows in surprise. 'Then your memory serves you very poorly,' she chuckled.

'I recall very clearly how long you took—that's what made me think of the epergne—do you remember...?'

Her eyes twinkled at him and he returned a reminiscent grin.

'That I do, my lady,' he nodded. 'Nothing like an insurmountable barrier to raise a man's fighting spirit! Will he ask her, do you think?'

'Aye, he will,' interposed Ramsey. 'He's already spoken to me—and he received Sarah's blessing earlier, I ken.'

Beldale regarded him pensively. 'How will you feel about losing your granddaughter as soon as you've found her?'

Ramsey's smiling eyes travelled to his daughter's face. 'I've won one major prize, man,' he said gruffly. 'It'd be a might greedy to demand two, and besides—' he lifted his glass and tossed off the contents '—I've no intention of losing her. I got yon laddie's promise that he'd make a yearly trek to Craigburn!'

Out on the terrace Harriet was leaning thankfully against the parapet, contemplating the moon's reflection in the lake across the park. Deeply conscious of Sandford's presence beside her she did not speak, afraid that her voice would betray her emotions. His remarks to Lord William had confused her and she still was trying to make sense of them when he spoke.

'I'm not sure that I wouldn't prefer to wrangle with you, O Silent One!' His still husky voice sounded nervous. 'Have you nothing to say to me, Harriet?'

'Wh-what would you have me say to you, my lord?' she stammered.

'Don't start that again, for God's sake!' he exclaimed impatiently. 'I'd have you say plenty of things to me, Harriet, but that isn't one of them!'

Confronted by her further silence, he took a deep breath. 'You can't keep doing this, you know—you must make up your mind!'

'M-make up my mind?' she repeated. 'I'm afraid I don't follow you.'

'You can't keep reeling me in and throwing me back, Harriet,' he said drily. 'Am I such a poor fish?'

She gasped. 'I haven't—I wouldn't...!'

Gently he turned her to face him, raised her chin and gazed searchingly into her eyes. Then, sighing, he removed his hand from her face.

'You really do have no idea of the effect you have,' he said, with a crooked smile. 'I keep forgetting how young you are!'

'Is that why you're always so angry with me?' she asked in a small voice. 'I shall get older, I promise! Some people say I'm very mature for—'

With a strangled groan he pulled her towards him, burying his face in her hair as his good arm tightened about her. She could feel the unruly beating of his heart against her cheek and was conscious of a burgeoning sensation within which was threatening to overwhelm her. As her hands crept up to curl themselves involuntarily around his neck, she raised her head until her eyes locked shyly with his and at his expression her own heart almost stopped in its tracks.

'Harriet?' he breathed hoarsely, afraid that the moonlight must be playing tricks with him, for he could not allow himself to believe what he was seeing.

'Robert?' came her soft reply as her fingers caressed the hairs at the nape of his neck and, with a little gasp, he possessed himself of her lips in a most ungentle manner, crushing her to him in an embrace so tight that she could scarcely breathe until, revelling in the sweet bondage of his arms, she found herself returning his kiss with a passion that equalled his own.

With difficulty, he forced himself to break away from her lips, but only to rain further kisses upon her brow, her eyelids and her cheek, whilst murmuring foolish endearments into her ear, all of which were pure delight to her.

'Do I take it that you still consider yourself betrothed—*my lord*?' she said mischievously, when he at last paused to take breath. 'Surely our arrangement is no longer necessary?'

'Necessary?' He gave a shaky laugh. 'Absolutely imperative now, my little warrior, unless you have a fancy to see your grandfather take his whip to me!'

'But it was agreed that one of us would cry off as soon as he arrived,' she reminded him, her bright eyes dancing.

'Well, let me assure you here and now that it won't be me!' he said fiercely, as his arms closed around her once more. 'Dearest heart, I fell totally in love with you the moment I rounded that corner and saw you rising like a naiad out of the waters, with your irresistible eyes and your flaming mop—and that was the really ''unexpected complication'' which dished Lady Butler's plans—and why I shall be forever indebted to her and her incompetent henchmen!'

'I said such awful things to you!' she cried, contentedly snuggling closer to him. 'I said you were not the man for me—and I know now that you always have been!'

His arms tightened convulsively and he pressed his lips to her hair. 'I was damnable to you! Can you ever forgive me?'

'If you promise that you never *will* be a pattern of perfection!' she teased him, her cheeks dimpling at his sudden grimace of recollection. 'For I'm sure it must be very difficult to live with such a paragon!'

'That, fortunately, is something neither of us is ever likely to find out,' he said with a wicked grin, as he once more lowered his lips to hers. 'You are about to discover that I can be quite as impetuous as you are, *my lady*!'

* * * * *

MY LADY ENGLISH
Catherine March

Falk de Arques got more than he bargained for when King William ordered him to take an English bride.

Lady Julia of Foxbourne wanted to hate the Norman knight who had invaded her home. But Falk, a fierce warrior on the battlefield, wasn't about to let this spirited and stubborn woman defeat him! How long would it take for Julia to surrender to her growing desires and become his Lady English…?

Norman knight…English lady

**Introducing Catherine March
an exciting new voice in medieval historical romance**

A MOST UNSUITABLE BRIDE
Gail Whitiker

The mysterious heavily veiled woman Edward Thurlow, Lord Garthdale, meets on his early morning rides in Hyde Park intrigues and then utterly charms him. What dark secret could possibly force her to hide away from society in such a fashion?

An eligible catch, Edward has eluded the marital net until now. So why, just when he's resigned himself to finding a wife, should this most unsuitable woman keep invading his thoughts?

HISTORICAL ROMANCE™

LARGE PRINT

A CONVENIENT GENTLEMAN

Victoria Aldridge

The bank won't lend Caroline Morgan the money she so
desperately needs until she gets herself a husband.

Caro finds Leander Gray, the younger son of an
aristocrat and the only eligible man in town, collapsed in
a local bar. He grudgingly agrees to a paper marriage
and Caro is left wondering what she's got herself into.
But when the gambler turns gentleman her feelings
begin to change…

**New Zealand
Love rush – Gold rush**

A VERY UNUSUAL GOVERNESS

Sylvia Andrew

Edward Barraclough's happy bachelor existence is thrown
into a spin when he is forced to look after his two
orphaned nieces. Employing the right governess is vital
and as unassuming and a little dowdy as Miss Petrie may
appear, he suspects she's neither so humble nor
respectful underneath!

Independently wealthy Lady Octavia Petrie is on the
verge of confessing that Edward's mistaken her for
someone else. Then, in a moment of sheer madness,
prompted by his cynical attitude, she finds herself
accepting the temporary position.

MILLS & BOON®

Live the emotion

HIST0904 LP

HISTORICAL ROMANCE™

LARGE PRINT

THE WIDOW'S BARGAIN
Juliet Landon

When her Scottish home is invaded by a dangerous band of reivers, Lady Ebony Moffat's first thought is to keep her young son safe. For his sake she is prepared to make a bargain with the men's leader—her body for her child's life.

Sir Alex Somers is intrigued. In a reiver's guise he has raided Castle Kells, seeking out traitors at the behest of the King of Scotland. Alex means no harm to the boy. But with his desire for Ebony so intense, he can't help but be drawn by her offer…

Robert the Bruce
…Scottish borders, raiding parties, endangered lovers…

THE RUNAWAY HEIRESS
Anne O'Brien

Miss Frances Hanwell effects a daring night-time escape—in the Marquis of Aldeborough's carriage! Mistaking her for a kitchen servant, Hugh only realises his grave error the next day. With scandal imminent, a reluctant marriage seems the only course of action.

Reluctance turns to respect when Hugh uncovers the brutal marks of the unhappy life she's been leading. Suddenly, he will do all in his power to protect her…especially now, as an unexpected inheritance threatens to take Frances from him…

MILLS & BOON®

Live the emotion

HIST0204 LP